I0781158

OSCAR

ALSO BY MARY ROMASANTA

Avīci Sagga
The Eternal Secret
Infestation
Oscar
La Llorona: The Awakening
Deliver Us: True Stories of Possession, Oppression, and Spiritual Warfare

For previews of upcoming books and information about the author, visit
www.MaryRomasanta.com.
Follow her on Instagram @AuthorMaryRomasanta.

OSCAR

A NOVEL

MARY ROMASANTA

Sagga Publishing House LLC

SAGGA PUBLISHING HOUSE LLC, SEPTEMBER 2025

Library of Congress Control Number: 2025903779

Premium Mass-Market Hardback ISBN: 978-1-964642-06-2

Premium Mass-Market Paperback ISBN: 978-1-964642-05-5

eBook ISBN: 978-1-964642-10-9

Published in the United States by Sagga Publishing House LLC, San Antonio, Texas.

This book is a work of fiction. Names, characters, businesses, organizations, places, events, and incidents either are the product of the author's imagination or used fictitiously. Any resemblance to actual persons, living or dead, events, or locales is entirely coincidental.

Cover design by Damonza.com

Visit the author's website at www.maryromasanta.com

Printed in the United States of America

For Lucas, Seth, and Jeremy.

May your fears fuel your passion and purpose.

Preface

As with each of my novels, the story behind *Oscar* was born from a wellspring of raw emotion. It came from the deep recesses of my childhood—memories of something outwardly innocent that became the source of profound, inexplicable fear.

Puppetry has a long and complex history, often intertwined with faith. In the Middle Ages, puppets were used to teach scripture to largely illiterate audiences, transforming abstract moral lessons into living stories. Even in modern times, puppets continue to captivate young audiences, carrying messages of faith and virtue.

I grew up immersed in that tradition. My father, a retired pastor, once brought home a hand puppet named Oscar. He was red-haired, dressed in a striped sweater and blue pants, with hollow eyes and a too-wide smile. At three or four years old, I remember staring at him in silent terror—a fear so deep it spilled into tears. My older brother felt the same, though we never spoke of it. Oscar unsettled us in ways we couldn't explain.

This novel is my reckoning with that fear. It asks whether Oscar was simply an uncanny object—or whether he became the vessel for something darker. More importantly, it's a story about the way fear embeds itself in memory, how it shapes us, and how we might reclaim power over it.

For my brother and me, Oscar will always remain a haunting presence. For you, dear reader, I hope he becomes something more—a reminder of the strength we each hold to confront our darkest fears.

Happy Reading,
Mary Romasanta

P.S. Turn to the end of the book for a glimpse of the real Oscar—*the puppet that inspired this story.*

OSCAR

Prologue

ELARA LINGERED AT THE EDGE of the University of Chicago quad, the cold cutting through her sweater like invisible claws. Above her, banners cracked in the wind—*Justice Now. Silence Is Complicity.* The fabric snapped and writhed, not like cloth at all but like something alive, summoning her closer.

"I don't want to—" Elara whispered, the plea threadbare.

Her mother's hand brushed her arm, light but firm, a tether she couldn't escape. "Stay with me."

Chants rolled across the quad in waves, not words anymore but a vibration that rattled her ribs. She tried to breathe past the thrum, but her heart beat louder, desperate, like prey cornered in the dark.

Her mother's profile burned in the gray light—chin lifted, eyes blazing, every step sure, as though fire itself carried her forward. Elara thought of her father then, the gentleness in his eyes when he had once pleaded for her to come with him, away from all this. But her mother's grip had been stronger. Always stronger.

"Mother, please," she pleaded.

The crowd devoured her words whole. They pressed in. The air reeked of sweat and smoke, acrid enough to sting. Strangers brushed her shoulders, their heat clinging to her skin until she couldn't tell where her body ended and theirs began. Her mother carved a path toward the front, magnetic, unyielding, dragging Elara—helpless—in her wake.

"Raise your voice," her mother commanded, already flinging hers into the storm.

Elara shook her head, throat tightening until the words strangled on her tongue. Heat flared up her neck, a fever not her own, as though the chants had already invaded her blood. When she finally opened her mouth, her voice split apart—a brittle sound swallowed instantly by the thunder. But the rhythm caught her anyway, winding around her lungs, dragging the sound out of her. Weak at first, then stronger. Louder. Until the voice pouring from her lips no longer felt like hers at all.

What's happening?

The thought skittered across Elara's mind, desperate, but her lips trembled as if she might say it aloud.

The crowd surged. Signs snapped upward, rhythm pounding like drums of war. For a moment, the fire caught inside her too. Her skin tingled, every nerve lit with an energy not her own. Borrowed. Stolen. Terrifying.

"You'll see," her mother said without turning, her voice taut with triumph. "This is who we are."

No, this isn't me, Elara thought. But the words shriveled, strangled by the chant.

Faces blurred, mouths wide, eyes gleaming too bright, fever-bright. The air quivered with their voices—no longer human cries for justice but something darker, an invocation that pulled at her marrow. The chant wound itself around her like a chain, dragging her down.

A shout, jagged and unnatural, cracked the cadence. Another followed, sharper, angrier. The crowd convulsed. A shove. A bottle shattered, glass scattering like teeth across the ground. The chant disintegrated into screams.

Elara's vision blurred as the mob transformed. No longer a crowd but a single monstrous thing, writhing, violent, alive. She fought for breath as it swallowed her whole, its pulse pounding inside her skull.

Yet in the press of bodies, in the roar of a thousand voices, she had never felt more alone. Every shoulder slammed against her, every hand shoved past her, but none of them touched *her*. She was only a fragment swallowed by the mass, a ghost inside the living beast. The others moved as one, bound by fury and faith, while she drifted at the center—untethered, hollow, unseen.

Her mother's hand clamped onto hers—iron-strong, inescapable. The pressure tightened until it no longer felt human, fingers burning like shackles seared into her skin. Elara tried to pull back, but the grip held with a will that wasn't her mother's.

When their eyes met, her breath caught. Her mother's gaze no longer belonged to her—it shimmered with something vast and merciless, the same fever-light that blazed in the mob around them. Elara felt the truth sink into her bones: this wasn't just a protest, not even just a crowd. Something older, hungrier, had awakened inside their voices, wearing her mother's face, speaking through her body.

The fight was no longer outside her—it had seeped into her marrow, claiming every beat of her heart. No choice. No escape.

Chapter One

GHOSTLY REMNANTS OF THE STORM clung to the air. Rainwater pooled in the gutters, glistening on the slick asphalt as the Windy City exhaled in uneasy silence. Traffic crawled along the stretch, brake lights flaring red against the gray.

Brianna's hands tightened on the steering wheel, her grip unsteady, betraying both her inexperience and the jittering pulse beneath her skin. Her gaze locked on the scene ahead—a violent rupture in the quiet neighborhood. Shattered ornaments and torn wreaths lay scattered across the pavement, glittering fragments of something once whole.

Headlights cut through the mist, revealing flashes of carnage. A red sedan lay crumpled against an electric pole, its frame twisted into a grotesque tangle of metal. Shards of glass littered the wet asphalt, catching the dim winter light like fractured stars. The air hung thick with the acrid tang of burnt rubber and leaking oil, a toxic blend that coiled in her lungs and turned her stomach.

Firefighters moved with grim precision, their shouts slicing through the murmur of engines and the hiss of lingering rain. A yellow tarp fluttered faintly in the cold breeze—a stark, haunting punctuation to the devastation. Brianna gripped the wheel tighter, fighting the unease clawing at her. The wreckage wasn't just a tragedy. It felt like a warning.

Relief came as the bottleneck of traffic began to ease. But it was short-lived.

Brake lights flared ahead—sudden, blinding. She slammed her foot down, tires skidding on the slick pavement. Her seatbelt snapped taut, cutting off her breath.

From the corner of her eye, a blur darted across the road. A figure in the mist. *Emma.*

Clutching a battered black case, Emma's frantic steps cut through the chaos, her breath visible in the icy air. Her wide, darting gaze met Brianna's for a heartbeat before snapping back toward the wreckage.

Brianna didn't think—she acted. She yanked the window down, cold air slapping her face. "Get in—now!" she barked, voice sharp and urgent.

The icy wind whipped into the car as Emma flung open the door and stumbled into the passenger seat. "Thanks," she muttered breathlessly, slamming it shut.

"What the hell were you thinking?" Brianna snapped, her voice vibrating with frustration.

Her gaze shot to the case on Emma's lap. Its surface twitched—thumping faintly, like a heartbeat trapped inside.

"What is that?"

Emma's fingers clenched around the worn edges. Her breath hitched. "I—I don't know."

Then, almost a whisper: "But whatever it is... it's alive."

Brianna's pulse quickened. "Alive? Well, what are you waiting for? Open it!"

Emma hesitated, breath shallow, hands hovering above the latches. The look in her eyes made one thing clear—if this thing was going to be opened, Brianna would have to do it herself.

Frustration surged. Brianna sucked in a sharp breath, yanked the wheel, and floored the gas. The tires spun, fishtailing before she pulled them back under control, speeding toward the church parking lot. Gravel crunched as she braked hard, the engine humming into the tense silence.

"Hand it to me," she said, her voice firm, edged with impatience.

Emma hesitated, then surrendered the case. It vibrated against Brianna's palms, the relentless thumping gnawing at her nerves.

Her fingers trembled as she unclasped the first latch.

Click.

The sound cracked through the hush of the car, like glass splintering in silence.

She moved to the second latch.

Click.

The third latch resisted, then snapped open with an ominous *crack*.

She flipped the lid back. A wave of rot rolled out—thick, cloying, rancid. The stench clawed at her throat.

Brianna recoiled, gagging, as a fat fly burst free, zigzagging past her face. The odor was unbearable, as though something dead had been festering inside for weeks. Instinct took over. She slammed the lid shut, sucking in quick, shallow breaths.

Emma shoved open the door, gulping in frigid air. One hand clamped over her mouth, her eyes watered as she fought the urge to vomit.

They climbed out together, the cold gnawing at their skin. Clouds of breath curled upward as they circled to the front of the car, boots crunching on damp pavement.

Brianna set the case on the hood. She drew in a deep breath, planting her feet, though her weight shifted restlessly from side to side. Her hands hovered over the latches, fingers twitching, poised as though about to disarm a bomb.

"Brie, don't," Emma urged, her voice frayed with tension. "Maybe we should—"

Brianna didn't let her finish. She flipped the case open, bracing herself. The smell was still vile, but less suffocating in the open air. She buried her nose in her elbow and forced her eyes to the contents.

Her breath hitched.

A puppet.

It lay eerily still, like something unearthed from a shallow grave. Strands of bright red hair sprouted in wiry clumps, matted and greasy, a garish crown against its sickly pale fleece skin. The black marble eyes bulged too far from the sockets, their glossy sheen catching the light as though wet. They stared past her, unblinking, lifeless—yet somehow watchful.

The grin was worse. Stretched too wide, the stitched mouth curved upward in a grotesque parody of cheer, puckered at the seams where the thread strained against old fabric. The expression looked permanent, cruelly forced, as if whoever had sewn it had wanted the face locked in mockery.

Brianna hesitated, then reached inside. Her fingers brushed the fabric—cold, clammy. Not the soft, familiar give of a child's toy, but a leathery stiffness that clung to her skin as she lifted it. The puppet dangled limply, its striped sweater and red pants sagging with damp weight.

"Brie, don't!" Emma's plea was sharp, almost panicked. "You don't know where it's been."

She held it up. Its head lolled sideways on the limp neck, the grin catching the dim light so that for a heartbeat it seemed to widen.

"Harmless," she said, but her own voice betrayed her with the smallest quiver.

Emma stepped back, arms wrapping around herself. Her wide eyes stayed locked on the puppet, fear radiating off her. Her gaze had dropped back into the case. "Brie, there's something else in there."

Chapter Two

EMMA STEPPED BACK INSTINCTIVELY as Brianna placed the puppet gently on the hood of the car. Her shoes crunching on the gravel, unease prickling across her skin as if the thing might twitch to life at any moment.

"Be careful, Brie," she whispered.

Brianna's fingers slid into the shadows of the worn case, digging past the velvet lining. Emma edged farther back, her body rigid, as though distance could shield her from whatever Brianna was about to draw out.

The silence stretched heavy, her pulse hammering in her ears as her eyes locked on Brianna's hand disappearing deeper inside.

With painstaking care, Brianna eased her hand out of the case, her movements deliberate, as though each inch mattered. When her fingers finally emerged, they revealed the limp, mottled body of a dead amphibian.

Emma's nose wrinkled, and the word slipped out before she could stop it.

"Gross," she muttered, her voice tight with revulsion.

A shiver ran down her arms, raising gooseflesh beneath her sleeves. The dead creature wasn't just disgusting—it unsettled her. Something about the way it sagged in Brianna's grip, the dull sheen of its skin, the sightless eye rolling toward her, stirred a chill deep inside. Emma couldn't name the reason, couldn't pin it to anything real, but the unease lingered all the same—like a whisper of danger brushing past the edge of her mind.

She hadn't grown up like most kids her age. While her friends drifted off to sleep with fairytales, she was lulled into uneasy dreams with stories of serpents coiled in gardens, whispering temptation. She learned early that curiosity led to exile, that a single bite of forbidden fruit could doom an entire world. And as she grew older, the stories didn't stop. They evolved.

Her father told her of his own experiences—things he swore were true. Shadows that moved when no one was there. Whispers curling through empty rooms. Cold hands pressing against his back in the dead of night. He spoke of omens and signs, of figures standing at the foot of his bed, watching, waiting. Of doors that locked on their own—not to keep something out, but to keep something in.

And beneath each story was something more than superstition—each tale was a lesson wrapped in a warning. Emma came to understand his words weren't for entertainment, not the harmless fireside fables her friends grew up with, but signposts marked with danger.

She watched as Brianna cradled the stiff, bloated toad in her palm. Its leathery skin sagged against her hand, swollen and unnatural.

"Brie, I'm not sure that's a good idea," Emma said.

Brianna murmured to the dead amphibian, "You must have been trapped all alone in there."

Emma froze as a realization struck like a shard of ice—one of her father's warnings clawing its way back from the shadows of memory.

"Don't touch it!" she burst out. "Put it down!"

Brianna jolted, nearly dropping the toad.

"Relax," she muttered, irritation creeping into her tone. She stepped toward the shrubbery. "I was going to put it down anyway."

Emma held her breath as Brianna crouched near a pink rosebush and laid the bloated creature beneath its petals, its pale hide stark against the dark soil. She scooped a handful of damp earth and pressed it over the body, patting it down as though tucking it in for the night.

"Leave it already!" Emma shouted.

Brianna turned, eyes flashing with annoyance.

"What part of 'don't touch it' don't you understand?" Emma snapped.

Brianna folded her arms, her tone clipped. "What's the matter with you? It just died. Have a heart, for God's sake."

Emma's gaze drifted back to the puppet sprawled on the hood of the car. The sight unsettled her in the same way her father's stories always had—warnings that clung like shadows, never fully gone.

"I think it's cursed," she said flatly.

Brianna scoffed. "Don't be ridiculous."

"Brie, I'm not joking," Emma blurted, her voice tight. "My dad told me about this kind of thing—toads are used in curses."

Brianna exhaled through her nose, arms still folded. "I see." The skepticism in her tone was undeniable.

Emma's voice lost its edge of panic and shifted into something rigid, almost mechanical, as though she were reciting lines she'd been drilled on since childhood.

"He said if I ever found a dead toad under strange circumstances, never touch it. Leave it alone. Tell him right away."

The words came out flat and rehearsed, like a script etched into her memory, and the eerie calmness of it only made the warning heavier.

Emma's eyes flicked to the battered case, dread pooling in her stomach. "I never would have picked it up if I'd known what was inside."

Brianna shoved the puppet back into the case with a sharp exhale. "Well, nothing we can do about it now," she said. "Let's go tell your dad about it."

Emma nodded. "We can tell him about the puppet, but don't mention the toad."

Brianna's brow creased, her tone edged with impatience. "I don't understand. You just said—"

Just—drop it,' she said. Heat prickled at the back of her neck. The words came out harsher than she intended, but she couldn't—wouldn't—entertain another question. Not when they clawed too close, scraping at the edges of truths she had spent her entire life keeping buried.

Chapter Three

T HE MATCH FLARED TO LIFE with a hiss, its sulfur bite clawing at the air. Emmanuel held it steady, the flame trembling in the dim room as though reluctant to be born. He lowered it toward the wall heater's pilot light.

Whoosh.

Gas ignited in a sudden rush, a bloom of warmth radiating outward. Emmanuel exhaled slowly, letting the heat bleed into his skin. For a moment, the room seemed to breathe with him. He slipped the spent match back into its worn cardboard box, his fingers lingering over the edges as if reluctant to let it go.

Crossing to his desk, he lowered himself into the chair. The Bible lay open before him, its pages splayed wide, whispering in the restless draft. His pen hovered above the paper, stalled over a half-finished line of notes.

A light knock on the door.

"Come in," Emmanuel shouted.

Emma shifted, glancing toward Brianna as the door creaked open. Emmanuel caught the beginning of her whisper—too faint to fully make out:

"Remember, don't say any—"

Teenagers and their secrets, he thought.

Part of him wished he could decode everything Emma was up to—to understand her world, to protect her from whatever shadows lurked at its edges. But there was another part of him wanted no insight into the mind of a seventeen-year-old girl.

"Good morning, ladies," Emmanuel said.

"Morning," they responded in unison.

With a heavy thud, Brianna set the case down on Emmanuel's desk.

"What's this?" he asked. "Are you taking up the violin?"

Brianna offered no response, not even a smile.

"Open it," Emma said, her expression stoic—detached, unreadable. Certainly not the look of someone presenting their father with a gift.

Emmanuel unclasped the case and lifted the lid. His eyes widened as they landed on its contents. He glanced at Emma. She stood rigid, her arms pressed tight across her chest, her expression flat but her eyes darting toward the case with unmistakable unease.

Suddenly, her posture made sense. Emma was about to graduate high school, teetering on the edge of adulthood, but in many ways, she was still the little girl he remembered. Her fear of puppets was one of those ways—an old quirk, something she had whispered to him about in the dead of night years ago after waking from another dream. Back then, he would kneel at her bedside, stroking her hair, promising that the puppets on TV or in Sunday school were harmless, just cloth and stitching, no more threatening than her stuffed animals. He had assumed she'd long outgrown it—and he wasn't about to bring it up now.

Emmanuel ran his fingers over the battered case, studying its worn edges. "By the looks of it, it must have fallen off the back of a truck."

He lifted the puppet, turning it over in his hands. His fingers followed the stitching that snaked along its seams, the fabric worn but crafted with unsettling care. Under the dim light, its glass eyes glimmered, unblinking, above a grin frozen in an eerie, almost knowing leer. His brows lifted, his curiosity shifting into admiration.

"Oscar," he murmured, tracing the name stitched onto a frayed label inside the puppet's shirt.

The letters were uneven, worn with time, but still legible. Just beneath it, a faded stamp bled through the fabric: *Women's International.* His mind drifted back to what he had learned about the power of puppetry—how, for centuries, it had been more than just entertainment. Puppets had been used to captivate, to teach, to influence. In churches, they turned scripture into something a child could see and touch, transforming abstract lessons into stories that lived and breathed. In the right hands, a puppet could break down barriers, soften hardened hearts, and make faith feel tangible in young minds.

This puppet had been a gift, he thought.

A smile stretched across his face.

Emma and Brianna exchanged uneasy glances.

"Please don't tell me you're thinking what I think you're thinking," Emma said.

He chuckled, sliding his hand into the puppet with a practiced flourish. "Meet the newest member of our children's program," he announced, wiggling his fingers to bring it to life.

The puppet's mouth flopped open and shut in exaggerated, jerky movements, its stiff fabric resisting just enough to make the motion feel unnatural.

He caught the way Emma's mouth fell open before she whispered, "Do we have a say in this?"

Irritation flared in Emmanuel's chest, sudden and hot. His expression darkened, the sternness of a father whose authority had been challenged. His posture stiffened, lips parting—then his gaze flicked to Brianna.

The reminder that Emma wasn't alone was enough to steady him. He stopped, swallowing the words before they escaped. Drawing a slow breath, he smoothed his features, forcing the sharp edge of his voice back down where it belonged. The reprimand—firm, corrective—dissolved on his tongue, leaving only a faint bitterness.

But as his eyes met Emma's again, he knew she had seen the shift. And no matter how carefully he smoothed his features, no matter how much he softened his voice, the reprimand stuck. Even unspoken, it hung between them, sharp as if he'd shouted it.

"You can choose," he said softly, "which one of you gets to be the puppeteer."

Emma crossed her arms, rigid, jaw tight as she fixed her eyes on the wall. To Emmanuel, it looked like protest, loud even in silence.

Brianna stepped forward. "I'll do it," she said, her voice steady. "She's not a fan of puppets."

"Perfect," Emmanuel said with a grin, the puppet's floppy mouth mimicking his satisfaction. "You start next Sunday."

"Wait, what?" Brianna said, her voice rising in disbelief. "That's too soon. We need more time to prepare."

"You're smart girls," he replied, waving Oscar's hand playfully as he stepped out of the room. "You'll figure it out."

Chapter Four

T HE CHILL FROM OUTSIDE hit him instantly—sharp, bracing, needling his skin. He didn't shy from it; he welcomed the cold, let it cut through the heaviness that clung to him inside, a shock of air that felt almost cleansing. He needed the clarity, the space to shake off whatever had unsettled him inside. He inhaled deeply, the icy air stinging his lungs as his gaze drifted over the quiet churchyard. The world outside felt still, undisturbed—yet that same unshakable feeling clung to him, threading through the crisp morning air like an unseen presence.

Movement caught his eye.

A stray dog darted along the edge of the rose bushes, its paws clawing at the frozen ground and its nose pressed low as if searching for something buried beneath the frost. Its movements were quick, almost frantic. Mid-motion, it froze. Its body went rigid, tail dropping between its legs as a low whimper escaped its throat. The dog's ears flattened; its gaze locked onto something in the dirt.

Emmanuel stepped toward it, his breath curling in the frigid air. His eyes followed the dog's line of sight until they landed on it:

A toad.

It lay motionless on the cold, brittle grass.

The sight of it sent a cold spike of unease through Emmanuel's gut.

A toad out in the open in the dead of winter?

The thought alone made his stomach tighten. That in itself was unnatural. But a dead toad, found like this, practically revealed to him, carried a deeper weight. It was an omen, a harbinger of something sinister.

"Dios mío," he muttered.

Emmanuel turned his gaze heavenward, his breath visible in the icy air. The sky stretched gray and empty above them, the sun muted behind thick clouds. No birds. No sound. Just the wind, whispering through the bare branches like something unseen had been disturbed.

There was no going back inside. Not now. He had to deal with this.

He lunged for a shovel. The blade cut into the frozen earth with a dull scrape, and he worked in silence, his mind racing with scripture, searching for the right words.

Psalm 91.

Deliverance.

Protection.

Whispering prayers under his breath, he lifted the toad with the shovel and lowered it into the shallow pit. From his pocket, he pulled a small box of matches, his fingers numb from the cold as he struck one. The tiny flame sputtered, then flared to life—fragile, flickering in the wind, a lone beacon against the darkness pressing at the edges of his mind.

The fire caught instantly, racing across the toad's body in an unnatural blaze, as if the creature had been soaked in fuel. Smoke poured upward, thick and acrid, twisting into writhing tendrils that seemed almost alive, as though resisting their own destruction. The scent that filled the air was wrong—not merely the stench of burning flesh, but something fouler, deeper, steeped in rot.

Emmanuel's prayers grew louder, more urgent.

"Deliver us from evil. Protect us from that which seeks to harm. Let no darkness take root here."

The flames danced higher, crackling, before suddenly snuffing out. No lingering embers. No smoldering remains. Not even ashes left behind.

The air in the Sunday School room felt heavy, charged with unspoken tension. What was usually a refuge of laughter and joyful chaos now seemed hollow, stripped of its warmth. The children's voices—normally bright and bubbling with wonder—were subdued, dulled to uneasy whispers.

Brianna moved carefully among them, her smile practiced. On most days, her presence could turn worry into giggles, fear into play. But today, their unease pressed down on her too, thinning the confidence she usually carried with ease.

Her gaze drifted to Jonah. The boy's stillness unsettled her. Normally, he was a whirlwind of energy—his small frame always in motion, words tumbling out as if his thoughts were too big to be contained. Now he sat cross-legged on the floor, strangely still, his eyes fixed on nothing. The spark that usually lit him was gone. He looked weighed down, older somehow, as if something pressed on him that no child should carry.

"Hey, bud, you doing okay?" Brianna asked, crouching beside him. She smoothed a hand through his chestnut curls, hoping to ease whatever shadow hung over him.

Jonah's hazel eyes flicked up, wide and anxious. His fingers twisted at the hem of his overalls. "Is Oscar really going to be in here with us... in this room... next Sunday?"

Brianna forced a smile, though it wavered at the edges. "Yes... isn't that exciting?" she said softly, her tone careful, fragile—like the wrong inflection might shatter the thin veneer of reassurance she was struggling to hold together.

Even to her own ears, the words rang hollow, the cheer brittle.

Jonah scrunched his nose and gave a small shake of his head. His voice dropped to a whisper, as though speaking too loudly might make the puppet hear him. "I really, really, really don't like him."

"That's only because you don't know him," Brianna replied, her tone light but stretched thin. "Once you get to know him, I think you'll absolutely love him."

She flicked a glance at Emma, silently begging for backup—a nod, a smile, any lifeline to prop up her faltering reassurance.

"Isn't that right, Emma?" she asked, urgency threading her voice.

But Emma sat stiffly, shoulders tight, gaze distant. To Brianna, it was as if she hadn't shaken off the puppet's shadow. Brianna nudged her gently, her own smile faltering.

"Emma? Isn't that right?" she repeated.

Emma blinked, her head jerking sharply, like someone startled awake. When she spoke, her voice came louder than intended, brittle at the edges. She cleared her throat and forced a smile. "Right."

Brianna's gaze wandered to the walls, plastered with drawings in cheerful disarray. Crayon suns, stick figures, and rainbows overlapped in a patchwork of color—but her eyes caught on the whales. Dozens of them, shaded in every blue and gray, each one signed in Jonah's wobbly handwriting. The repetition tugged at her. She seized on it, leaning closer, as if anchoring herself in something familiar.

"Hey," she said gently, "you like to draw, don't you?"

Jonah gave a quick nod, his small fingers still twisting the hem of his overalls.

"How about we skip the lesson today and go straight to the fun stuff?"

His face brightened, eyes widening. "You mean I can draw? Now?"

"Yes! Go ahead, what are you—"

She didn't even finish before Jonah bolted across the room, his earlier unease falling away in an instant. He skidded to a stop at the activity table, where stacks of construction paper and a rainbow of crayons waited like treasure.

Brianna exhaled, a flicker of relief loosening her chest as Jonah settled in. But the calm barely had time to take root.

A gentle tug at her leg pulled her back. She looked down to find Janie staring up at her, wide brown eyes shimmering with worry. Small fingers clutched at Brianna's shirt like an anchor in a storm.

"I'm scared," Janie whimpered, her plump cheeks drawn tight with concern.

Brianna knelt beside her, brushing away a stray tear. "What are you scared of?"

Janie hesitated, then raised a trembling finger toward the mural painted across the wall—Noah's ark, animals paired off in frozen play.

"The giraffe," she whispered. "Its teeth look mean... and its neck is too long."

Brianna gave a soft chuckle. "Tell you what—want a piggyback ride?"

Janie's face brightened, and she nodded eagerly.

"Come on, saddle up," Brianna said, lifting her effortlessly onto her back. Janie giggled, arms wrapping tight around Brianna's shoulders, her small weight warm and grounding.

"Let's go check on Jonah."

She carried her across the room, but the girl's laughter trailed off as they neared Jonah at the activity table. He hunched low, his small frame rigid, a crayon carving across the page in jagged strokes. The sound grated—too hard, too deliberate—like scratching from something desperate to break free.

Relief flickered again in Brianna's chest. At least Jonah was busy. At least he wasn't whispering about Oscar.

But then her gaze dropped to the page.

Her relief curdled.

The drawing twisted in front of her, unsettling in a way she couldn't name. A heaviness pressed against her chest, growing with every second she stared, as though the paper carried something it never should.

Her breath caught. The words tore out before she could stop them—sharp, urgent:

"Emma! I need you to come look at this—now!"

Chapter Five

THE DEEP RUMBLE OF THE BASS GUITAR vibrated through the packed sanctuary, its steady pulse reverberating off the walls like a heartbeat. The faint squeal of guitar strings blended with the low murmur of the congregation, a quiet prelude to the coming service. Onstage, musicians moved with focused precision, adjusting their instruments, testing notes that hung briefly in the charged air before dissolving into the expectant hush. Families shifted in their seats, whispered conversations crackling softly—like static before a storm.

The room was thick with expectation, tension woven into the familiar rituals of Sunday morning as the congregation waited for the service to begin. The hum of voices faded, replaced by a reverent stillness. Emmanuel stepped up to the podium, his stride quick and purposeful, exuding a quiet authority that needed no announcement. Reaching the lectern, he gripped its edges, fingers pressing into the worn wood. The sound of his polished shoes tapping softly against the carpeted stage was nearly inaudible over the hush.

Brianna and Emma stood from their seats in the first row. The movement was subtle, but Emmanuel noticed the children stir, as if recognizing the unspoken cue to follow them to Sunday School. They began to rise, eager chatter blending with the soft rustle of fabric.

Emmanuel's voice cut through the room—commanding, firm. "Hold on—stay put, kids."

The microphone carried his words with undeniable weight, silencing the room in an instant.

The children froze, puzzled glances darting between them.

Emmanuel cleared his throat and adjusted the microphone. "This will just take a moment," he said, his gaze sweeping the congregation. "I have an exciting announcement, and I want the kids to hear it."

Announcements were usually saved for the end of the service, a quiet formality before dismissal. The fact that one was coming now jolted the congregation from routine. A ripple of curiosity stirred through the pews, faint at first, then spreading outward in waves. Heads tilted, whispers flitted between neighbors, and questioning glances darted across the sanctuary as anticipation swelled.

A small smile tugged at Emmanuel's mouth. He had their full attention now.

"We have a new member of the congregation I'd like to introduce to you," he said.

Around the sanctuary, heads turned, eyes scanning for an unfamiliar face. Emmanuel followed their searching looks, anticipation curling tighter in his chest.

He bent down behind the lectern, his hand disappearing briefly before he rose again. With practiced ease, he slipped his arm into the hollow end of the puppet, anticipation humming inside him. He was excited about the unveiling, confident in its purpose.

"This is Oscar," he said, lifting it for all to see. The puppet's black, vacant eyes stared out over the congregation, its grin frozen, unsettling. Its garish red hair swayed slightly with his movement, the striped sweater draped loosely over its rigid frame.

The room fell silent.

The energy shifted—sharp, uneasy. No laughter. No amused smiles. Just wide, unblinking eyes fixed on the puppet in stunned, almost unnerving quiet.

Emmanuel's confidence wavered, but he pressed on. "I'm happy to announce that Oscar is joining Emma and Brianna in our children's ministry."

A sharp cry split the silence.

A woman in the front row jolted to her feet, clutching her four-year-old daughter tight against her chest.

"I'm so sorry," she murmured, her face pale as she hurried toward the exit. The little girl whimpered, fingers knotted in her mother's sweater, her gaze fixed unblinking on the puppet.

Their footsteps faded, the child's sobs echoing long after the doors closed. Emmanuel blinked, struggling to make sense of it.

It couldn't possibly be because of the puppet.

With a forced smile, he pressed on.

"Emma and Brianna will be preparing Oscar with engaging content for the kids, starting next week."

Another wail pierced the air...

Then another.

The sobs spread like wildfire, cascading through the pews.

Emmanuel's smile faltered. He turned to Emma and Brianna. "You are dismissed," he said quietly, stuffing the puppet back into the lectern.

"Let's go, kids," Emma murmured, her voice soft but steady as she and Brianna guided the little ones out with gentle reassurances. He listened as their whispers faded down the hall, the sanctuary seeming suddenly quieter, emptier.

The children were gone now. Emmanuel swallowed hard, throat dry as his hands tightened on the podium. For a moment, he steadied himself against the wood before lifting his eyes to the congregation.

"I have to admit—that wasn't the response I was expecting," he said, his attempt at humor weak.

A few nervous chuckles rippled through the room.

Now you laugh, he thought bitterly.

His gaze shifted to the musicians, instruments in hand, waiting. But the tension in the air kept him rooted.

Straightening, he forced authority back into his voice. "I want to remind everyone that we're all human. We make mistakes."

"Amen," came a scattered reply, the energy still subdued.

"Perhaps I went about this the wrong way. I should've consulted with you about the puppet first, and for that, I apologize."

His gaze swept the pews, searching for a response. Silence stretched, heavy, pressing against the walls.

A hand lifted slowly.

Emmanuel exhaled, relief loosening the knot in his chest. "Brother Byron, yes?"

Byron cleared his throat as he rose, his tall frame commanding attention. "If I may, Pastor," he said carefully, voice deep and measured. "The puppet just caught me off guard, that's all."

Murmurs rippled through the pews—low, uncertain, tinged with agreement.

Byron rubbed his jaw, then gave a deliberate nod. "But I think Oscar will be good for the kids."

The words lingered, smoothing the edges of tension just enough. A few heads bobbed in agreement.

Emmanuel nodded, some of his tension easing.

Another hand lifted near the front.

"Yes, Sister Jillian?" he said.

Jillian smiled nervously. "I agree... And I'm sorry again about Janie crying earlier. She's just been fussy lately. Probably going through a growth spurt."

Emmanuel felt a flicker of hope. "Very well, then," he said, voice steadier. "Let's give it a shot. And spread the word—Oscar might just be the shake-up this church needs."

He stood at the lectern as the congregation's mood began to lighten—shoulders loosening, chuckles softening the air, hesitant smiles forming. Yet, beneath the surface, Emmanuel couldn't shake the sense that something was off. Subtle, almost imperceptible. Like a ripple beneath still water.

A shift.

He exhaled sharply, pushing the thought aside. Straightening his shoulders, he cleared his throat.

"Let us continue with the service," he said. "Brother Daniel will be delivering this morning's teaching."

Polite applause followed as Daniel rose and made his way to the lectern.

Emmanuel clasped his hand firmly.

"Sorry about Janie," Daniel murmured. "Jillian and I will talk to her when we get home."

"No worries," Emmanuel replied, though the words felt automatic. He exhaled slowly, the weight in his chest refusing to lift. "I need some air. I'll be back in a minute."

Chapter Six

THE DINING ROOM WAS QUIET, broken only by the faint clink of cutlery against porcelain. Late afternoon light slanted through the tall windows, gilding the tablecloth in a pale, fading glow. Brianna sat across from Emma, her fingers circling the rim of her glass in restless silence. Emma barely touched the turkey sandwich and side salad Brianna had prepared, pushing the food around her plate more than eating it.

Brianna told herself not to stare, but she couldn't help it. The silence between them carried weight, heavy and unspoken. She felt it pressing in, seeping into her chest the way Emma's moods always did—like secondhand smoke she couldn't stop breathing in. Emma's shoulders were too tight, her eyes fixed too carefully on the plate.

Brianna's pulse quickened. She needed to know.

"What did your dad say when you told him about Jonah's drawing?" Brianna asked.

She leaned in across the table, elbows brushing the wood as she tried to catch Emma's eyes, searching for something—an explanation, reassurance, anything. But the image of that drawing clung to her mind, sharp and invasive. The heavy lines, the jagged shapes—none of it looked like the clumsy scribbles of a child. That drawing wasn't normal. And Emma's silence wasn't, either.

"Well? What did your dad have to say?"

"I haven't told him yet," Emma replied.

"Em, why not?" Brianna asked, disappointment bleeding through her voice.

Emma exhaled sharply. "Relax, I intend to. He was busy."

Brianna blinked, thrown off balance. Confusion prickled at her, a tangle of frustration and disbelief. Her brows knit as she leaned back slightly, searching Emma's face for a clue, for some logic that would make sense of it. Why Jonah's strange drawing seemed safe to bring up, but something as ordinary as a toad was treated like forbidden ground.

"You're going to tell him about Jonah's creepy drawing, but you won't mention the toad?" She shifted in her seat, restless, her knee bouncing under the table. "I don't get it, Em. Help me understand what's off-limits."

Emma flinched, the reaction small but sharp. Her fork stilled halfway to her plate, fingers tightening around the handle. She looked up, eyes flashing, and the words snapped out:

"You think I know what's off-limits?" Her voice trembled, equal parts anger and exhaustion. "You think I can—what—hand over a list of topics to avoid?"

"No, Em—that's not what I mean. I just meant—"

"I wish you would have stood up to him," Emma interrupted, her voice quieter now, words laced with something raw. "I wish you could have done it for me."

Brianna's stomach twisted, a knot of unease tightening until it was hard to breathe. She had thought about it—standing her ground, pushing back when Emmanuel gave his quiet but absolute orders about working with the puppet. The words had burned on her tongue more than once, ready to spill out. But when the moment came, her courage faltered.

He was her pastor. He was Emma's father. A man she respected, even admired. Defying him felt unthinkable, like stepping out of line in a place where the rules weren't hers to question. The weight of that reverence pressed against her ribs, hot and smothering, until guilt seeped through her chest like smoke.

Her eyes dropped to the table, unable to meet Emma's. "I'm sorry," she murmured, the words barely audible. "It's just... it's not my place. He's not my father."

Even as the words left her mouth, they tasted hollow. A shield. An excuse. And she hated herself for it.

Emma lowered her gaze, but the tension still radiated from her. Brianna felt it instantly, the storm beneath the surface—silent, but undeniable. She always caught these shifts, the currents no one else seemed to notice.

Her mother had once called it empathy, even a gift. To Brianna, it had always felt more complicated. What sounded mystical in childhood had, over time, revealed itself as a double-edged sword. She could feel what others felt with startling intensity, her own emotions blurring with theirs until it was hard to tell where one ended and the other began. At its best, it was a bridge—allowing her to comfort, to understand, to connect in ways few people could. At its worst, it was a burden she carried whether she wanted to or not—especially in moments like this, when Emma's emotions clawed at her as though they were her own.

"I just wish you could talk to him," Brianna said. "Tell him you don't want to do this. He can't force you."

Emma raised her brows. "Oh, can't he?" she said incredulously.

My dad would never force me, Brianna thought.

"You know we don't have to do this, right?" she said, her voice softer now, threading through the thick tension that clung to the air. "I mean, he can't force us both."

The words hovered between them, an invitation to step back, to escape before they crossed a line they couldn't return from.

Brianna's eyes followed Emma's, landing on the case sitting before them. Emma's gaze was heavy, unblinking, fixed on it as though it were a coffin—sealed, inescapable. Brianna's throat tightened at the sight, at the hollowness in Emma's face, the way she looked emptied out, already mourning what came next.

Emma's voice, barely more than a whisper, cut through the silence. "You have a choice. I don't."

Chapter Seven

BYRON SAT IN THE WORN ARMCHAIR of Jonah's mother's living room, gripping the boy's drawing in his hands. A shadow figure loomed on the page, drawn almost entirely in thick black crayon. Jagged red slashes tore across its head, rising like flames—a crown of fire etched in frantic strokes. Its spindly fingers stretched downward, poised to snatch the stick-figure boy huddled beneath it. The boy was little more than a handful of lines, yet his tiny arms were flung upward in desperate protest. The drawing was crude, childlike—but not innocent.

Across the coffee table, the drawings sprawled in chaotic layers, edges curling, pages overlapping. Each one carried the same image—again and again. Sometimes the boy cowered, arms raised. Sometimes he ran, stick legs stretched in frantic escape. But the shadow was always there. Always looming. Always crowned in fire.

"There are hundreds of them," Byron murmured.

"He started drawing them when we got home from church today," Jonah's mother said, her voice frayed and trembling. "He hasn't stopped. I've tried everything—I yelled, begged, bargained, bribed—but he won't stop. Not even to eat."

Byron watched her carefully as she spoke.

Her shoulders sagged, her frame folding inward, hands tugging absently at the hem of her sweater. Her face looked drawn, pale, dark circles carved beneath her eyes. She seemed like a woman hollowed out by fear and fatigue, barely holding herself upright. The sight struck him with an almost physical force, too familiar. He recognized it—the look of someone haunted, helpless, teetering on the edge. The same look that had stared back at him in the mirror when his own daughter had been sick. The memory gnawed at him, twining with the present until it was hard to breathe.

She turned to Emmanuel.

"Pastor, do you think something demonic is going on?"

Emmanuel's voice was gentle, almost soothing. "Children often create imaginary friends."

But Byron caught the way his gaze lingered on the fiery crown etched across the page. The pause stretched too long, the look too intent. His words urged caution, but his eyes betrayed something else—unease.

Byron wanted to agree, to accept the easy explanation. But the sheer number of sketches made his stomach knot. Logic faltered under the weight of that repetition.

He cleared his throat. "Has he ever acted like this before?"

She hesitated, her eyes flicking toward the corner.

Jonah sat hunched at his activity table, small shoulders rigid. His head drooped forward, casting his face in shadow, and his hand moved feverishly across the page. He gripped the crayon too tightly, carving frantic lines. Not the free strokes of play, Byron thought, but something urgent. Desperate.

"Nothing like this," she whispered.

"Has Jonah said anything about these drawings? Why he's making them? What they mean?" Emmanuel asked.

"Only that he has to keep drawing," she said, her voice brittle. "He says if he stops, the monster in the pictures won't leave."

"May we speak to him?" Emmanuel asked.

She nodded, stepping aside.

Byron followed Emmanuel to the table, careful not to break the taut quiet of the room. Jonah's hand kept moving, paper scraping under the crayon's force.

They leaned in closer.

The shadowy figure reemerged on the page, larger now—its limbs stretching unnaturally wide, clawing at the edges of the paper as though it wanted out.

Above it, the fiery crown blazed brighter, strokes of red and orange exploding outward in violent bursts.

Then Byron's eyes caught on something else. Smears. Dark, wet blotches staining the page—too thick for crayon, too raw for marker.

His gaze shot to Jonah's hand. Crimson streaked across his small fingers, glistening in the light.

"He's bleeding!" Byron's voice ripped out, ragged with panic.

Jonah's mother bolted toward the kitchen, footsteps pounding against the tile. She returned almost instantly, clutching gauze and bandages in trembling hands. The supplies slipped, nearly tumbling to the floor as she lunged for her son.

"Stop, Jonah! Please, stop!" she cried, voice cracking as she tried to catch his flailing wrists. His small arms lashed wildly, slick with blood, scattering streaks across the paper and desk.

"I can't!" Jonah shrieked, his voice high with desperation. His eyes blazed with feverish intensity as he fought against her grip. "I need to keep drawing!"

Byron moved without thinking. Instinct carried him forward, arms wrapping around Jonah and hauling him up. To anyone watching, it might have seemed effortless—a grown man lifting a five-year-old. But the illusion shattered the moment Jonah twisted in his grip.

The boy's strength was far more than he had bargained for. Muscles strained beneath small limbs, his body bucking with a ferocity that made Byron's teeth clench. He held tighter, bracing himself, but the fight felt less like restraining a child and more like grappling something older, darker, wearing a child's skin.

A guttural growl ripped from Jonah's throat—raw, feral. It vibrated against Byron's chest, more beast than boy. Jonah's head snapped from side to side, violent and unnatural, teeth flashing, saliva catching in the light.

"Hold him steady!" Emmanuel barked, moving in to catch Jonah's arms.

Byron tightened his hold, muscles straining. Sweat beaded at his temple. "He's stronger than he looks," he ground out.

"Just focus," Emmanuel urged. "He's just a child."

Jonah's mother hovered nearby, fumbling with the gauze, tears spilling freely. Her pallor was stark, her breaths ragged. Byron caught the way her fingers slipped, the bandages tumbling to the floor.

Emmanuel hissed as Jonah's nails raked across his arm, crimson welling instantly. Still, the pastor pinned the boy's wrists down with steady determination. "Don't worry about me," Emmanuel said, though urgency sharpened his tone.

Jonah's screams rose to a piercing wail, rattling the air, vibrating through Byron's chest. His body convulsed, eyes rolling white before fixing on nothing Byron could see.

"I'm done! I'm done!" Jonah's mother gasped, finally knotting the bandage.

Byron eased his grip. Jonah tore free, bolting back to the table. He moved with a feral speed that froze Byron in place. The boy sat, calm now, gripping a red crayon in his bandaged hand. He bent over the page, as if nothing had happened, as if nothing else in the room existed.

Byron's pulse pounded. He had restrained plenty of grown men in his time, but nothing compared to that.

Emmanuel crouched low, his voice measured. "Tell me, Jonah. Why so many drawings? Don't you think you've made enough for one day?"

Jonah's hand stilled. Slowly, his head turned. His eyes met Emmanuel's with a hollow intensity that made Byron's skin prickle.

"I'm not done yet," Jonah said flatly.

Byron's stomach dropped.

Emmanuel's voice softened. "If not now, then when?"

"When he's out of my head," Jonah replied.

Silence gripped the room.

Byron felt it press against his ribs, heavy, suffocating.

Emmanuel asked quietly, "Who's in your head, Jonah?"

The boy blinked, lips parting. "The man with the fire hair," he said. He cocked his head slightly, as if tilting his ear toward some whisper the others couldn't hear. "He says I have to keep drawing."

Byron shivered. The air felt colder, shadows stretching longer, the light dimming around them.

The crayon slipped from Jonah's hand and rolled off the table, hitting the floor with a dull, final thud.

"No," Jonah said, his voice flat, unnervingly calm. "He's in control."

Chapter Eight

THE RUMBLING OF THE APPROACHING STORM deepened, rolling through the night like distant thunder. Wind whistled against the windows, rattling them faintly—a familiar sound, one that usually lulled Daniel into sleep. But tonight, something was different. His eyes shot open at the sharp creak of metal cutting through the quiet.

The house was prone to moans and groans, a symphony of age he'd long since accepted. But this was different.

He exhaled slowly, squeezing his eyes shut, unwilling to abandon the fragile embrace of rest. Maybe it was nothing. Maybe, if he ignored it, the sound would vanish beneath the wind and thunder.

Then it came again. A long, slow creak—closer this time—jagged and intrusive.

Daniel's eyes flicked open. His hand groped for his phone on the nightstand. The screen lit with a soft glow:

11:30 PM.

He turned his head toward Jillian. Normally a light sleeper, she lay undisturbed, her breathing deep and even. The stillness unsettled him. She always woke at the faintest sound—except now.

The creaking persisted, sharper now, like an old hinge straining. Daniel swung his legs over the mattress, the cool floor grounding him. He strained to listen. Under the bedroom door, a thin band of light cast faint, erratic shadows.

Someone's in the house, he thought, pulse quickening.

He rose carefully, each step measured to avoid the betraying creak of a floorboard. The room felt unnaturally still, the only sound the storm beyond the walls. His breath thinned as he neared the door. His hand hovered over the knob, fingertips grazing the cold metal. His pulse drummed in his ears.

"Get a grip," he whispered. But the words did little to steady him.

The light under the door was steady now. No shifting shadows. He tightened his grip on the knob, twisting it slowly. The latch released with a soft click.

His body jolted.

Janie.

She stood just outside the door. Relief rushed him, a quiet chuckle escaping under his breath. His mind had spun shadows into menace again. Maybe it was the old house next door that haunted him still, Emmanuel's place, with its whispered history. The memory of that night—what they had faced—never fully left him. It lay dormant, waiting for the quiet hours to stir. Still, he reminded himself, not everything that came from that house was dark. It had brought him to Jillian, after all.

"What are you doing up, sweetheart?" he asked softly, stepping closer.

She didn't answer.

Her long brown hair hung in messy strands across her face, arms limp at her sides. Her small figure stood unnervingly still in the glow of the hallway nightlight. He brushed her hair back. Her cheeks were warm and dimpled, lips soft and rosy. But her eyes... her gaze didn't land on him. It passed through, unfocused, fixed somewhere far beyond.

"Janie?" he said, crouching low.

Her lips parted. No words—only breath.

Slowly, she lifted her arms, fingers quivering as though tugged by invisible strings. The hem of her nightgown shifted with the movement, brushing against her legs and catching a faint shimmer in the lamplight. Not a word escaped her lips. She drifted past him, each step deliberate, unnervingly stiff, as though her body no longer belonged to her. Without hesitation, she climbed into his bed, her motions rigid and mechanical, the mattress sighing beneath her slight weight.

She's sleepwalking.

He stepped back into the room, his gaze fixed on Janie as if looking away might break some fragile tether. Crossing to the corner, he lowered himself into the wooden rocking chair—Jillian's old relic, its joints creaking in quiet protest. His eyes never strayed, tracking the small rise and fall of Janie's chest.

Daniel waited, minutes dragging like hours, before deciding he couldn't leave her there. Outside, the storm swelled. Rain hammered the windows, wind keening through the eaves, the glass rattling with a fury that felt less like weather and more like a warning.

Janie lay curled atop the blankets, her limbs wound tight, her body too rigid for sleep. No soft sighs, no shifting beneath the covers—only a tense stillness, as if she were bracing against something unseen pressing in from the dark.

With a quiet exhale, Daniel rose. He moved carefully, careful to silence the groan of the rocking chair, careful not to stir Jillian. Step by step, he closed the distance. His hands steadied as he leaned over the bed, reaching for Janie.

His fingers brushed her arm.

Janie's eyes snapped open.

For a heartbeat, Daniel froze. His mind refused to process what he was seeing—her pupils blown wide, swallowing the whites, her gaze fixed straight through him as if he weren't there at all. The room seemed to tighten around them, the storm outside fading beneath the sudden roar of his own pulse.

No flicker of recognition. No sleepy confusion. Just that unblinking stare.

A chill spread through his chest, sharp and immediate.

"Janie?" Daniel whispered. His pulse thundered. "Sweetheart?"

She didn't blink. Didn't move. Just stared—through him, not at him. For a moment, he thought she might still be asleep, trapped in a waking dream.

Then her expression shifted. Slowly. A frown spread across her face, too deep, too deliberate.

"Help... me," she whimpered. Her voice was hollow, as if echoing from somewhere distant.

Jillian stirred, her voice groggy but edged with concern. "Is Janie having a bad dream?" She pushed up, eyes narrowing against the low light.

"I... I don't know," Daniel stammered. He glanced between wife and daughter. "It seems like she's awake."

"Help me," Janie cried again, sharper now, her voice breaking through the storm's relentless battering.

Daniel's breath caught. The hair on his arms rose.

Her cry twisted, shifting into a sound no child should make. A jagged braid of laughter and sobs spilled from her lips, starting as a faint giggle before rising into a shrill, maniacal pitch. Daniel's stomach turned. That wasn't Janie's laugh. Not the bubbling giggles of his little girl. This was warped, sharp, wrong.

Her body shuddered, limbs trembling as if caught in an unseen struggle. Her chest heaved, breaths rasping in jagged bursts. Then came the exhalations—long, guttural, dragging out of her small body as if something older, darker, forced its way through.

"Something's wrong," Jillian said, her voice tighter now.

"I... I don't know," Daniel whispered, frozen. His hands hovered inches from Janie's trembling shoulders, terrified to touch her, terrified not to.

"I'm not asking—*I'm telling you*," Jillian said. "Something's wrong!"

Chapter Nine

EMMA SHIFTED IN HER SEAT, skin prickling as her gaze locked on Oscar at the head of the table. Its head lolled at an unnatural angle, the painted grin stretched too wide—a parody of joy and emptiness. Its striped sweater seemed to twist and writhe, an illusion of movement. The chandelier light flickered across its glossy black eyes, catching just enough to make them shimmer—as if something behind them was shifting. She blinked hard. A trick of the light. A reflection. That's all. But the feeling refused to fade.

"Let's get this over with," Emma said, her stomach churning.

She usually felt safe at Brianna's—the cozy house, the easy laughter, the unspoken understanding. Sometimes it felt more like home than her own. But tonight that safety was gone. The air pressed in, the walls seeming to lean closer. Each breath took effort, like pulling air through water.

"I feel like it's watching me," she whispered, her voice thin and frayed.

Across the table, Brianna swallowed—hesitation flashed in her eyes. "It's just a puppet," she said, but the words sounded brittle.

Emma couldn't pull her gaze from the puppet, every nerve waiting for Oscar to betray her dread.

And then it did.

Her chair clattered backward as she scrambled up, a ragged gasp tearing free. She hit the floor hard, palms smacking the boards.

"Em!" Brianna rushed toward her. "What happened? What's wrong?"

Emma fought for air as she rasped, "It moved."

Brianna's eyes darting to the puppet, still perched on the chair.

"You're saying Oscar moved?"

"I'm telling you—I saw it. It turned its head and looked right at me."

"No," Brianna said sharply.

"Why would I lie about this?"

"I'm not saying you're lying," Brianna snapped. "I'm saying the mind sees what it expects to see."

"What the hell is that supposed to mean?" Emma shot back.

"It means our minds fill in the gaps. It's natural."

Emma scoffed. "Science, of course. Hate to break it to you, but science doesn't explain everything."

"I beg to—"

"I'm going to be sick," Emma cut in.

"Em, come on—"

Emma shoved herself up, knees trembling as she staggered down the hall. Her bare feet slapped the hardwood, sharp against the hush between thunderclaps outside. Panic hauled her forward—half-running, half-stumbling—until she reached the bathroom. She twisted the knob and fell to her knees at the toilet.

Brianna appeared behind her, breathless. One hand gathered Emma's hair, pulling damp strands from her face; the other steadied her shoulder through the spasms.

"I saw it move," Emma choked between heaves. "I know what I saw."

"Okay, okay," Brianna said quickly, smoothing Emma's hair with a shaky hand. The words came too fast, too soft—soothing, not agreeing.

Emma lifted her gaze, searching Brianna's face. She knew her well enough to catch the cracks: the quick slide of her eyes, the tight press of her mouth. Brianna wasn't agreeing. She was placating.

"It's top-heavy," Brianna added. She handed over a towel. "Don't you think it's at least feasible that gravity had anything to do with it?"

Emma yanked the towel a little too hard, the fabric twisting between damp fingers. She pressed it to her mouth, mind racing as she stared at the tile. Brianna's neat explanation hung in the air like a bow tied around something too messy to contain.

It reminded her of childhood—her father leaning down, steady-eyed, reasoning away shadows in her room or the cold under the door: *It's just the house settling. Just the pipes. Just your imagination.* But she remembered those nights, the gooseflesh, the certainty that something unseen was there.

And now Brianna echoed him. Logic where logic didn't belong.

Emma's grip on the towel tightened until her knuckles ached. What she'd seen wasn't nerves. The way Oscar moved—slow, precise, deliberate—made her doubt her own sanity.

Still, her voice softened. "I guess it's a possibility," she said at last, the words tasting like ash.

Brianna cleaned quickly, the lemon spray stinging the air. "What was that about?" she asked.

"Nerves, I guess," Emma muttered.

"So are we going to do this?" Brianna's tone sat somewhere between daring and weary.

"Like I said—I don't have a choice," Emma said. Heavy words, but they got her on her feet.

Reluctantly, she followed Brianna back down the hall. Each step toward the dining room tightened the knot in her stomach.

At the table, Brianna reached for Oscar. Its limp body sagged, the striped sweater crumpling like dead weight. The head tilted; the grin stayed fixed. Brianna swallowed and set it between them.

"It needs a voice," she said, her tone clipped.

Silence stretched. Emma's mind scraped for words and found none. Brianna didn't speak either.

"Just wear it," Emma said finally, flat and resigned. "See what comes to you."

Brianna drew a breath and slid her hand up the back of the sweater. "Shit!" she yelped, jerking away. Her elbow slammed the table edge, glasses rattling.

"Not funny, Brie," Emma snapped.

Brianna held up her hand. Angry red flushed across her skin, swelling as Emma watched.

"Holy— We need to get you to the ER," Emma blurted, nearly toppling her chair.

Brianna shook her head, breath unsteady. "No. I just need cold water." She stumbled into the kitchen and opened the faucet.

Emma grabbed a bowl. "I'll get you some ice."

"No," Brianna said quickly. "My mom says ice makes burns worse. You're supposed to use cool water."

Emma stared at the swelling. "How did this even happen?"

"I don't know," Brianna murmured, though her eyes cut toward Oscar.

"Maybe static electricity?" Emma offered, clinging to the very logic she'd mocked minutes earlier.

Brianna shook her head, voice flat, almost clinical. "Static electricity isn't capable of this." She turned her hand slowly, studying the angry skin as if it were someone else's. The absorbed focus read more analytical than afraid.

Emma's phone chimed, slicing the silence. She fumbled it out, pulse still ragged. "Hi, Dad."

"Mija," her father said—calm, weighted. "You'll be staying at the Browns' tonight."

Emma's stomach knotted. "A sleepover? Why?" It came out sharper than she meant. He never allowed sleepovers. Not when she was little and begged. Not at Brianna's, not anywhere. Home at night—that was the rule. Permission felt less like freedom than warning.

"Yes," he said evenly. "I'll be out late with Byron, and I don't want your mother driving to pick you up in this weather."

"Where are you going?" Unease bled into her voice.

"We're going to Daniel's for prayer. It may be a late night."

Her heart skipped. "Why?"

Silence.

"Dad?"

"It's Janie," he said at last.

Emma's breath caught. "Janie? Is she okay?"

"She's fine," he answered quickly, but the pause before told on him. "She's probably just having a nightmare. You know—first-time parent stuff."

"But Jillian's no first-time parent," she said, low but firm. "I've known her a long time. She's great with kids. If Daniel's worried enough to call you, something's really wrong."

"You know, Janie was really shaken up today at church," Brianna said. "I've never seen her like that."

Emma glanced at her. Concern tightened Brianna's brow; her mouth set in a thin line. Not just worry—recognition. Something was wrong.

"Wanna check it out?" Brianna asked, grabbing her phone and keys.

"What about your mom? Won't she worry if we're not here when she gets home?"

"She's on the night shift. We'll be back before she is."

Emma hesitated, then nodded. "Okay. Let's go."

The words sounded braver than she felt. They moved toward the door, the quiet of the house pressing close. Outside, the storm groaned through the eaves, rattling the windows as if warning them back.

Emma's gaze slid toward the dining room, a cold unease crawling her spine. Yes, her father had warned against driving in this weather. But the storm outside was danger she could see. Inside was danger that was watching.

Chapter Ten

S NOW HAMMERED EMMANUEL'S WINDSHIELD, the wipers squealing as they fought to keep pace with the storm. The road ahead stretched desolate and narrow, flanked by skeletal trees whose branches clawed at the night sky, lit only in fractured flashes by his headlights. Gravestones surfaced in the beam—brief, ghostly shapes—before sinking back into darkness as he passed Mount Carmel Cemetery. The sight chilled him, though whether from the cold or something deeper, he couldn't say. The cemetery stood as a grim landmark, a mute reminder that Daniel's house lay close.

Emmanuel eased the car alongside Byron's, the headlights casting pale beams across the snow-blanketed yard. He turned into the driveway, tires crunching through fresh powder until the car rolled to a stop.

Daniel stood on the porch hunched against the cold, arms wrapped tightly around himself. Even from the car, Emmanuel noted the sag in his shoulders, the pallor of his face, the heaviness in his posture. He looked worn down, like a man pressed under something unseen.

Clutching his Bible, Emmanuel stepped out of the car. The frigid air stole his breath before he trudged up the porch steps.

"How are you holding up?" he asked.

Snow clung to his coat, but before he could brush it off, Daniel opened the door with quiet urgency and ushered him inside.

"I'm okay. It's just... it's hard to see her like this," Daniel said. "Thank you for coming."

Late-night calls for prayer were nothing new. Over the years, Emmanuel had grown used to the phone ringing after midnight, each call a reminder that darkness crept in during quiet hours. Sometimes the voice on the other end was steady but desperate, sometimes ragged with sobs—but always heavy with unraveling lives. House calls, though, were rarer. They were for nights like this, when words over the phone could not pierce the weight pressing on a family.

"Where is she?" Emmanuel asked.

"She's in the bedroom," Daniel replied.

Emmanuel's tone stayed even, almost clinical. "How long has it been going on?"

"Hours now, and it's not letting up."

"Let me see her."

They moved down the hushed hallway, their footsteps muffled against the worn floorboards. Emmanuel felt the air grow heavier with each step. At the bedroom door, Daniel paused. His hand hovered over the knob, fingers trembling. His breath came shallow.

"Brace yourself," he whispered, before pushing the door open.

The acrid stench of urine hit Emmanuel at once. His eyes fixed on Janie—her small body convulsing, sweat plastering hair to her damp skin. The sheets beneath her were soaked and foul, the mattress groaning under the force of her thrashing.

At the foot of the bed, Jillian stood motionless. Her arms hung limp at her sides, her face streaked with tears. She looked hollowed out, her stillness almost unnatural.

"Get away from me!" Janie screamed.

Her voice was raw, jagged with terror. Her body twisted violently against the bed, limbs jerking as though wrenched by something unseen.

Between ragged breaths, a guttural growl tore from her throat. Her face contorted, features warping into an expression so dark it made Emmanuel's stomach clench.

"I don't wanna play!" she cried again, her eyes wide. They darted wildly, tracking empty corners of the room with frantic precision.

With a sudden, unnatural crack, Janie's head twisted toward Emmanuel. Her eyes fixed on him—hard, glassy, unblinking. The weight in that stare hollowed him out. It wasn't a child's gaze. It was older. Hungrier. Something ancient peering from behind her small, innocent face.

"You're a bad guy," she hissed, her voice warped, brittle as broken glass. "Stop pretending you're not."

Her hands jerked up, fingers curling in grotesque spasms, clawing at the air. The motion was puppet-like, stiff and jerking, as though she weren't moving herself at all but being manipulated by something unseen.

The words struck sharper than he expected, needling straight into his gut. Emmanuel had read enough case files, experienced enough accounts to know the tactic: in true possession, the entity never wasted energy on meaningless threats. It went for the jugular. It cut deep with lies wrapped in slivers of truth, personal barbs meant to unravel a man's focus. He had seen hints of it in others—but here, in Janie's trembling body, it carried a venom that chilled him.

Still, he forced a slow, steady breath through his lungs, willing his thoughts into order. He would not give it ground. He would not let the words draw blood.

"I've never seen anything like this," Byron said quietly from the rocking chair, a steady presence amid the chaos.

"She's talking—maybe we can figure out what is going on in her mind," Emmanuel said, voice low. He turned to Jillian. "Has she said anything else in this state?"

Jillian didn't respond. Tears streamed unchecked down her face.

"She said, 'Help me,' before" Daniel answered hoarsely. "And I just feel so helpless, because... I don't know how.

"Don't blame yourself," Emmanuel said. "You need to be strong for her. She's fighting something."

"Fighting something?" Byron asked, his voice weighted. "Are you saying she's fighting a demon?"

"I didn't say that," Emmanuel replied. His voice carried calm authority, though his heart twisted. He wouldn't name it, not aloud, not with Janie lying there. To call it that would feel like surrendering hope—and he couldn't do that.

"Children have fears, anxieties, struggles inside them, just like anyone," he said gently. "Who knows what she's facing. Demon or not, she needs our help."

"How do we help if we don't know what she's dealing with?" Byron asked.

Emmanuel took a breath, drawing the Bible tight to his chest. "The only way we know how," he said. "We pray."

Chapter Eleven

BRIANNA EASED THE CAR along the curb and parked across the narrow street from Paul's house. The tires crunched through frozen slush, the sound sharp in the muffled hush of the storm. She cut the engine, and the headlights dimmed, their glow sinking into the snow like a fading pulse.

Leaning forward, she squinted through the windshield. The driveway was crowded, but the storm had swallowed everything in white—cars buried so deep their identities had been erased, their edges softened until they looked more like mounds of snow than machines. She strained to make out details, searching for a familiar silhouette, but the storm's icy veil blurred every line, rendering the world a shifting mirage of shadow and frost.

"Are you sure we're in the right place?" she asked, glancing in the rearview mirror. Beyond her reflection, the cemetery loomed at the edge of sight, headstones jutting against the snow like jagged teeth gnawing at the horizon.

"I used to live next door—I would know," Emma said, reaching for her phone. She lifted it, the cold glow of the screen lighting her face as she aimed the camera toward the house.

"Can you see anything?" Brianna asked.

"Not a thing," Emma muttered, frustration creeping into her tone. "This thing can't zoom in close enough." With a sigh, she lowered the phone and set it on her lap, the glow of the screen dimming as it slid against the fabric of her jeans.

"Let me try," Brianna said. She dug into her bag and pulled out her sleek new phone. She couldn't hide the flicker of pride as she held it up. "I just got it. It's the Sony Ericsson K800—the same one James Bond had in *Casino Royale*."

"Of course you have the James Bond phone," Emma muttered, disbelief coloring her voice. She gestured toward the house. "Aim it over there—at the window with the pink curtains. It used to be her son's room. I'm guessing it's Janie's now."

Brianna flipped the phone sideways and activated the camera. The screen's glow bled into the darkness, washing the car's interior in cold, artificial light.

Emma leaned closer, her breath fogging the glass, neck craning to see. "Do you see anything?"

"Not yet." Brianna's voice was taut, every syllable strained with focus. Her thumb swept across the controls, steady despite the faint tremor running through her hand. The blurred shapes on the screen sharpened, lines resolving into something more than shadow.

"There's a sliver between the curtains," she whispered. Her pulse quickened. "I think I can make out what's—"

The words died in her throat. Her breath caught, sharp and involuntary. The glow of the screen seemed to pulse brighter, mocking the sudden stillness that had gripped her.

Her heart slammed against her ribs as the scene inside took form.

∘ ∘

Emmanuel stepped closer to Janie, Scripture already burning at the edge of his tongue—ancient words he had summoned in other nights of darkness.

"In the name of the Father, the Son, and the Holy Spirit," he declared, his voice steady, unyielding.

"Stop! Stop! Stop!" Janie shrieked, her cries slicing through the room like shattered glass hurled against stone. Emmanuel's chest tightened at the sound. This wasn't the voice of a child—it was something deeper, raw, primal. A sound that clawed at the soul.

Her small frame convulsed violently against the mattress, limbs jerking with unnatural strength. The springs beneath her groaned in protest, metal grinding as if straining to hold her down. Emmanuel forced himself to steady his breathing, even as every instinct screamed that what he witnessed was more than fever, more than fear.

Beside him, Daniel lurched forward. Emmanuel's eyes tracked the man's trembling hands—hovering inches above his daughter, twitching, curling into fists and unfurling again. The conflict was written in every movement: a father torn between the desperate urge to protect and the terror of making things worse. His whole body shook, grief and helplessness radiating like heat from a furnace.

Emmanuel lifted his gaze and caught the movement. Calm washed over his features, authority rooted in every syllable as he spoke.

"She's okay. Be strong."

Daniel hesitated, chest heaving, then gave a tight nod and drew back, folding himself again into the fragile circle of prayer.

A guttural growl rumbled from deep in Janie's chest. Her body arched taut, limbs straining so violently it looked to Emmanuel as though unseen chains bound her.

His voice grew stronger, defiance rising with every word. "We come before you, Lord, Heavenly Father, asking that you be with Janie, that you comfort her, that you fight for her."

Each phrase left his mouth with the force of conviction, faith cutting against the dark weight pressing into the room.

"Your Word says You will fight for us—we need only be still. For the Lord our God goes with us, to fight for us against our enemies and to give us victory!"

The storm outside raged, wind clawing at the windows, snow pelting the glass in relentless bursts.

"God is our refuge and strength, an ever-present help in trouble," Emmanuel declared. He laid his Bible gently over Janie's chest. The book's weight seemed to still some of her movement, her spasms grinding slower, heavier, as though resistance dragged against them.

She writhed beneath it, but the fight was changing. The violence dulled, her limbs dragging instead of snapping.

Emmanuel drew a small glass bottle of oil from his pocket. As he twisted the cap, a sharp, earthy fragrance filled the air, cutting through the sour staleness. He poured a few drops into his palm, rubbing them warm, never taking his eyes off Janie.

"We are not afraid or discouraged," he said steadily, "because this battle is not ours, but God's."

Leaning closer, he lifted his hand. With reverence, he traced the sign of the cross with his fingertip across her damp forehead. The oil glinted in the flickering light as he pressed his palm to her brow, his other hand resting firmly on the Bible across her chest.

Janie writhed once, then slackened. The violent thrashing ebbed into tremors. Her small body still shook, but less wildly now. A fragile hush settled over the room.

Emmanuel raised his head.

"Pray with me."

Daniel and Jillian stepped forward, hands trembling as they stretched them over their daughter. Byron followed, lips moving in silent plea. Together they formed a circle, their faith pressed outward like a shield.

Emmanuel's voice softened, taking on the cadence of love and pleading.

"Lord, let your light fill this room. We ask for peace—for calm—for Your unending love to surround Janie. Grant her comfort, protect her, and drive out all that is not of You."

Their voices rose together, weaving prayer through the air. Emmanuel felt a shift, the heaviness lifting, the shadows drawing back. Yet even as the room eased, he sensed it still—lingering at the edges...

Whatever had come for Janie had not gone far.

Chapter Twelve

T HE PHONE SLIPPED FROM BRIANNA'S grasp, tumbling to the floorboard with a muted thud that seemed unnaturally loud in the storm-muted silence. Emma flinched at the sound, but Brianna didn't move to retrieve it. She didn't move at all. She sat rigid in the seat, her posture frozen, fingers splayed limp across her lap as though the strings that held her together had been cut.

Her eyes stared forward—glassy, vacant, hollow—glistening with a faraway sheen. Not the look of someone lost in thought, but of someone dragged elsewhere, pulled into a place Emma couldn't follow.

A ripple of dread crawled down Emma's spine, each vertebra sparking with cold unease. Her voice slipped out low, steady in tone though her fear betrayed her in the cracks. "What did you see?"

The silence pressed back, thick and impenetrable.

"Brie?" she tried again, sharper this time.

Still nothing. Not a blink.

Emma leaned closer and snapped her fingers sharply in front of Brianna's face.

"Hey—snap out of it!"

The sound cracked through the car's stillness, sharp as a whip, but Brianna didn't even blink. The silence grew unbearable, pressing against Emma's ears until she swore she could hear her own pulse pounding.

Then, all at once, Brianna jolted—a ragged gasp tearing free, violent and desperate, like someone surfacing too quickly from dark water. Her breath came jagged, uneven, chest hitching as her shoulders shuddered under the weight of something Emma couldn't see, something that clung to her like invisible chains.

"What did you see?" Emma demanded, the question sharper now, her patience fraying, fear threading her voice whether she wanted it to or not.

"I... I don't know," Brianna whispered. "I mean, I'm not sure."

Emma bent down, retrieved the phone, and angled it toward the house. Her grip tightened as the frame steadied, the image sharpening slowly. She could see her father and the others, hands linked, forming a circle around the bed.

"It's just a prayer chain," she muttered, more to herself than to Brianna.

"I've never seen anything like it," Brianna whispered.

Emma turned to her. Normally, Brianna never cracked—always collected, always steady. But now her face was pale, her eyes wide. She looked shaken in a way Emma had rarely seen, and Emma felt sure this was no ordinary prayer circle.

"What did you see exactly?" Emma pressed, urgency creeping into her tone.

"I... I don't—" Brianna stammered. Her mouth opened and closed, words refusing to form.

"Did you see Janie?" Emma asked.

Brianna gave a small, shaky nod. "She was on the bed."

"Was she thrashing? Kicking?"

Another nod.

"Showing her teeth?"

"I... I don't know. It's possible." Brianna rubbed her temples, eyes squeezed shut as if replaying the scene burned her from the inside. "She was thrashing a lot. It was hard to tell."

That was enough. Emma felt her suspicions harden into certainty. This wasn't some midnight prayer call for a bad dream—it was one of *those nights*. The kind her father had whispered about in scripture and silence. The kind she had grown up knowing were real, even if no one else wanted to admit it.

She looked at Brianna, pale and rattled, hands still shaking as though the image had clung to her skin.

The truth was, Emma felt it too—the same fear, the same unease coiled tight in her chest. She had just learned to bury it, to shove it deep where no one could see. That didn't make it vanish. It festered there, raw and unhealed, a storm that never really stopped.

Her voice softened. "Do you want me to drive back? You seem... out of it."

Brianna gave a small nod, and together they unbuckled. They switched seats in silence—Emma sliding behind the wheel while Brianna moved to the passenger side, her motions slow and unsteady.

For a while, neither spoke. The silence pressed heavy as Emma turned the key. The engine rumbled, the wipers swept in steady rhythm, and the storm churned outside.

Emma's eyes stayed on the road, but her thoughts slipped elsewhere. She remembered other nights like this—the phone ringing, her father rising from bed, his voice low and urgent in the next room. She'd caught whispers: an addict pleading for salvation, a dying soul begging for one last prayer.

Those were the easy calls—the ones that ended in peace.

But there were others. Nights when his voice sharpened, when his prayers cut like steel. He never said the word around her, but she'd heard enough in the silences to know.

Demonic possession.

She knew he had faced it, cast it out. The details were always hidden, but she'd pieced together enough from fragments and the heaviness in his eyes when he came home.

Beside her, Brianna's shaky breath broke the quiet. "What do you think is wrong with her?"

Emma glanced at her. "Are you serious? Isn't it obvious?"

"No, Emma, it's not."

Emma exhaled sharply, her breath loud in the car. She chose her words carefully; Brianna already looked close to unraveling.

"Listen," she said gently. "My dad knows how to handle this. Janie's going to be okay."

Brianna turned her head toward her. The dashboard lights carved shadows across her pale face. "What kind of thing?"

"You know…"

"No, Emma, I clearly don't. So just tell me already."

Emma hesitated. They were talking about Janie—sweet, bright-eyed Janie. She'd hoped Brianna would connect the dots herself, but that hadn't happened.

"Demonic possession," Emma muttered at last, eyes fixed on the dark ribbon of road. The words came out flat, almost calm—and that calmness chilled her most. "I know it sounds bad," she added quickly, "but it's not like Janie's on her deathbed or anything."

Brianna snapped her head toward her. "Em, that's seriously messed up. You're joking, right?"

"No, I'm not joking," Emma said, voice steady, almost flat. "That's the kind of thing my dad deals with. This isn't the first call—and it won't be the last."

Silence pressed into the car. Emma kept her eyes on the road, but she knew Brianna too well—the quiet wouldn't hold.

"It's just… so messed up," Brianna said finally, her voice tight. "That you'd even suggest something like that—and seem so unbothered." She shifted, fingers twisting in her lap. "I don't like this side of you. I've never seen you like this."

"Like what?" Emma asked, eyes fixed on the dark road unraveling ahead, headlights slicing through sheets of falling snow.

Brianna hesitated, then whispered, "So… *cold.*"

The word cut deeper than Emma expected, sharper than Brianna could have known. Her jaw clenched, teeth grinding. She wanted to fire back, to explain, to insist Brianna didn't understand—but nothing came. The truth swelled in her throat like a stone she couldn't swallow.

She was right. I am cold…

But not by choice.

Hardened by nights when evil had a face, a voice, a presence she could *feel*. Hardened by whispers of demons, by the weight of her father's prayers bleeding through the walls. This wasn't metaphor. It was real—pressing against her life like a shadow she could never outrun. It had carved itself into her, reshaped her until there was no space left for softness.

"You call it *cold*," she said. "But it's just the way the world is."

Chapter Thirteen

T HE NIGHT PRESSED CLOSE, cold and merciless, wrapping around Brianna like a tightening noose. Her hands shook as she fumbled with the key, the metal slick with sweat despite the chill. It slipped once, twice, scraping the lock uselessly.

"Damn it!" The word tore from her, jagged and raw, her breath clouding in the darkness. Her pulse thundered in her ears, every beat louder than the last, drowning out reason.

"Brie, calm down," Emma said. Her voice was low, steady on the surface, though Brianna thought she caught something uneasy beneath it. A hand settled on her shoulder, grounding. "Trust me—you'll feel better once you process it."

Brianna froze.

The key stilled, but her shoulders stayed rigid. Slowly, she turned, eyes wide, her voice sharp.

"Process what? That my best friend thinks a sweet, innocent little girl is possessed?"

Emma shook her head. "You saw it. That wasn't normal, Brianna—and you know it."

Brianna had never seen anything like it—at least not with her own eyes. Whispers, stories, rumors in hushed tones she'd heard before, but this... this was different.

It was real.

Terrifyingly real. Janie's contorted body branded itself into Brianna's mind—spine arched at impossible angles, limbs thrashing with violent abandon. The image refused to loosen its grip; it clung like barbed wire, cutting deeper each time she tried to force it back. It wasn't just a memory of what she'd seen—it was as if she had stood in that room herself, caught in the storm of it. She could almost feel Janie's desperation coursing through her veins, her fear crawling under her skin, her anger and frustration battering against her ribs like a trapped animal.

Her hand shook as she jammed the key toward the lock, the metal scraping against the plate. *Come on. Focus. Just focus.* She tried again, teeth gritted against the tremor in her fingers. This time, the mechanism gave. The bolt slid back with a heavy clunk, the door groaning into the dark.

They stepped inside, the tension following them, thick and clinging as the winter chill outside. Emma's words echoed in Brianna's head. What unsettled her most wasn't the claim itself but the *certainty* in Emma's voice, as if demonic possession were as ordinary as the flu.

"I need to figure this out for myself," Brianna muttered, her voice tight.

She strode into the dining room, footsteps sharp and deliberate. Each one felt like an effort to ground herself. Flipping open her laptop, she hovered over the keys, then finally typed: *demonic possession.*

The screen lit with results—scientific articles, sensational headlines, contradictory accounts. Brianna clicked through them one by one, frustration rising with every inconclusive answer. Alleged cases of children being possessed were rare, most riddled with doubt. Nothing offered certainty. Nothing offered relief.

"Just give me an answer!" Her voice cracked under the strain.

Emma slid into the chair beside her. She didn't speak at first. The silence pressed heavy until finally she asked, "You believe in God, don't you?"

Brianna folded her arms, narrowing her eyes. "You know I do."

"And the Bible? Good and evil?"

"Yes." The word came out heavier than she intended. "What's your point?"

"Then you have to believe in demons."

Brianna's mind darted to Janie—the little girl she'd watched grow up week after week. She saw curls bouncing as she raced down church aisles, giggles ringing like bells. She saw the shy toddler clinging to her mother's hand, the bright-eyed child whose smile softened every stern face.

I've grown attached, she realized, startled by the depth of it.

And now that same little girl is writhing in terror...

The thought twisted something deep inside her.

"I'm not questioning the existence of demons," Brianna snapped. "I'm questioning why you think Janie is possessed—and why you're talking about it like it doesn't matter. We're talking about Janie."

She glared at Emma, waiting for something solid. Emma said nothing.

"Fine." Brianna's voice turned tight. "Let's say it's possible. Why Janie? Why her?"

"Little kids are the most susceptible," Emma said. "They haven't built up defenses. Janie's the youngest in the church."

The explanation slid under Brianna's skin. She wouldn't admit it, but it made a frightening kind of sense.

"Where did it come from? Why now?" she asked.

"Demons can attach themselves to objects," Emma said.

Brianna followed her gaze to Oscar, still perched on the table. Her stomach lurched.

"You've got to be kidding me."

"Janie reacted to that thing," Emma said firmly. "We both saw it."

The certainty in Emma's tone left Brianna off balance.

This is absurd. Science can explain it. It has to.

Yet Emma's calm conviction made the impossible feel disturbingly plausible.

And Emma had grown up in it—faith, sermons, scripture. Things Brianna's family only brushed against in passing.

Maybe she knows more than I do, Brianna thought, uneasy.

"If demons can possess animals," Emma said, "what makes you think they can't—"

She stopped short, but the unfinished word hung heavy.

Brianna's mind raced, dredging up sermons she'd half-dismissed. One surfaced clear: Jesus casting demons into a herd of pigs.

Her pulse stumbled. A cold tremor slid through her veins. The story no longer felt distant—it pressed close, tangible.

"Demons can possess animals," Brianna whispered. Her gaze stayed locked on the screen, but the thought coiled tighter.

The laptop's glow painted Brianna's face in pale light, the only illumination in the dining room. Emma had drifted asleep on the couch, her breathing steady in the dark. But Brianna's eyes burned, bloodshot from hours of searching. She couldn't stop. Not now.

Her mind spun between two worlds—the grounded certainty of science and the impossible weight of Emma's words. *Demons can possess animals.* And the toads—Emma had claimed they were used in curses. It sounded primitive, absurd. Yet the image gnawed at her: the toad she had found.

Her jaw clenched. She remembered it clearly.

One second it was moving—alive, wriggling. The next, stiff and bloated.

The contradiction refused to let her go.

"It didn't make sense," she whispered, voice hoarse.

Her fingers flew over the keyboard: *stages of toad decomposition.*

The screen filled with biology journals, veterinary reports, field studies. She devoured them, scrolling through diagrams of decay:

Fresh stage: body limp, soft tissues intact.

Bloat stage: gases swelling, eyes clouding, skin loosening.

Active decay: tissues liquefying, the stench of rot overwhelming.

All measured in hours. Days. Not seconds. Nothing matched what she had seen. No natural process explained how a living creature turned from breathing to grotesque stillness in a blink.

Her stomach churned. She pressed her knuckles to her lips. Science promised order, rules, timelines. What she had witnessed defied them all.

The cursor blinked at the edge of her search bar, patient, waiting. And in the silence, Brianna admitted the thought she had fought all night:

Maybe Emma wasn't wrong after all.

Chapter Fourteen

THE FIRST LIGHT OF MORNING bled through a ceiling of heavy clouds, washing the world in a dull gray that felt more like dusk than dawn. Frost rimmed the edges of the windshield, melting in thin rivulets as the heater pushed back against the cold.

Brianna flicked a glance sideways. Emma sat stiff in the passenger seat, arms locked tight across her chest as though bracing against more than the chill. Posture rigid. Gaze pinned to the window. Silence weighted with disapproval.

She steered onto the church grounds. Gravel crunched beneath the tires like brittle bones. The lot lay empty—except for Emmanuel's car parked near the church doors. The church loomed ahead, its steeple cutting into the cloud-heavy sky, its windows dark and unwelcoming in the weak morning light.

Brianna's voice sliced through the silence.

"We're here. Stop the tantrum and get over it."

Emma's head snapped toward her, eyes narrowing.

"This is a bad idea." The clipped tone, absolute, carried the weight of a warning meant to bar the door on whatever waited ahead.

Brianna didn't flinch. She kept her gaze forward, jaw set. "I'm sorry you feel that way," she said, each syllable hard as stone. "But we need to exhume the toad."

At first, the notion Emma had planted—that the toad was cursed—had seemed absurd, laughable even. But the image refused to let go. Its bloated body, skin mottled and stretched unnaturally tight. The way decay had advanced too quickly, impossibly so. And above all, the fact that it had been sealed inside the case at all.

"What exactly do you think you're going to find?" Emma asked.

"If I knew that, there wouldn't be a need to exhume it, now would there?"

She hadn't questioned it then. But now the very notions she'd dismissed—curses, toads, demonic possession—refused to let her go.

"The condition it was in when we found it doesn't make sense," Brianna said. "It should have occurred to me sooner."

Now, questions circled, relentless. How had it gotten into the case? Why had it decomposed so quickly, when moments before it had still been moving? She'd tried to reconstruct the scene, force it into logic. But the details refused to align.

I have to go back.

I have to dig it up.

Emma shifted, her eyes flicking to the case in the back seat. Brianna caught the subtle recoil, the way Emma's shoulders folded inward—as if the very sight of the thing sickened her.

The plan was simple now: dig up the remains, snap a few photos with her phone, prove they hadn't imagined it. She pulled the device from her purse, pushed the door open, and stepped outside.

A rush of cold morning air sliced into the car, stinging her skin.

She glanced back over her shoulder. "Are you coming or not?"

Emma's door creaked open. She stepped out at last, arms still locked across her chest.

They crossed the churchyard, shoes sinking into sodden ground. The storm had left the earth swollen, the air still faint with rain and rot.

Brianna dropped to her knees beside the rosebush, the blossoms' sweet perfume clashing with the sour churn of wet soil. She dug in without hesitation. Fingers clawed through the muck, tearing at roots, raking up clumps of blackened earth. Mud slicked her palms, packed beneath her nails, streaked across her jeans.

Emma lingered a few paces back, arms tight at her sides, shifting her weight as though the ground itself might swallow her whole.

"Don't just stand there. Help me," Brianna muttered, tearing at the earth with raw impatience.

Emma sighed but crouched anyway, shoving up her sleeves before plunging her hands into the muck beside her.

A minute dragged by.

Then another.

Their fingers churned through the sodden soil, scooping and scattering, snow sucking at their skin. Still—nothing. No toad. No sign it had ever been there.

"It's not here," Brianna said at last.

Disappointment knotted in her chest.

"Why are you making a big deal out of this?" Emma asked. "Like you said before—it's just a toad."

"The big deal," she pressed, "is the case Oscar was in was moving when we found it. Which means the toad must have been alive just before we got to it."

"So?"

"So if it had just died, its body should have been fresh."

Emma wrinkled her nose. "But it was already rotting. I can still smell it."

"The cold should have slowed decay," Brianna said. "It should have been preserved—maybe perfectly."

Emma rose, brushing damp earth from her palms. "Well, there's nothing here. Let's go before my dad catches us."

They trudged back to the car in silence, shoes squelching in the snow.

Inside, Brianna gripped the wheel but didn't turn the key. "The toad couldn't have made the case move on its own," she said. "There's no way."

She waited—for a word, a question, anything.

Nothing.

No blink.

No flinch.

Brianna's gaze hardened. "But you already knew that, didn't you?" She slid her phone onto the dashboard with deliberate care.

Emma's fingers clamped the edge of her seat, knuckles whitening. Her lips parted, a shiver catching in her breath—the start of a confession clawing its way out.

The car groaned. A low tremor rattled through the frame, subtle at first—like something unseen pressing against it.

Then Brianna's phone lurched. It skidded across the dashboard and slammed into the passenger door with a sharp crack.

Glass and plastic exploded in a violent spray. The sound reverberated through the car like a gunshot.

They froze. Wide eyes locked. Breath held. Bodies rigid with shock. Brianna's pulse thundered in her ears, drowning out thought.

"What the hell was that?" Emma's voice cracked.

"I don't know." Brianna barely whispered, afraid a louder word might summon it back. "Whatever it was, we should tell your dad."

Emma nodded quickly, scrambling out of the car.

Brianna reached into the back seat, her fingers closing around the case. The frayed edges bit into her skin, heavier than she remembered—dense, oppressive. She tightened her hold and hurried to catch up.

As they neared the church doors, Emma pulled her back, grip iron-tight on her wrist.

"Remember—don't mention the toad." Her voice was taut, almost desperate.

Brianna saw it then—the hesitation, the plea behind her eyes. She seized it.

"I won't," she said evenly. "But only if you tell me what you're hiding."

Emma stiffened. Her fingers twitched, then released. She chewed the inside of her cheek, gaze flicking to the heavy doors like she was calculating escape. Then, with a sharp exhale, she ripped it out.

"My dad knows I don't like puppets. If we tell him about the toad, he'll think I planted it—to get out of this."

Brianna's mouth fell open. Disbelief hit first, then anger.

"Are you serious?" Her voice spiked, sharp enough to cut. "You think he'd actually accuse you of that?"

Emma didn't answer. She didn't need to. The slump of her shoulders, the way her eyes dropped, the shame tight around her mouth—they said everything.

Heat surged through Brianna. Not just at Emma's father, but at Emma herself—for the way she shrank under a weight that was never hers to carry. She hadn't done a single thing wrong, yet she wore the blame like a cloak, shoulders rounded as if she deserved it. She had already surrendered, already accepted the accusation before it had even been spoken, as though she'd been rehearsing guilt her whole life. And somehow, that was worse than the accusation itself.

Chapter Fifteen

T HE OFFICE DOOR BURST OPEN, slamming against the wall with a force that rattled the framed certificates hanging nearby. The crash tore Emmanuel from his focus, his pen skidding across the page and gouging a jagged streak of ink that bled into the paper like a wound.

Emma staggered in first, her hand clutching the doorframe as though it were the only thing keeping her upright. Behind her, Brianna pushed through, her arms wrapped tight around Oscar's battered case, the frayed leather pressed hard against her chest as if the puppet inside might escape if she loosened her grip even slightly.

"Girls, what's going on?" Emmanuel asked, rising from his chair.

"Dad," Emma gasped, pressing a trembling hand to her chest. "It's Oscar."

Brianna stepped forward, dropping the battered case onto his desk with a thud. "You have to do something," she said urgently. "We think it's cursed."

The corners of Emmanuel's mouth twitched, fighting an impulse to dismiss it with a chuckle. He'd always known Emma disliked the puppet, but this felt... extreme.

"Girls, calm—"

"What happened to your arm?" Emma cut in.

"Nothing. Why?" His reply came too quickly, rehearsed. Beneath his sleeve, the scratches burned, raw and fresh despite the bandage he'd wrapped on in haste.

Emma's eyes narrowed, her hand lifting to point at the dark stain spreading across his shirt. The blood had seeped through—vivid, damning—an unbidden confession of what he had tried to hide.

"Oh, I…" Emmanuel cleared his throat, fumbling for a lie. "I brushed my arm against a rose bush." His voice cracked, just slightly—enough to betray him.

Emma said nothing. Her silence weighed heavier than accusation. Emmanuel forced a breath and dragged his gaze away from her, fixing instead on the battered case. He reached for authority, for logic.

"Mija," he said, low, almost pleading, "it's just a puppet."

"But Jonah drew something—Oscar got in his head."

Emmanuel's brows furrowed. "Excuse me?" His tone was even, but edged with steel. "What are you talking about?"

Emma hesitated, then pressed on. "Yesterday, during Sunday School, he drew this… figure. Black. Twisted. With bright red hair. I was going to tell you," she admitted, her voice unsteady.

Red hair.

The words clawed at his memory, dragging him back to Jonah's drawings—the endless sketches, page after page, each one shadowed in dark charcoal. And always, always that crown of fire. Not flames in the literal sense, but hair rendered as a burning halo, jagged streaks that seared across the paper like a warning. It had haunted Jonah's art, relentless.

No.

Emmanuel forced the connection shut, gripping it like a vice.

Don't let your mind go there. Jonah's drawings have nothing to do with the puppet.

He smoothed his expression, pulling on a mask of warmth he didn't feel. The smile he offered Emma was thin, practiced. "Mija, it means nothing," he said gently, though the hollowness in his voice betrayed him. Even to his own ears, it sounded like dismissal.

Emma's jaw tightened. "No, Dad. You don't understand. Brianna burned her hand when she tried to wear it. Her phone—it moved on its own and shattered. And Janie…"

Her words tumbled out in a rush. Emmanuel heard her voice, but most of what she said slid past him like water skimming over stone.

"And Janie—"

That got his attention. "What about Janie?" he asked sharply, suspicion hardening his tone.

Brianna stepped forward, her voice steady. "I followed my dad to Daniel's house. I saw you in the room with Janie."

Emmanuel's jaw tightened. His temper flared hot and immediate. His gaze snapped to Emma, sharp as a blade. "You left the house—when I had just told you—"

"I went alone," Brianna cut in quickly. "Emma was in bed. I didn't even tell her I was leaving."

The room fell taut with silence. Emmanuel's gaze moved between the two of them, suspicion burning. He wanted to press, to tear through the cracks in their story. But Brianna's explanation left him no ground to stand on.

He scoffed, though unease flickered in his chest. "Janie is fine," he said, shaking his head. "She was having night terrors." He glanced at Emma, who looked away, lips pressed tight. "I'll admit her behavior that night was... unsettling. But Janie is fine."

He turned back to Emma, softening his tone. "Do you remember that toy you had, around her age? The one you were terrified of?"

Emma shrugged. "Maybe."

"I remember," Brianna said.

"Emma made me throw it out," Emmanuel said, almost wistful. "She wouldn't even let me donate it."

"And let it torment some other kid?" Emma snapped.

"So you do remember." A hollow chuckle escaped him. "You had nightmares. Sleepwalking. Talking in your sleep. Saying strange things at all hours."

Emma's glare burned into him. "And you never proved that toy wasn't haunted, did you?"

His expression hardened. "That's enough, Emma."

"But, Dad—"

"I said enough!" His voice thundered, filling the room with a pastor's authority.

Emma dropped her head, and for a moment Emmanuel thought the matter settled—until Brianna stepped forward.

"You have to admit there's at least a possibility that Oscar had something to do with whatever was going on with Janie."

Emmanuel hesitated, caught in their desperate stares. *It's fear. That's all. Fear weaving lies out of shadows.* But something in their eyes twisted his gut.

He drew in a long breath, reached for the case, and snapped open the clasps. Each metallic click cracked through the silence like a gunshot.

Emma and Brianna stiffened, their bodies rigid, as Emmanuel lifted the lid.

Oscar stared up at him, its marble eyes catching the light in a way that made the puppet seem disturbingly alive.

Emma took a step back, her breath hitching.

Emmanuel's intention had been to reassure them, to prove there was nothing to fear—but staring into Oscar's vacant eyes, a sliver of doubt slipped beneath his defenses.

"See? Nothing to worry about," he said, though his voice sounded strained even to his own ears.

"You're not listening," Brianna snapped, frustration sharpening her tone.

"Brie, save your breath," Emma muttered.

"No, he needs to hear this." Brianna thrust out her hand, palm red and raw. "I burned myself trying to wear it. And my phone—it moved on its own. That's not a coincidence."

Emmanuel exhaled sharply, eyes rolling skyward. Skepticism etched plain across his face. But before he could finish dismissing their fears, the stack of papers on his desk erupted upward—caught in a violent gust from nowhere.

The room fell into a stunned hush. Emmanuel scrambled for logic.

No windows. No vents. No reason...

A sudden thud split the silence.

His head whipped toward the sound.

Brianna lay sprawled on the floor, eyes shut, motionless.

"Brianna?" Emmanuel's voice cracked as he lurched forward. He dropped to his knees, nearly skidding on the scattered papers, hands fumbling to reach her.

Before he could steady her, her eyes snapped open—glassy, unfocused, stripped of recognition.

Her body arched violently, a guttural roar clawing its way out from deep within. Her head lolled, eyelids fluttering as though caught between waking and a nightmare. Growls broke into gasps, jagged and raw, as her body convulsed. Foam frothed at her lips, streaked with blood that trickled down her chin.

Emma stood frozen, limbs locked, terror pinning her in place.

Emmanuel slid his hands under Brianna's head, lifting it gently as her body seized. Wet, strangled sounds rattled from her throat. Her eyes rolled back, swallowed by white.

"Emma!" Emmanuel's voice cracked like a whip, sharp and commanding. "Call 911—now!"

Chapter Sixteen

B RIANNA'S EYES FLUTTERED OPEN, vision wavering, the world tilting in and out of focus like a warped film reel. The fluorescent lights above flickered erratically, their sterile glow stabbing at her eyes. The hum from the fixtures wasn't steady anymore—it droned and faltered, insect-like, as if something unseen were feeding on the current.

She swallowed hard. Her throat was raw, her tongue thick with bile. The air reeked of vomit, sharp and sour, making her stomach clench. She tried to lift a hand to wipe her face, but her limbs felt heavy—pinned down, as though invisible hands pressed her into the mattress.

A mechanical beep pulsed steadily beside her. Alive. Yes. But the reassurance rang hollow. Beneath her, the ambulance engine rumbled low, vibrating through her bones. Beyond that—the siren wailed, its rise and fall warped, broken, like a scream stretched and strangled, trapped in a loop.

Her blurred gaze landed on Emmanuel's silhouette. "What happened?" she rasped, her voice jagged, every word scraping her throat raw.

He leaned closer, his face drawn, his voice steady but frayed. "I'm not sure. But you're okay." His hand hovered just above her shoulder, close but not touching.

For a heartbeat, his presence anchored her. Then a metallic clang split the air. A pan skittered across the floor, clattering to a stop as if shoved.

"Easy on the brakes!" the paramedic snapped.

"I didn't brake!" the driver barked.

The sharp edge in their voices made her pulse race. *Something's wrong. Something's in here with us.*

Brianna shivered beneath the oxygen mask, breath quickening. The memory came rushing back—Oscar, the arguments, Emmanuel's evasions. She wasn't Emma. She didn't run from confrontation. Her eyes fixed on him, burning with accusation.

"Oscar is responsible for this, isn't he? Tell me."

Emmanuel hesitated. His brow creased, eyes flicking away then back. For a moment, she saw it—fear. "You fainted. You convulsed. That's what I know."

"I understand." Her voice cracked, but her will held. "But did Oscar have anything to do with it?"

His head shook, but the movement lacked conviction. "No... I don't know. But whatever's behind this, we'll figure it out. I promise."

Brianna's fists curled, nails biting into her palms. *Empty words. He doesn't believe them himself.* The siren's warped cry and the flicker of the lights told her what he would not.

It wasn't coincidence. If Emmanuel wouldn't act, she would.

∘ ∘

The ambulance siren wailed in broken, uneven bursts, its faltering cry rising and falling like a wounded animal. Each violent lurch of the brakes pitched Emmanuel forward, churning his stomach. The chaos of the ride could have been chalked up to rough roads or poor maintenance—but the gnawing in his gut told him otherwise. *This isn't just mechanical failure. Something else is in here with us.*

"Brianna, I'll be right back," Emmanuel said, rising to his feet. He steadied himself against the rail, moving deliberately toward the front, every muscle braced against the swaying ambulance.

The driver startled as Emmanuel appeared beside him, his voice cracking. "Hey—what are you doing up here?" His foot twitched on the pedal.

"May I ride up front with you for a moment?" Emmanuel asked evenly.

The man snapped his head toward him, disbelief etched in his features. "What? No, sir—you need to—"

But Emmanuel was already lowering into the seat. "Forgive me if I startled you."

"Yeah, well, you did," the driver muttered, knuckles white on the wheel. "You need to get back there. Now."

"I will," Emmanuel said calmly. "But first, I need to ask you something."

The man groaned, exasperation flashing across his face. "And I'm guessing you won't take no for an answer?"

"You're correct."

A long breath hissed between the driver's teeth, his eyes darting upward as though appealing to the ceiling. "Fine. I saw you locking up back there—was that your church I picked you up at?"

"Yes."

"In that case, call it a favor. I'm a man of faith myself. Name's Leroy Johnson. You tell Him that."

"Believe me," Emmanuel said, lips tugging faintly, "He already knows."

Leroy gave a thin chuckle, but it carried no warmth. "Alright then. What's your question?"

"Earlier," Emmanuel said, his tone sharpening, "I heard you swear you didn't brake."

Leroy's eyes flicked to him, then snapped back to the road. "I don't know what the hell is happening. But yeah—I didn't touch the brakes."

As if summoned by his words, the windshield wipers screeched to life, thrashing wildly across the glass. Windshield washer fluid burst from the nozzles, smearing the view into a foamy blur.

Leroy's shoulders jerked as he fought the wheel. "See? Did you see that? That wasn't me!"

Emmanuel's pulse hammered. The explanation on his tongue—*electrical problem*—felt hollow, absurd.

Machines don't behave this way. Not on their own.

"I've driven these rigs for years," Leroy said, panic edging his voice. "Never had anything like this."

"What issues?" Emmanuel pressed, though dread already coiled in his gut.

"First the brakes pumping by themselves. Then the siren cutting in and out. Now this." Leroy jabbed a finger at the frothing windshield. "I just want to get to the hospital and get the hell off this death trap before whatever's riding with us decides it's not done."

Chapter Seventeen

B YRON BURST THROUGH THE HOSPITAL DOORS, his breath ragged, pulse hammering like a war drum in his ears. The cold, sterile air slapped him, sharp with antiseptic and edged with something metallic—blood. His stomach lurched, nausea curling at the edges, but he shoved it down. There was no room for weakness.

His shoes squeaked against the polished floor as he tore down the corridor, every muscle wound tight. Fluorescent lights blazed overhead, glaring and merciless, turning the hallway into a tunnel of white heat. He had driven like a madman to get here—stoplights, horns, angry drivers blurring past in a haze. None of it mattered.

Only her.

He slammed to a stop at the front desk, gripping the counter like it was the only thing tethering him to the ground. "Where is she?" The words tore from his throat, sharp and raw, carrying the weight of desperation.

The nurse flinched but kept her composure, voice careful, controlled. "Sir, please—"

"Where is she?" he demanded again, louder this time, his fists curling tight. "My daughter—Brianna Brown."

A voice cut in behind him. Emmanuel. "The doctors are with her. Diane's inside."

Byron spun. "Have they said anything? Do they know what caused it?"

Emmanuel's eyes flicked away for the briefest moment before returning. "They think it might have been triggered by... a phobia."

Byron's brows snapped together. "Phobia? What phobia?"

"Pupaphobia—fear of puppets." Emmanuel's voice was low, reluctant. "I was wearing Oscar when it happened. The girls... they were shaken."

"That's absurd." The words rumbled from Byron's chest, closer to a growl than speech. "She doesn't have a phobia. That doesn't make sense."

Emmanuel exhaled, steadying himself. "Her brain scan showed massive neural discharges. The doctors said an intense emotion—fear—can disrupt neural rhythms. They compared it to a switch flipping the wrong way, firing in patterns that caused... this."

Byron's legs wavered beneath him. He stumbled into the waiting room and collapsed into the nearest chair. Exhaustion bore down like iron, disbelief grinding into his bones. His fists clenched white as his head shook, refusing the words he'd just heard.

I'd know if Brianna had a phobia, he thought fiercely, his voice rasping out low and broken.

"She's fearless," he said.

And with that certainty, a memory surged up, unbidden—clawing its way out of the dark.

Byron sat in the living room, half-absorbed in a book, when a low, menacing growl shattered the quiet. His head snapped up. He rushed to the window—and froze.

A massive dog prowled the yard, its fur matted and wild, lips pulled back in a jagged snarl. Abandoned, most likely—driven half-mad by hunger, fear, or both.

Byron's stomach dropped. Out in the yard, Brianna and Emma stood rooted in place, no older than ten, their small bodies rigid, eyes wide, locked on the beast. The dog crept closer, towering over them, its bloodshot gaze darting between the girls with a hunger that twisted into something darker.

Panic surged hot and urgent. Byron lunged for the door, fumbling with the lock, fingers trembling as he yanked it open—then stopped cold.

Brianna had stepped forward. Tiny shoulders squared, skinny legs planted, she placed herself in front of Emma, her small frame a fragile barricade against the hulking menace.

"Go!" she barked. The word cracked the air with a force that didn't belong to a child.

The dog's growl deepened, muscles coiling, jaws snapping in frustration. But Brianna didn't move. She held its gaze, chin high, eyes burning with something fierce—something far beyond her years.

"Go!" she commanded again, stabbing a finger toward the street.

The animal faltered. Its ears twitched back, its snarl wavering. And then—Byron's breath caught—Brianna barked. A raw, guttural sound tore from her chest, so primal it rattled through the air.

The dog stiffened, lips sliding back over its teeth. Step by step, it retreated, eyes locked on her as if weighing the risk. Then, with a final reluctant growl, it slunk away, swallowed by the fading afternoon light.

Byron stood stunned in the doorway, his pulse hammering. *How had she done that?* How had his little girl—barely ten years old—stared down a beast that could have torn them apart? That bark still echoed in his ears, unnatural and powerful, crawling over his skin long after the silence returned.

Something about Brianna was different. And whatever it was... it had just saved them.

Chapter Eighteen

T HE AIR IN THE HOSPITAL cafeteria was heavy with unspoken tension. The usual hum of clinking trays and distant conversation seemed unnaturally loud, every sound sharp against the silence at the table. A stale mix of microwaved cheese, day-old bread, and overbrewed coffee lingered in the air, clashing with the sterile tang that marked this place as what it was: a waiting ground. Meals weren't meals here—just necessities, swallowed between worry and exhaustion.

Emmanuel's gaze lingered on Byron and Diane across the table. Neither spoke. Byron traced the rim of his paper cup in slow circles, the motion restless, almost compulsive. Diane kept her hands folded, her composure taut, her eyes occasionally flicking toward the case as though it might shift on its own.

"Byron, is everything okay?" Emmanuel asked finally. His voice came softer than intended, edged with the unease he couldn't shake. "I mean... given the circumstances?"

Byron let out a weary breath. "Physically, so far so good. We're just waiting for the all-clear from her brain scan so she can be released."

Emma's voice cut in, sharp and sudden from where she sat off to the side. "What do you mean physically?"

The question snapped the fragile balance. Emmanuel felt the weight in the room tilt as all eyes turned to her.

Byron shifted, his answer halting. "She'll be undergoing a psychiatric evaluation... and Diane thought it would be helpful if Oscar was here for it."

"Why?" Emma's tone was clipped, demanding.

"Strange things have been happening," Byron admitted. "Lights flickering, objects moving. And Brianna—" he hesitated, "she just doesn't seem like herself when we bring up Oscar."

A cold shiver edged Emmanuel's thoughts.

The ambulance. The siren, the wipers.

Diane caught the flicker on his face. "Emmanuel, did you see something too?"

He hesitated. To deny it felt dishonest. To admit it felt reckless.

Finally, he nodded. "There were... complications in the ambulance. The siren cut in and out. The wipers switched on by themselves. At first, I thought it was just an electrical issue."

Byron's gaze hardened. "At first? And now?"

Emmanuel exhaled slowly. "I'm not sure."

Byron folded his arms, tension plain.

Diane's voice sliced through. "What about the burn on her hand? Do either of you know how she got it?"

Silence hung heavy.

"I do," Emma said. Her fingers twisted together, her shoulders rigid. "It was Oscar... We think it's cursed. It started with Janie, and now Brie."

"Mija, I already explained—Janie is fine, Emmanuel said."

Byron leaned closer to Emma, gentler now. "Sweetie, we need you to elaborate. What exactly makes you think Oscar is cursed?"

"Brie was trying to wear Oscar for practice. Then she screamed. Oscar burned her. I don't know how, but it did."

Emmanuel's heart thudded hard. A puppet causing burns—it was absurd.

And yet, why does that doubt refuse to leave me?

"There has to be another explanation," he said, though his words lacked the conviction he wanted.

"I agree," Diane said immediately.

Her firmness startled him.

"There must be a scientific explanation," she continued.

Emma crossed her arms. "Like what?"

Diane leaned forward. "What else were you doing before she was burned? Anything unusual?"

Emma searched her memory, eyes flicking upward as though trying to pin down the right words.

"I got sick—must have been something I ate," she said finally. The answer came too fast, too light, and Emmanuel caught the strain in her tone. *That's not the whole truth.*

Diane reached across the table, her voice soft but probing.

"Sweetie, it's okay. You can tell us."

Emma's shoulders slumped, her gaze falling to her lap. When she spoke again, her voice was quieter, stripped of its earlier edge. "Oscar makes me nervous," she admitted. "I threw up."

Guilt pressed into Emmanuel like a blade.

He softened. "Mija, I'm so sorry. I should've—"

Diane cut him off. "Did you make it to the bathroom?"

Confusion tightened in him.

Why does this matter?

"Yes," Emma said quickly. "I made it to the toilet. But, don't worry, we cleaned up."

Diane shook her head gently. "Sweetie, it's fine."

Emmanuel studied her. The steadiness of her gaze only unsettled him more. *She's circling something. But what?* He leaned in, voice low. "What exactly are you getting at, Diane?"

Chapter Nineteen

P ROBLEM-SOLVING WASN'T MERELY A SKILL Diane had sharpened through years of nursing—it was marrow-deep, an instinct stitched into her very being. Where others saw panic, she saw patterns. Where uncertainty paralyzed, she found entry points, threads to follow until sense emerged from the tangle.

Logic and explanation were her lifelines, the anchors she clung to in the storm. Every crisis, every patient, every sleepless shift had trained her to look past the noise and into the heart of the matter.

"You're not in any trouble, Emma," Diane said, her tone calm but probing. "I just have a few questions, that's all."

Emma gave a small nod, the motion so slight it might have been missed, but it carried the weight of reluctant trust.

"Did Brianna clean up after you?"

Another nod.

Diane wasn't surprised. Brianna's empathy often put her in caretaker mode, especially when someone was unwell. She leaned forward slightly, softening her tone.

"Do you remember which cleaning product she used?" she asked.

Emma's brows drew together as she searched her memory.

Diane's face remained neutral, though her mind was already turning, piecing together fragments of an unspoken puzzle.

"I'm not sure... some kind of spray? It smelled lemony," Emma said at last.

Mmm-hmm.

Diane's thoughts snapped into place. Her mind was always working, dissecting the world, searching for understanding—even in the mundane. That detail triggered a memory—a case she'd read about where static electricity had ignited a cleaning agent, causing severe burns.

"What does this have to do with Brianna's burn?" Emmanuel asked.

"All the cleaning products we use at home are natural, free of harsh chemicals," Diane said.

She paused, letting the weight of her next words sink in. "Except for the bathroom."

"So?" Byron asked.

"So... if Brianna used a harsh, flammable cleaner right before putting her hand inside the puppet—"

Emmanuel's eyes widened. Realization hit him. "It could have caused a flash burn."

"No way," Emma whispered.

Diane nodded firmly. "It's rare, but it's possible. I read about a woman who was cleaning a plastic container sprayed with a substance called Ambersil. Static electricity ignited the chemical. She suffered severe facial burns."

"How does that even happen?" Byron pressed, skepticism edged with curiosity.

"Static electricity usually carries too little current to harm anyone," Diane explained, slipping into clinical mode. "But when flammable substances are involved—especially aerosol cleaners—the spark can be strong enough to cause a flash burn. Even something as simple as friction, like pulling your hand from a glove or puppet, can generate a charge."

Byron leaned back, the weight of her explanation settling in. "So you're saying this was an accident? Not something... supernatural?"

Diane gave a small nod. "If Brianna had been cleaning the bathroom right before wearing Oscar, it's entirely possible—if not likely—that static caused the burn."

"That explains the burn," Emmanuel said. "But what about everything else? The lights flickering? The objects moving?"

Diane didn't have an answer. Not yet. Not even close.

The burn had a rational explanation—she was certain of that. But it couldn't explain what she had felt in the hospital room. Lights flickering weren't unusual.

The way the air thickened… the sudden chill pressing against me as if the walls themselves were closing in—that was different.

Her mind replayed that moment: Brianna shooting upright, her movements too sharp, too sudden—like a puppet yanked by its strings. And her face.

That wasn't pain. That was something distant.

And then there was Byron.

Diane hadn't missed the fear in his eyes—the way he looked at his daughter like she was a stranger. Even in her pursuit of logic, she wasn't blind to the inexplicable. She had seen enough as a nurse to know that some things refused neat, scientific explanations. And that unsettled her most. While she clung to reason, a part of her—the part that had felt the air shift in that room—knew she might be up against something beyond her understanding.

"I don't know," she admitted finally, her voice low, speaking more to herself than to the others. "Emmanuel, do you have anything to contribute?"

Emmanuel drew a steadying breath.

"Are you asking me to address the elephant in the room?" he asked,

Diane tilted her head, riddled with confusion. "What elephant?"

"Demonic possession," he said—cold, clinical, as though naming a simple diagnosis.

The words landed like a thunderclap.

Chairs scraped the floor as everyone shifted, discomfort rippling around the table.

Diane's lips thinned, disbelief warring with dread. "Surely you're joking."

"It's not Brie that's the issue—it's Oscar," Emma blurted.

Byron raised a hand, calm but firm.

"Ladies, hold on. Let's hear Emmanuel out."

Emmanuel leaned forward, gaze steady. "I assumed it was already on everyone's mind."

"It was on mine," Byron admitted.

"Not mine," Emma muttered.

Diane glowered at Emmanuel, her voice rising despite herself. "Do you seriously think my daughter is demonically possessed?"

Emmanuel met her glare with quiet resolve. "I don't know," he said.

His tone was steady, but seemingly burdened.

Diane's frustration flared, sharp. "How could you not know?"

"I'm human, Diane," Emmanuel replied. "I don't have all the answers yet."

Her shoulders sagged. "I'm sorry."

The air seemed to constrict, the silence weighted, expectant. All eyes shifted toward him.

Diane felt the pressure most of all. It was as if Emmanuel were waiting—seeking her permission to go on. Yet her throat tightened, her will faltering. She couldn't bring herself to grant it, even as the question hung there between them, heavy and inevitable.

Byron broke the silence. "Of course. Please, go ahead," he said.

Emmanuel's gaze swept the table. "As far as you know, has Brianna participated in any occult practices? Spirit boards, card readings, séances—anything like that?"

The denials came quickly, sharp.

"She would never," Diane said, her tone steady, protective.

"You never know," Emmanuel countered. "Especially with teenagers. They hide things."

His eyes flicked toward Emma.

Emma stiffened, shoulders taut. Diane caught it instantly.

"She's right. Brianna would never," Emma said quickly. "*We* would never. Honest to God."

Her voice rang with conviction.

Diane's voice cut in, sharp.

"So does that settle it? Can we all agree my daughter isn't demonically possessed?"

Her gaze swept the table, searching for an anchor—confirmation, reason, someone, anyone to put the madness to rest. But the silence that followed stretched long and suffocating, as though even the walls were holding their breath.

"Not yet," Emmanuel said firmly.

Frustration bubbled up in Diane's chest, hot and uncontrollable, threatening to spill into anger. She wanted this discussion to be over. She wanted the very *idea* of possession buried and gone, excised from the conversation like a cancer.

She forced herself to breathe, to rein in the edge of desperation, and chose her words with surgical care.

"What do you need," she asked slowly, "to eliminate the possibility?"

"Take me to see her," Emmanuel replied.

Chapter Twenty

"MAY I SPEAK TO HER... alone first?" Emmanuel asked as they stood just outside of Brianna's room.

Byron's gaze darted to Diane, searching her face.

She gave a single, measured nod. Only then did Byron ease the door open.

Emmanuel stepped inside.

The door closed behind him with a dull *thud*.

Brianna turned at the sound. Her movements were smooth, almost mechanical.

"Hola, Brianna," he said gently, keeping his tone warm but cautious.

Her dark, hollow eyes fixed on him. She was there—present in body, but appeared absent in every other way.

He recognized the look, but experience had taught him to tread carefully—never rushing to label it demonic possession, no matter how disturbing the behavior. He had seen too much. What appeared supernatural was often born of fear, trauma, or the fragile architecture of the human mind.

Janie had been the most recent reminder. Her screams had split the night, her body convulsing, eyes glazed and unseeing. The memory still chilled him, the kind that clung long after the moment passed. Yet he knew better. Janie hadn't been possessed. She had been trapped inside her own mind, her anxiety twisting dreams into nightmares so vivid they erased the line between reality and imagination.

Lord, I pray that you let Brianna's case prove the same.

"How are you feeling?" he asked, stepping closer.

She shrugged. The gesture was casual, indifferent. Jarring.

"Fine," she said flatly. "I just want to go home."

He studied her face, searching for the girl he knew. There was no fear. No confusion. None of the emotions he expected. The terror that had brought her here was gone, replaced by something cold, detached.

"I understand," he said. "But first, can we talk for a bit?"

Brianna's lips twitched into the faintest smile—tight, mocking. "Sure," she said, her voice flat as stone.

As Emmanuel lowered into the chair beside her, the lights flickered—a quick, stuttering pulse overhead. He glanced up. The hum wavered, then steadied before silence reclaimed the room.

Brianna didn't react. She didn't even look up.

"I don't know why they keep doing that," she said.

His pulse quickened.

The flicker isn't random.

Through the door's small window, he caught Byron mouthing, *Do you want me to come in?*

Emmanuel gave a small, deliberate shake of his head before turning back to Brianna.

Not yet.

"I'm sorry about what happened," he said carefully, trying to bridge the gulf between them. "If I had known how uncomfortable you were with Os—"

The change was instant.

Brianna snapped into focus, her gaze sharpening into raw, unfiltered rage. Her hands gripped the bedsheets, knuckles white, her frail frame coiled like a spring. The intensity in her eyes was too much—unnatural. The kind of look he'd only ever seen in those lost to something darker, something beyond control.

"Brianna," Emmanuel said, forcing his voice calm, "I didn't mean to upset you."

Her lips stretched, warping the innocent smile he once knew into a grin that felt wrong—sharp, cruel. "Of course you didn't," she whispered, voice soft but venomous. "Just like you don't mean to upset Emma."

The sound of Emma's name hit him like a blow.

What does Emma have to do with this?

The question tore through his mind, but he had no time to dwell. He needed to stay present.

The lights wavered again.

She was watching him.

Waiting.

His gaze dropped to her hand—the burn. The mark he had only heard about but never witnessed with his own eyes.

"Let's pray together," he said softly, reaching for her hand.

The words bore a double edge—comfort in the ritual, yes, but also inquiry masked as devotion. He wasn't simply inviting her into prayer. He needed to see the burn mark for himself, to study whether it carried a significance hidden from the untrained eye.

She pulled away before his touch could land, slipping from his grasp like a deliberate act of defiance.

"I don't want your prayer," she growled.

She tilted her head, lips curling into a cold, mocking sneer, her narrowed eyes locking on him.

The words lanced through him, sharp, dismissive.

She leaves me with no choice.

Emmanuel steadied himself, speaking with deliberate precision. "In nomine Patris, et Filii, et Spiritus Sancti," he intoned, the ancient Latin prayer rolling off his tongue.

Brianna leaned back, arms crossed in exaggerated indifference, her expression flickering between amusement and disdain. A laugh slipped from her—soft, mocking.

"Are you kidding me?" she said, her tone dripping contempt. "You think I'm the problem?" She scoffed. "What are you going to do—throw holy water at me next?"

The door swung open, startling Emmanuel with its suddenness. He jolted, turning to see Byron and Diane step inside, their faces drawn tight with tension.

Byron crossed the room and stopped at Brianna's bedside as the air hummed with tension.

"Is everything okay in here?" he asked.

Brianna's gaze flicked to Emmanuel.

"Fine," she replied flatly. Her voice carried no warmth, each word dropping like dead weight. She sat rigid in bed, hands folded neatly in her lap.

Emmanuel hesitated, his eyes lingering on her before scanning the room. The curtain near the window stirred though the air was still. He brushed his fingers over its threadbare fabric. Beyond the glass, city lights fractured into hazy halos, distorted by rivulets of condensation sliding down like silent tears.

An electrical outlet sat beneath the sill. The pristine plastic stood in stark contrast to the faded wall. Emmanuel crouched, pressing his palm against it, the cold surface slick beneath his fingertips.

"What are you doing?" Byron asked, confusion sharp in his voice.

Emmanuel withdrew his hand.

"Poor insulation," he murmured. "Explains the temperature shift."

When he turned back, Brianna was watching him—silent, still, unreadable.

"Brianna, I'm very sorry about Oscar," Emmanuel said lightly, as though it were nothing. "I didn't think it would bother you so much."

"It didn't," she answered too quickly.

Her jaw set, a flicker of unease sparking in her eyes before vanishing.

"Emma's the one who's bothered by it."

The words sharpened the air. Emmanuel felt it—a crackle, like static before a storm.

The lights dimmed. Flickered. A shadow crossed her face, distorting it just enough to make his breath hitch.

"Brianna, whatever this is—whatever's going on with you—I want to help," Emmanuel said.

Her lips curled into a sneer, warping the innocent smile he once knew into something cruel.

"Help me?" Her voice was soft, venomous. "You can't even help your own daughter."

The words reverberated through him, dragging to the surface what he had long buried—truths he had refused to see, or perhaps, more damningly, what he had chosen never to acknowledge.

Byron laid a firm hand on Emmanuel's shoulder and gave a subtle nudge toward the door.

"She needs her rest," he said. "Let's talk outside."

Chapter Twenty-One

B YRON STARED DOWN THE STERILE hallway, polished floors gleaming beneath the fluorescent strips, as they waited for the nurse to emerge with Brianna. He avoided Emmanuel's eyes, knowing what needed saying would cut deeper here, in this place where silence pressed heavier than words. He needed a moment, space to line up the truth, but there was no disguising it. What he'd witnessed was too stark, too raw to ignore. And from Brianna—who almost never let anger touch her face—it was impossible to dismiss.

"Boy, is she mad at you," he said finally, his voice low, weighted with certainty.

He couldn't shake the image of Brianna's face—the way her lips had curled into a sneer, her tone clipped, her eyes sharp. Predatory, coiled, ready to strike. He had seen that look only once before—when she was ten years old, standing between Emma and the dog that could have torn them both apart.

Emmanuel shifted, shoulders uneasy. "I sensed it too," he admitted.

Diane tilted her head, gaze locking onto Emmanuel like a pin through paper. "Do you know what you may have done to upset her?"

Emmanuel's mouth parted, but Byron cut in before he could shape an excuse. His tone came out flat, decisive.

"I don't think Brianna is the one that's upset here—not really," Byron said. "Those feelings belong to Emma. Brianna's just the one who exposed them."

The words struck home. Emmanuel's head dropped, shame weighing him down until it showed in the slump of his shoulders.

"I imagine so," he said at last. "Emma has had this irrational fear of puppets since I can remember." His voice nearly faded to nothing.

From the corner of his eye, Byron caught Diane's expression harden. Pity gave way to frustration, bubbling hot beneath her steady voice.

"With all due respect, just because you call it irrational doesn't make it any less real," she said.

Her words landed, but Byron didn't let them hang. He pressed, his own voice slicing in.

"So you never got Emma any professional help? And you expected her to what? Just deal with Oscar?"

Byron's mind flicked to the puppet. He pictured its glassy eyes that never blinked, the jerky way its head lolled as if alive. Even to him—a grown man who had never feared puppets—it was unsettling, the kind of thing that crawled under the skin if you stared too long.

Emmanuel nodded, quiet and broken. "I prayed for her. And the nightmares stopped. She never mentioned it again. I thought it was behind us. But when Brianna and Emma brought Oscar to me, I recognized the fear in Emma's eyes and I ignored it. Pushed her silence into service of my will."

The admission was damning. Byron's eyes narrowed. "You're saying she respects you too much to speak up?"

Emmanuel nodded once, slow, pained.

Byron felt the weight of it settle.

"That's not respect, Emmanuel," Byron said. "That's fear."

Emmanuel's throat worked, voice breaking as he forced the words out. "I'm a fool."

No one corrected him. The silence between them was agreement enough—unyielding, absolute.

Diane's phone chimed, slicing through the stillness.

"It's the neurologist," she said quietly. "They want to discuss Brianna's brain scan results."

Without another word, Diane turned and walked quickly down the hall, her pace brisk, almost clipped.

Byron excused himself from Emmanuel with a quiet nod, then hurried after her. He struggled to keep pace; she moved ahead with single-minded determination, her strides sharp and unrelenting.

"Diane," he called out.

She didn't slow.

He quickened his steps until he was beside her. "Diane," he tried again.

Her eyes stayed fixed ahead, sharp with resolve.

"Diane, why the rush?"

"If the results were normal, they would have said so over the phone," she answered.

They reached the neurologist's office. Diane squared her shoulders and knocked—three sharp, insistent taps that echoed down the hall.

"Come in," the doctor's voice called from inside.

She pushed the door open. Byron followed, pulse quickening as they stepped in.

The doctor sat behind a desk cluttered with folders and medical charts, his expression grave but composed. "Mr. and Mrs. Brown, good to see you. Please, have a seat," he said, gesturing to the chairs across from him.

Byron had barely settled when Diane cut through the pleasantries. "What did you find?"

The doctor paused, gaze steady. "She has a brain cavernoma."

Byron's mind flashed back—Brianna at five, nearly lost in the vastness of a hospital bed. Wires coiled around her fragile body, machines chiming their cold, mechanical rhythms. That was the moment the word *cavernoma* invaded their world—a word he never escaped, only learned to endure.

Byron exhaled sharply, relief spilling through him. "We already knew that," he said quickly. "The doctors said surgery was too risky. We agreed to leave it alone."

He turned to Diane. "But he should already know that, right?"

The doctor didn't flinch. "I wasn't finished. Her brain scan shows a high level of neuronal activity—neurons firing in rapid bursts—around the cavernoma."

Dread pressed closer, talons hooking deep. "What does that mean, exactly?" Byron asked.

Diane answered before the doctor could. "It means massive electrical discharges in the brain, which is common during a seizure."

The doctor nodded grimly. "Yes. But again—I wasn't finished. The neurons are firing around—and quite possibly *within*—the cavernoma."

Diane's face paled, her composure faltering. "Oh," she whispered, voice hollow.

Byron's stomach sank. The words slid past him like smoke, leaving no clarity. His eyes darted between Diane and the doctor, desperate for plain meaning. "Again, what does that mean exactly?" he asked.

The doctor leaned forward, clasping his hands. "The neuronal activity could be her brain's way of trying to relieve stress caused by the cavernoma."

"This neuronal activity... is it deadly?" Diane asked.

The doctor's eyes softened, but his words did not ease the weight in the room. "We'll need to do more testing to understand what we're dealing with."

"What kind of tests?" Diane asked, barely steady.

"fMRI and PET scans," the doctor replied.

The words hung, cold and clinical.

More tests.

More waiting rooms.

More sleepless nights waiting for test results.

More dread gnawing at me with every passing second.

Beside Byron, Diane's worried expression mirrored his own.

Her hand brushed his arm briefly—fleeting, but enough for him to feel the tremble in her fingers. She was trying to be strong, like always, but he knew better.

She's just as afraid as I am.

"How soon can we get started?" Diane asked, urgency breaking through her composure.

"Right away," the doctor said, steady as ever. "I just need your consent."

Byron and Diane exchanged a glance. No words—just a nod. Agreement. Resolve.

"Very well," the doctor said, turning to his computer.

The soft clatter of keys broke the silence, each stroke precise, deliberate. To Byron, they sounded less like typing and more like the tick of a clock, a countdown he couldn't stop.

The doctor lifted the phone. "Hello, Dr. Ellis," he said briskly. "You should have received the orders for Brianna Brown. She's ready for you."

Chapter Twenty-Two

DIANE REFUSED TO SIT IDLY in the cold limbo of the waiting room with Byron while Brianna lay in some sterile room down the hall. She needed to be near her daughter, to see for herself—even if it meant confronting the unknown head-on. Each step across the neurology floor dragged her closer to a revelation she wasn't sure she was ready to face. Her feet felt heavier with every stride, her breath catching as memories clawed their way up—endless tests yielding no answers, long nights in antiseptic rooms, helplessness pressing down like a shroud.

She slipped into the monitoring room, the faint creak of the hinges swallowed by the steady hum of machinery. The air carried the sharp tang of antiseptic mixed with the warmth of overworked electronics. Rhythmic beeps filled the small space, sharp and unrelenting—a ticking countdown. On the video screens, patterns of electrical activity flared in erratic bursts, a jagged symphony of spikes and valleys. It reminded her of a one-man NASA command center, chaotic yet purposeful. She didn't fully understand what she was seeing, but she couldn't look away.

"What do you see?" she asked, her voice clipped, professional.

The technician jumped. "You startled me. You're not supposed to be in here."

She stepped closer, eyes on the screens. "I work here," she said—fact, not excuse. Her arms crossed tight, her stance clinical, controlled.

He hesitated. "I—I really can't share—"

"You can, and you will." Her tone dropped, firm, the same one she used when residents fumbled under pressure.

He swallowed, then gestured toward the screens. "There's increased neuron activity. See those spikes?"

"I see them," she said.

"They're... unusual. I don't usually see this intensity firing from mirror neurons."

Her brow furrowed. "Define unusual."

"Elevated," he said carefully. "Concentrated near the cavernoma. It could indicate stress... or something else."

Don't dance around it—what are you not saying?

"Is it dangerous?"

"I can't say," he stammered, shrinking under her gaze.

Her attention shifted to the one-way mirror.

Beyond the glass, Brianna sat small and still on the exam table, electrodes crowning her head. The sterile light washed her out, making her look even more fragile.

The door opened. A woman entered—mid-40s, folder in hand. "I'm Dr. Ellis," she said, brisk, controlled. She closed the door behind her.

"Hello," Brianna said faintly, voice tinny through the speakers.

The technician leaned closer to the monitors. "Ah, see that?" His fingers flew across the keys, each rapid *click* punctuated by the sharp *snip* of a screenshot being taken.

Diane followed his line of sight. On the screen, clusters of light pulsed across the scan, firing in jagged bursts. The patterns rippled, then seemed to echo themselves—one flare sparking, another answering a heartbeat later, like reflections in a hall of mirrors.

"It's mirroring activity," she said, eyes wide.

"I'm going to show you a few images. Just look at them. No need to describe what you see," Dr. Ellis said, his posture rigid, tone brisk as he sat across from Brianna.

Diane shifted, her eyes sliding from the restless glow of the monitors to the glass that separated her from her daughter. She fixed on the scene inside the room—Ellis, controlled and clinical, and Brianna, so small in the bright, sterile room.

"Not much of a nurturer, is she?" Diane muttered.

"Nope," the technician replied, eyes glued to the monitors.

Inside, Brianna shifted, tugging at the wires. "You'll be monitoring how my brain responds to the images through these electrodes, right?"

She nodded. "There are no wrong answers."

Dr. Ellis lifted the first card—a house.

Brianna's eyes locked on it, her face eerily still. No blink. No twitch. Nothing but silence. Yet the monitor flared.

"Good," Dr. Ellis said. "Next image."

A baby. Round cheeks, tiny fingers, a tooth peeking from the gum.

Brianna's gaze lingered, then flicked to Dr. Ellis.

"Do you want to talk about it?" she asked suddenly.

The technician froze, fingers hovering above the keyboard. "That's... unusual."

Dr. Ellis blinked, caught off guard. "Excuse me?"

"Your baby. Do you want to talk about it?"

The doctor's lips pressed into a thin line. Her eyes flickered away—brief, telling.

"I'm sorry," Brianna added softly. "I didn't mean to upset you. I just... got the impression you wanted to talk. Maybe get something off your chest."

Dr. Ellis inhaled sharply. "And what gave you that impression?"

"That you had a baby... or that you wanted to talk about it?"

Dr. Ellis's eyes glistened, her mask of professionalism faltering.

"Both," she whispered.

Brianna exhaled, her voice low, steady. "I sensed it."

Dr. Ellis stiffened. "Sensed it? Sensed it how?"

"The way someone can sense when something isn't right. Intuition, I suppose."

The technician turned to Diane, wide-eyed.

"Did you tell her about the baby?"

Diane shook her head, a chill crawling her spine.

"No. I didn't know myself."

"I wouldn't think you did—Dr. Ellis is private," he murmured. His tone softened. "Her daughter was born with an underdeveloped heart. She died last year. On her first birthday."

Diane's breath caught.

The technician's fingers flew, capturing more data. "Her brain is reacting intensely," he said. "Look—these spikes are off the chart. She's processing more than we can capture."

Diane's gaze snapped back to Dr. Ellis. Tears pooled in the woman's eyes. The stoic mask was gone, stripped away.

Brianna tilted her head, slow and deliberate. "It's okay," she murmured, gentle but certain. "You don't have to carry it alone."

Chapter Twenty-Three

DR. ELLIS BURST INTO THE ROOM, her voice slicing through the hum of machines like a blade.

"Did you see that?" she asked, moving with a force that made the technician flinch. Her momentum faltered when she noticed Diane standing by the monitors—an intrusion into a space that should have been sealed.

"What are you doing here? And why aren't you in scrubs?" Dr. Ellis asked.

"I'm here on personal business," Diane replied evenly. "Brianna is my daughter."

Your daughter?

The words stalled Dr. Ellis for half a beat.

The flicker of shock threatened to soften her, but she buried it beneath the armor of professionalism.

"I see," she said, her voice edged, yet tempered.

"I thought you knew," the technician muttered.

"I didn't, and I don't care," Dr. Ellis snapped, dismissing the exchange with a flick of her hand. Her eyes locked back on the monitors, scanning the jagged spikes. "What I care about is what the hell just happened in there."

She stepped closer, heels clicking, eyes narrowing on the chaotic tracings. "This... this is extraordinary."

"I'm sorry for your—" Diane began softly.

Dr. Ellis raised a hand, cutting her off. "Don't."

The silence stretched. Dr. Ellis folded her arms, her fingers tapping in agitation.

Not empathy. Not simple mirroring. Something sharper. Something invasive.

"The level of mirror neuron activity is unprecedented," she muttered.

"I've known Brianna's an empath," Diane said. "That would explain it, wouldn't it?"

Dr. Ellis regarded her carefully. She could see how Diane might reach for that connection—it was a comforting explanation, neat and familiar. After all, it was widely known that highly empathic individuals often exhibit stronger mirror neuron responses; their brains light up more vividly when observing the emotions of others.

But Dr. Ellis's gaze slid back to the monitor, to the jagged tracings pulsing across the screen. This wasn't simply heightened activity. This was orchestration—rhythms too precise, too relentless to be dismissed as the byproduct of empathy.

"This is far beyond empathy," Dr. Ellis said at last, her voice cool but edged with a weight Diane couldn't miss.

"But wouldn't that explain—"

"Explain what? That your daughter's some kind of mind reader?" Dr. Ellis snapped.

Her voice was sharper than she intended. The moment the words left her mouth, regret followed. Her nerves were frayed—still raw from what she had just endured behind the glass wall with Brianna. Normally, she kept her composure sealed tight, but now the seams were showing.

She had trained herself to compartmentalize her grief. The loss of her daughter was a wound she locked away, never exposed, never spoken of. In her world, grief was weakness, and weakness was dangerous. Still, the pressure of it pressed at her ribs, straining against the armor she had built.

"I'm sorry," Dr. Ellis said at last, her tone quieter. "It's just—"

Diane cut in gently, surprising her. "No need to explain."

Their eyes met for a fraction of a second, and though neither woman named it, something passed between them—recognition, maybe even a sliver of compassion. Then, just as quickly, the moment was gone, each retreating back behind her walls.

The technician spoke hesitantly. "Maybe her brain isn't pruning synaptic connections?"

Dr. Ellis scoffed. "If that were true, neurons would be firing everywhere, not in concentrated regions like we're seeing here."

"Maybe the cavernoma is affecting it," Diane said cautiously. "The activity is practically concentrated in that region—it can't be coincidence, can it?"

Dr. Ellis's eyes sharpened. Intrigued. Coincidence was a word she distrusted, though she had seen enough of them in her career to know how often they marked the edge of discovery. Some of the greatest breakthroughs had begun that way—Fleming stumbling upon penicillin when mold spread across a petri dish, Röntgen noticing the strange glow that became X-rays. Accidents. Anomalies. Coincidences—at first. But once spotted, science demanded they be pursued, tested, dissected until the hidden mechanism revealed itself.

"Go on," Dr. Ellis said, her tone clipped but curious.

"Cavernomas are malformed vessels. Abnormal, right?"

"Obviously." Dr. Ellis's nod was brisk, impatient.

"But what if the malformation disrupted pruning in that region?"

The words snagged her like a hook.

Dr. Ellis's gaze froze on the tracings pulsing across the monitor. Synaptic pruning—the brain's natural culling of excess connections. If malformed vessels had interfered—if pruning never completed—then faulty links might have persisted. Not just persisted. Multiplied.

Her breath caught. A chill threaded through her as the possibility crystallized.

"Overconnectivity," she whispered, the word leaving her lips like a diagnosis. "Brianna's brain might be overloaded with connections that should have been pruned away."

The technician leaned closer. "Are you implying her brain is over-wired?"

"Yes. But the precision of this? The way she's targeting emotion? It's not just abnormal—it's enhanced."

"Enhanced how?" Diane pressed.

Dr. Ellis turned to her, voice measured. "Imagine standing in front of a mirror wearing a trench coat. I look at it—what do I see?"

"Me in a trench coat," Diane said skeptically.

"Right. But when your daughter looks? She sees through the reflection. Straight into what's behind it."

Her chest tightened as the memory clawed its way up—her baby girl, pale and still, the sterile weight of the hospital room pressing down. The heart defect had slipped past every sonogram, invisible until it was too late. Doctors called it rare, almost unheard of, the kind of anomaly that defied both medicine and odds. To Dr. Ellis, it had felt less like science and more like a cruel riddle written into her child's body. She shoved the memory back into the dark where it belonged.

"She didn't just observe me in there," Dr. Ellis said, her voice thinner than she intended. "She reached inside, stripped the armor away, pulled grief I'd buried so deep I thought it was gone."

The room went still, the hum of machinery suddenly louder in the silence that followed her admission.

"Wow," the technician whispered, breaking the hush.

Dr. Ellis exhaled slowly. "Look, I don't know what we're dealing with," she said at last, voice low and measured. "But it's more complex than a cavernoma."

"What makes you so sure?" Diane asked.

Diane's knees buckled. Dr. Ellis moved without thinking, steadying her with a firm grip on her arm. "Sit," she ordered, her voice carrying the weight of command.

The technician hurried a chair into place, its wheels squeaking against the tile. Diane collapsed into it, her body rigid, fingers locking around the armrests until her knuckles blanched.

Dr. Ellis exhaled again. Normally, she would dismiss phenomena like this—reduce it to misfiring neurons, an anomaly to be cataloged. Normally, she'd say: *There's nothing we can do. I'm sorry.*

She couldn't bring herself to utter those words now. Instead, her gaze drifted to Brianna's file lying open on the desk. One word leapt off the page.

"Pupaphobia?" she muttered, almost to herself. "What does that have to do with anything?"

Dr. Ellis tapped the file, considering. "I can see how that might happen."

"The strange thing is," Diane added, lowering her voice, "she was never afraid of anything—until Oscar."

Oscar?

The name sharpened her focus.

"Is that the puppet?"

Diane nodded.

"Bring it in," Dr. Ellis said without hesitation. "I'd like to observe your daughter interact with it."

Diane stiffened. "Are—are you sure?"

"Why wouldn't I be?" Dr. Ellis replied, her voice cool, clinical.

"Because... strange things have been happening. Lights flickering, objects shifting. Brianna swears the puppet's involved."

"Strange things?" Ellis echoed, almost savoring the phrase as it left her mouth. Her gaze slid back to the monitors, their glow carving her features into stark planes of shadow and light. For a moment, her expression sharpened—not skeptical, but hungry.

"All the more reason to bring it in."

"What makes you say that?" Diane asked.

A smile ghosted across Dr. Ellis's lips—thin, deliberate. Not dismissive. Hungry.

"From my experience," she said, "the truth doesn't dwell in the ordinary. It lives in the strange."

Chapter Twenty-Four

D R. ELLIS HAD SPENT HER career sifting through patterns of electrical storms in the brain, but what she had witnessed in Brianna was unlike anything she had ever seen. The readings still pulsed in her mind—rows of jagged spikes marching across the monitor, waves rising and falling in perfect synchrony, as though Brianna's neurons were mirrors locked in a ceaseless hall of reflection.

The data should have thrilled her. It did, in a way—but it also unsettled her. Mirroring activity that precise, that relentless, defied everything she knew about neural architecture. Brains echoed. They adapted. They never copied with such unyielding devotion.

She had her theories—wild, unpublishable notions about consciousness folding back on itself, about some unseen force choreographing the patterns. But theories could only take her so far. The sterile lights of the lab, the hum of machinery, the antiseptic tang of bleach and plastic... none of it told her who Brianna was—or what she might be capable of—when she wasn't being measured.

A sharp knock fractured the quiet in her office.

Dr. Ellis exhaled, steadying herself before rising. She opened the door, her expression controlled, professional.

"Diane, Byron, Brianna. Thank you for coming."

Her gaze lingered on the case clutched in Byron's hand as they entered, their steps weighted with more than fatigue.

"I take it that's the puppet?" she asked.

Byron's nod was clipped.

"I want to see it."

A fractional hesitation. Then he unlatched the clasps. The case creaked open.

Ellis's eyes flicked upward as the overhead lights faltered, bulbs dimming with a sharp electrical buzz that seemed to crawl through the room.

This was what she wanted now: to see her subject beyond the cage of science. Like an ethologist trailing a jaguar through the jungle, she needed to watch Brianna in her natural environment—where no wires tethered her, no electrodes interfered, no controlled setting dulled the raw edges of her mind.

Dr. Ellis's gaze cut to Brianna. Her composure was chilling—dark curls tucked neatly behind one ear, arms crossed, chin lifted. Regal, unyielding. The tension in the air bent around her, unable to penetrate.

"It wasn't me," Brianna said flatly. "Oscar did it."

Oscar's garish red hair stirred faintly in the draft, its marble eyes glinting like black mirrors. For an instant, the puppet seemed to watch them.

Absurd, Dr. Ellis thought.

Yet the unease clung, tightening its grip.

"Brianna, enough!" Diane's voice cut through, her fist striking the desk.

Brianna's mask slipped—the faintest tremor. Lips pressed together. A nervous bounce in her leg. Vulnerability, quickly smothered.

"I must admit," Dr. Ellis began, her tone measured, "the lighting conditions are rather... irregular."

"Tell that to Oscar," Brianna muttered.

Dr. Ellis's eyes returned to the puppet—limp and wobbly, too flimsy to sit upright without support. Someone had meant for it to resemble a boy, but the attempt had gone wrong. The longer Ellis looked, the harder it was to dismiss the sense of distortion. It wasn't grotesque enough to be monstrous, yet it was nowhere near human. It lingered in that uneasy space between the two, the kind of imperfection that snagged on the mind.

"Please, have a seat," she said, gesturing toward the chairs arranged in front of her desk.

Dr. Ellis took her place last, sliding into the high-backed chair behind her desk. She adjusted her notepad and pen with practiced ease, the small ritual signaling the shift from conversation to inquiry. As the others settled, the soft creak of the chairs and the hush of fabric filled the silence—a fragile calm before the questions began.

"Brianna," Dr. Ellis said softly, "do you really believe Oscar is responsible for the... unexplained events your parents tell me have been occurring in your presence as of late?"

"I don't believe," Brianna murmured, her voice thinned to a knife's edge. "I know."

Something flickered at the edge of Dr. Ellis's vision.

Fatigue. Stress. A trick of perception.

She locked her gaze forward.

But then she saw it again.

Oscar's head tilted. Mouth parted—fractionally, impossibly—like the start of a whisper. The puppet toppled forward, its oversized head striking the floor with a sickening thud.

Byron recoiled, his chair screeching across the floor. "Holy—"

"See? I told you!" Brianna's words rang sharp, triumphant.

Dr. Ellis glanced at the puppet on the floor. For a moment she considered stooping to pick it up, to set it neatly back in its place. But something in her stilled the impulse. A faint, un-nameable warning pressed against her thoughts, urging her to leave it where it lay.

She returned her attention to Brianna.

"You said you weren't afraid of puppets," Dr. Ellis pressed gently. "Are you absolutely certain?"

"Yes," Brianna replied, even, unblinking.

"Not even as a young child? Nothing to be ashamed of—it's quite common."

"Never," Brianna repeated.

"And your friend Emma?" Dr. Ellis asked.

Brianna stiffened. "What about her?"

Dr. Ellis noted the shift immediately. At the mention of Emma's name, Brianna's shoulders went rigid, her spine locking as though bracing against an unseen blow. Her hands, which had been idle in her lap, suddenly gripped each other tightly, fingers knotting until her knuckles whitened.

"Does Emma fear puppets?" Dr. Ellis asked.

"She fears Oscar."

"Fear is putting it lightly," Byron interjected. "Emma is completely terrified of it."

"You can't blame her," Brianna snapped.

Another shift. A reaction too quick—too charged.

"I take it you and Emma are close?"

Brianna nodded. "She's like a sister."

A flicker of warmth softened her expression despite her defensive tone. Her eyes darted toward the floor for a fraction of a second before she forced them back up, the way someone does when a memory threatens to surface.

Dr. Ellis recognized it for what it was: the tension of a bond too deep to be easily spoken, the kind that left traces not just in posture, but in the workings of the mind. Whatever Emma meant to Brianna, it wasn't casual. It ran deeper—intimate, visceral—like a thread stitched into the fabric of her being.

"Earlier," she began, eyes steady on Brianna, "you mentioned you couldn't blame Emma for being afraid of Oscar."

She let the words hang, giving Brianna a chance to fill the silence.

Then, more carefully: "Why is that?"

"It's cursed," Brianna replied.

"You believe that?"

"Yes," Brianna replied without hesitating.

"Does Emma believe that, too?"

"Yes."

Brianna's answers were enough. Dr. Ellis had what she needed to draw a conclusion.

She let her pen rest against the pad, eyes lifting briefly from her subject to the parents.

Diane's face betrayed her—tight around the mouth, jaw clenched with frustration she couldn't quite swallow. Beside her, Byron's expression was different: brows drawn, lips pressed thin, his worry radiating in the small furrow between his eyes.

Dr. Ellis could have ended it there, closed the file, and walked away with her conclusions. But she couldn't leave them suspended in that silence, the mother's anger simmering, the father's fear pulling him taut. They had come here desperate for something, and though she had gathered what she needed, abandoning them now would only deepen the fracture.

"So who conjured it?" Dr. Ellis asked, her voice calm but direct.

Brianna blinked, as if the question had struck her from an angle she hadn't expected.

Diane leaned forward quickly, cutting in. "Dr. Ellis, you don't really—" she began, her voice taut with a mix of disbelief and alarm.

Dr. Ellis lifted a hand, palm outward, a subtle gesture that halted Diane mid-protest. Her expression stayed composed, professional, yet the movement carried quiet authority—*bear with me here.*

She turned her attention back to Brianna. "If Oscar is really cursed," she said evenly, "someone must have conjured the curse, correct? Curses don't just... appear out of nowhere. Right?"

Her tone was calm, almost conversational, but her eyes remained fixed on Brianna.

Brianna faltered, just as Dr. Ellis suspected she would. Her mouth parted, then closed again, the muscles in her jaw tightening. She shifted in her chair, fingers worrying at the hem of her sleeve, eyes darting toward the puppet on the floor before snapping back to Dr. Ellis.

"I... I really don't know," Brianna said at last.

Dr. Ellis caught Diane's eye. Neither spoke, but the look was enough. Diane's mouth softened into the faintest curve of relief. Dr. Ellis responded with a subtle lift of her brows—an unspoken *you're welcome.*

Chapter Twenty-Five

E MMANUEL TOOK HIS EYES off the road just long enough to take Emma in. She sat rigid in the passenger seat, shoulders squared, hands pressed flat against her lap. But it was her eyes that unsettled him—fixed not on the empty stretch of highway ahead, but on something far beyond it. Tension showed in the set of her jaw, the stiffness of her fingers, the way she blinked a fraction too slow, as if lost in a thought she refused to share.

She's holding back. I can feel it. Teenagers carry their secrets like armor, layered thick to keep the world out.

"Brianna's being discharged today," Emmanuel said, his tone deliberately light, trying to crack the silence that hung between them.

"I know." Emma's response was clipped, too quick.

"Aren't you happy?"

"Yes."

The word fell flat and hollow.

Her lips parted, then shut again. A flicker—*fear, or was it guilt?*—lit her eyes before she looked away, hands twisting in her lap. That brief hesitation spoke louder than words.

The silence thickened, not just absence of sound but distance. In the confines of the car, she was close enough to touch, yet impossibly far—like a figure behind glass, present but unreachable. And Emmanuel knew he had built that wall between them.

"I'm sorry about Oscar," Emmanuel said finally.

Emma's head snapped Toward him.

His throat tightened, but he forced the words out. "I should never have asked you to work with him. With it," he corrected. "At the very least, I should've given you a choice."

Emma's lips trembled, a breath away from speaking, but the words never came. Instead, she pressed them closed. Tears shimmered, heavy with things left unsaid.

Emmanuel waited.

The air between them vibrated with unspoken emotion.

Come on, mija. Say something. Anything.

But she gave him nothing.

"Can we talk about the toad?" he asked suddenly.

Emma froze. Her eyes widened.

"What toad?" she stammered, the words rushed, uneven.

He shot her a sidelong look.

"I mean—you know about the toad?"

"And evidently, so do you," he said. His voice was steady, but his grip on the wheel tightened. "I saw a dog digging near the rosebush outside the church. It stopped suddenly—like it was spooked."

"Spooked? By what?"

"That's what caught my attention." His eyes stayed on the dark ribbon of road, but the memory rose sharp in his mind. "It froze—like it saw something it couldn't understand. Then it bolted."

The unease crept back, crawling under his skin.

"I went to see what it had found," he continued, lowering his voice, as if speaking it aloud gave it more weight. "And there it was. A dead toad."

Beside him, Emma sat stiff, fingers tangled in her lap, twisting and untwisting in a nervous rhythm.

Finally, she whispered, "Brianna and I found it. In the case. With Oscar."

Emmanuel's stomach clenched.

He had been so blinded by his excitement over Oscar that he'd ignored the prickling unease at the edges of his awareness. The pieces had been there all along, scattered like a puzzle.

I found the toad the same day Oscar showed up.

But even as the weight of it settled over him, he wasn't willing to accept the blame alone.

His gaze snapped to Emma, frustration crackling in his voice.

"You didn't think finding the toad was important enough to tell me? So you just hid it?"

His voice rose, sharp, accusatory, the tension that had simmered now boiling over.

"We've talked about this! You had to know it mattered!"

Emma didn't flinch. Arms crossed, she didn't even look at him.

"Why didn't you tell me?"

His voice was harsher now, cutting through the quiet like a blade.

Emma exhaled slowly, her hands stilling at last. When she spoke, her tone was eerily calm, drained of all emotion.

"Because I knew you'd think I had something to do with it."

The words hit him harder than a shout. She didn't speak with anger or defiance, but with the weary certainty of someone who had accepted his disappointment long before this moment. And she wasn't wrong.

Emmanuel drew in a sharp breath, his fingers digging into the steering wheel as his gaze flicked to her, then back to the road. "Well, did you?"

Her head snapped toward him, eyes blazing with hurt and fury. "Of course not! I had nothing to do with it!"

The words burst from her, loud and defiant, but they barely had time to settle before Emmanuel's glare cut into her.

Her confidence faltered.

She swallowed hard, her breath shaky. "I mean... no," she said, softer this time, almost unsure—her voice no longer armor but something fragile, exposed.

"Why didn't you tell me?" he pressed.

"I knew what you would think," she whispered. "That I planted it there. That it was some kind of message. And I didn't... I don't know, Dad. I didn't know how to tell you without imagining you blaming me."

The realization cut deep, regret stabbing through him.

God forgive me. I've silenced my own daughter.

Emma turned fully toward him, her expression raw.

"What have I ever done, Dad? What have I ever done for you to think I'd be responsible for something like that? To force me to work with that thing? To make you think I'm a liar?"

Her words sliced through him.

He opened his mouth, but no sound came.

She's right. She's never given me reason to doubt her.

For a long moment, he stared at the road, the horizon stretching endlessly ahead. He exhaled slowly, forcing himself past the instinct to deflect, to downplay, to retreat.

"I'm sorry," he said at last, his voice heavy with regret. "You're right. I should have trusted you. I should've listened. I should have made you feel safe—like you can tell me anything." He swallowed hard. "I know I'm hard on you. That isn't an excuse. But I'm just trying to protect you from things I can't even explain—things I can barely face myself."

The confession hung in the air, raw and unguarded.

"But that doesn't excuse how I've treated you." He forced himself to meet her gaze, his eyes softened by regret. "Please forgive me, mija."

Emma studied him, unreadable at first. Then she exhaled, her shoulders lowering slightly, as if a weight had eased—not gone, but less crushing.

"Thank you," she said quietly, steady but trembling at the edges.

Her words were simple, but they struck him harder than any rebuke. He nodded, his grip on the wheel loosening.

"You said the toad was dead," Emmanuel continued. "Was it like that when you found it?"

Emma's eyes dropped to the floor, her voice small. "We're not sure... not completely. It looked dead, like it had been for a while, but... the case moved while the toad was inside."

Emmanuel's stomach churned.

"Are you certain it moved?"

She nodded, eyes wide with remembered fear.

"Yes," she whispered. "I'm sure."

A chill spread through him. His gaze flicked to the back seat—to the case where he'd placed Oscar.

Emma's voice broke the silence, shaky but certain.

"Oscar was trying to get out of the case—that's why the case was moving—isn't it?"

Chapter Twenty-Six

T HE FAINT TICKING OF THE wall clock punctuated the silence as Byron and Diane sat waiting in Dr. Ellis's office. The walls, lined with framed degrees and accolades, gleamed under the muted glow of the desk lamp. They should have reassured him, but instead loomed like trophies in a shrine—cold reminders of authority that felt more imposing than comforting.

"Where is she?" Byron muttered, glancing at his watch.

He leaned forward, broad shoulders folding inward, elbows braced hard against his knees. His hands, clasped in a white-knuckled grip, trembled. The blood had drained from his fingers, leaving them pale against his dark pants. Beside him, Diane sat rigid, spine straight as steel. Only her hands betrayed her, worrying the strap of her purse in a ceaseless rhythm. Her expression was composed, but her eyes carried a raw, unspoken weight.

The door creaked open.

Dr. Ellis entered, and with her came a shift—an almost physical pressure that thickened the air. Her steps were measured, deliberate. Each footfall echoed too loudly, stretching time taut, like a wire about to snap.

Byron exhaled, patience fraying. "Have you reached a conclusion?"

His voice was clipped, each word edged with frustration.

Dr. Ellis lowered herself into her chair with excruciating deliberation, folding her hands atop the desk.

"Yes and no," she said at last, her tone measured, somber. Her gaze moved between them, steady yet unreadable, as though weighing each word, balancing authority with empathy.

Byron's jaw clenched, a muscle twitching as he leaned further forward, fists planted on his knees. "Great," he muttered.

"Shh!" Diane snapped, the word cutting like a whip.

Byron blew air sharply through his nose but stayed silent.

Diane turned back to Dr. Ellis, posture rigid. "Please, go on."

Dr. Ellis steepled her fingers. "She does not appear to have any type of personality disorder—antisocial, sociopathic, obsessive, borderline. What we're seeing is rarer, more complex. Likely a case of *shared psychosis*."

Diane's eyes widened, recognition flashing. "Shared psychosis," she murmured. "Of course."

Byron straightened, confusion tightening his features. "Shared what?"

"Shared psychosis. Also known as *folie à deux*," Dr. Ellis explained. "It's when a delusional belief is shared between two or more people in close proximity. Typically, there's an inducer—the one experiencing the psychosis—and they influence others to adopt their belief."

Byron's thoughts raced. Emma had been convinced Oscar was cursed from the start. Brianna—who had never spoken of curses, who should have dismissed it first—now echoed her fears.

"Emma is the inducer," he said.

Dr. Ellis nodded, her expression unreadable. "In many cases, shared psychosis occurs among family members, often sisters."

"You mean siblings," Diane interjected.

"No, *sisters*," Dr. Ellis corrected. "Statistically, it's more common among females."

Byron's mind spiraled backward, fragments of the girls' past flashing in quick succession.

"What about the strange things that have been happening?" he asked, voice rising. "The lights flickering in your office. The puppet moving on its own. That wasn't imagined."

Dr. Ellis's lips pressed together. "I've considered that. What I witnessed doesn't fit any recognized psychiatric syndrome. There is, however, a phenomenon—though not widely accepted—called *psychokinesis*."

Byron leaned in. "Psychokinesis? Like... *Carrie*?"

Diane shot him a glare. "Byron, be serious."

Dr. Ellis didn't flinch. "Yes. Precisely. Psychokinesis is the supposed ability to move or influence objects with the mind. Not proven under controlled conditions, but studied for decades."

Byron swallowed, recalling fragments of the novel and film. "You're saying our daughter's anger or... something in her allows her to move things with her mind?"

Diane stiffened. "Of course not. Brianna isn't angry, and she hasn't suffered trauma."

"I'm not saying trauma is the cause," Dr. Ellis replied, leaning back, the leather chair creaking. "But think of Brianna's extreme empathy—her ability not just to mirror emotions, but to amplify them. Imagine the sheer energy that creates."

Byron's eyes narrowed. "You're saying emotions produce energy?"

Diane answered first. "They do. Neurotransmitters, electrical signals in the brain, adrenaline—every biological response uses and releases energy."

"Exactly," Dr. Ellis said, leaning forward, intensity sharpening her voice. "But let's move beyond biology. Consider this—"

She reached for a glass on the desk and set it before them. "This glass is a vessel. Just like you and me." She lifted a pitcher and began to pour. "The water is energy—our essence, our life force."

The room seemed to hold its breath as the liquid rose to the rim.

"Now imagine," Dr. Ellis said softly, "what happens when the vessel is full."

Water spilled over, rivulets sliding down the glass, pooling across the desk, dripping to the floor. She set the pitcher aside and watched it spread.

"Energy doesn't vanish. It shifts. Moves into another space. Another form. The question is—where does it go?"

Byron's voice was low, heavy with realization. "You're saying Brianna is the vessel?"

Dr. Ellis nodded once.

Byron's eyes dropped to the water creeping outward—deceptively simple, yet loaded with meaning.

"When a vessel overflows," Dr. Ellis continued, tapping the surface with her fingertips, "the energy doesn't disappear. It finds somewhere else to go. Some other form to inhabit."

Byron's throat went dry. "And you believe... that form is Oscar?"

Silence stretched, weighted, suffocating the space.

Dr. Ellis exhaled. "I believe something is using him as a conduit. Whether it's Brianna's subconscious, displaced energy, or something far darker..."

Diane pressed her fingers to her temples, her voice taut. "Then what do we do?"

Dr. Ellis picked up the glass, tilting it until water spilled into an empty one beside it. She set both down, eyes steady.

"Take her home," she said evenly. "And teach her to control it."

Chapter Twenty-Seven

T HE WORLD OUTSIDE RUSHED BY in streaks of muted color, but Brianna barely noticed. She sat hunched in the backseat as her parents drove her home from the hospital, the steady drone of the tires a hollow counterpoint to the storm in her mind.

Dr. Ellis's words clung to her like burrs—sharp, unrelenting, impossible to shake. No matter how she shifted in her seat, they pressed deeper, needling her from the inside out.

Brianna wasn't naïve. She knew exactly what Dr. Ellis was doing—layering doubt with that measured tone of hers, couching disbelief in questions that sounded almost reasonable. *Reverse psychology.* A trick meant to make her second-guess herself, to untangle conviction into confusion.

And maybe it worked on other patients. Maybe it was meant to work on her. But Brianna could see through the strategy, could feel the subtle way Dr. Ellis angled her questions toward appeasing her mother.

What Ellis couldn't have known was how her words would linger—sharp and barbed, twisting in Brianna's thoughts long after the conversation ended. No matter how she shifted in her seat, the echo of them pressed deeper, embedding themselves with every mile.

Who had conjured the curse?

She pressed her forehead against the window, the cool glass doing little to soothe the tension building beneath her skin, but the question looped relentless and raised other concerns.

Conjuring means incantations.

Rituals.

Spirits.

Witchcraft.

It was a world that had always hovered at the edges of stories, of sermons, of whispered warnings—but never her reality.

Until now.

She exhaled, a hollow breath that carried her powerlessness with it. This was a world she barely understood, one threaded with shadows and rules she couldn't name.

But she knew someone who did…

Brianna had learned early on that the world didn't make sense—stitched together with contradictions fraying at every seam.

Don't judge a book by its cover, they told her—right before reminding her that presentation was everything.

Be yourself, they preached—until someone actually stood out.

Rules, she realized, were fluid, bent to favor those who wrote them. Kindness was conditional. Justice wasn't blind—it was selective. The hypocrisy wasn't subtle; it lived in the way people moved, in smiles that reached their mouths but never their eyes.

By high school, Brianna had stopped questioning it. She played the game instead, slipping between cliques with practiced ease. Jocks, cheerleaders, band geeks, theater kids, even the ROTC crowd with their pressed collars and rigid posture—she could move among them all, calibrating her humor, her tone, even her posture just enough to belong.

But one group always remained out of reach:

The goths.

They weren't just another clique; they were an enclave—an order cloaked in mystique. They didn't ask for acceptance. They demanded it. Their boots struck the linoleum with heavy certainty, darkness clinging to them not as absence but as sanctuary. Their look was armor: spiked chokers, corsets laced tight, pale faces painted into masks. Eyeliner cut sharp as blades, hair dyed jet black, blood-red, cobalt—frames for expressions that revealed nothing.

They weren't hiding. They were daring the world to look.

Brianna admired that—their refusal to soften or conform. For all her adaptability, the goths were impenetrable. Until this year. Until Nadia.

Nadia's combat boots hit the floor in rhythmic defiance. Black leggings clung like a second skin beneath her studded leather jacket, glossy under the harsh fluorescent light. Her lips—painted the color of dried blood—curved in smirks but never in smiles. She wasn't just noticed. She was *felt,* a quiet gravity that shifted the air around her. Rumors followed her like smoke:

She worships Satan.

She performs rituals in abandoned parking lots.

She cursed Jason Simmons, and now he's failing algebra.

Brianna rolled her eyes at the clichés, but still—something about Nadia was magnetic. It wasn't intimidation. It wasn't fear. It was curiosity. Nadia's walls were high, her indifference unshakable. Brianna couldn't tell if they were meant to keep people out—or to keep something in.

She had tried before: a smile, a wave, a casual *hey.* Each attempt had earned her nothing more than a flick of kohl-rimmed eyes, cool and unreadable. Brianna wasn't used to being ignored. And that only pulled her in further.

But today was different.

It wasn't Nadia's armor that caught her eye. It was the object in her hand: a *Curious George* lunchbox. Bright pink. Innocent. So absurdly out of place it looked almost defiant.

Brianna's curiosity sharpened. The contrast was too deliberate, too revealing—as if a crack had opened in Nadia's carefully built façade. Maybe, just maybe, this was the opening.

She leaned forward on her desk, voice light. "Cool lunchbox."

Nadia scoffed, not even turning.

Brianna smirked. "No, really—look." She dug into her bag and pulled out a pencil topped with a *Curious George* eraser, twirling it between her fingers.

A beat of silence.

Nadia turned. Her gaze flicked from the eraser to Brianna's face, sharp eyes studying her.

And then—the faintest smile.

It wasn't much...

But it was a start.

Chapter Twenty-Eight

T HE TELEVISION FLICKERED IN THE dim living room, its bluish glow casting restless shadows across the walls as thunder rolled outside. Rain lashed the windows, each gust rattling the glass until it quivered in its frame. The storm wrapped the house in sound and shadow, as if the night itself leaned closer to listen.

Brianna sat cross-legged on the couch, a bowl of popcorn balanced in her lap. On screen, Nancy Downs sneered at the trembling boy in *The Craft*.

We are the weirdos, mister.

Nadia shot upright from where she lounged on the rug, her knee-high socks smacking against the coffee table. "Hell yes!" she crowed, punching the air. Her dark hair tumbled over her shoulder, a halo of midnight in the flickering light.

At the far end of the couch, Emma sighed like someone enduring torture. She hugged a throw pillow so tightly it looked in danger of bursting. "I still don't get why you two love this movie so much. It's ridiculous."

Brianna gasped dramatically, clutching the bowl to her chest. "Emma! Bite your tongue!"

Nadia twisted around, her smirk sharp enough to cut. "She won't. Emma has no respect for '90s feminist cult classics."

"I have respect," Emma snapped, rolling her eyes. "I just don't see the appeal of four teenage girls summoning demons in their free time."

"They're not summoning demons," Brianna countered. "They're claiming their power. Big difference."

"Except Nancy completely loses her mind," Emma shot back.

"And that's the point." Nadia's tone dropped low, her eyes glittering with conviction. "It's about pushing back when the world tries to crush you. About clawing back what's yours."

Emma arched a brow. "It's about throwing men out of windows and sprouting weird scars across your face."

"Details," Brianna said, flicking her hand dismissively before shoving popcorn into her mouth.

The storm roared louder, rattling the panes. Wind funneled down the chimney, groaning hollow through the house. The night was perfect for a midnight movie—dark, electric, the kind where even ordinary things felt charged with possibility.

On screen, the four witches stood in a circle, chanting. Candles flared. Waves crashed. The wind surged.

Manon, fill us!

The living room lights flickered.

They froze.

Emma's wide eyes darted to Brianna. "Please tell me that was just the storm."

Brianna swallowed.

Definitely the storm.

Nadia wiggled her fingers theatrically in Emma's direction, her grin wicked. "Or maybe..." She dragged out the words. "Maybe we just tapped into something real. Three powerful women in one room. You never know."

Emma groaned into the pillow. "I hate you both."

"No, you don't," Brianna teased, tossing a handful of popcorn her way.

The kernels bounced off Emma's shoulder. She sighed but didn't retaliate.

Nadia flopped onto her back, arms sprawled, eyes fixed on the screen like scripture. "Say what you want, Em, but one day you'll admit this movie is a masterpiece."

The storm battered the house, but inside, the three of them sat close—bound by banter, by differences, by something unspoken that only made sense in the space they created together.

From the kitchen doorway, Diane poked her head out, drying her hands on a dish towel. "Can I get you girls anything?" she asked, warm and casual.

Before anyone could answer, the doorbell rang.

All three jolted, the sudden chime cleaving through their laughter.

"Time for me to go," Nadia said quickly, pushing herself off the couch.

"Is that your mother?" Diane asked, brows lifting.

Nadia gave a reluctant nod.

"Stay put for a sec. I want to meet her," Diane said, her tone light but edged with curiosity.

Nadia hesitated, then sank back onto the couch, folding her arms tight across her chest.

"You think she'll come in?" Brianna asked, eyes darting toward the door.

Nadia shrugged, unreadable.

Byron strode in, his voice a low rumble. "Did I hear Nadia's mother is here?"

"Yes," Brianna said.

"Great. I want to introduce myself."

"I kind of want to meet her too," Emma added, curiosity sharpening her voice. "Nadia, is she like you at all?"

Nadia laughed, low and rough. "I am nothing like my mother," she said.

A beat.

"Maybe just a little."

Emma groaned. "God help us—two Nadias?"

A sharp voice cut in from outside:

"Nadia!"

Nadia stiffened. Her jaw set, though her eyes betrayed a flicker of something—dread, annoyance, maybe both.

"Uh-oh," she muttered. "That doesn't sound good."

Emma and Brianna started to rise, but Nadia waved them down.

"Stay. You can meet her another time," she said. "Justin must be in the car waiting, and I promised him a tickle fight when we get home."

For a moment, her armor slipped, and Brianna caught the tenderness beneath—a love fierce enough to soften Nadia's sharpest edges.

"A goth girl who loves tickle fights... you really are a *weirdo*," Emma said, crossing her arms and shaking her head.

"Damn right I am," Nadia replied. She swung her coat over her shoulder and lifted a single finger into the air—a slow, deliberate gesture.

Their gazes locked—an unspoken language passing between them, stronger than jokes, stronger than rumor. And Brianna knew:

Whatever storm had been summoned tonight, inside or out, it had already pulled her and Emma closer to Nadia.

Chapter Twenty-Nine

O N THE SURFACE, EMMA RECOGNIZED the three of them had never made sense together.

Brianna—the whirlwind, all sunlight and laughter, who could charm a brick wall into conversation. She squeezed joy from thin air, her warmth contagious, her courage reckless.

Nadia—the shadow to Brianna's light. Unapologetic. A razor smile beneath layers of black eyeliner, her lighter always ready to spark flame—whether for a cigarette, a candle, or an argument. Mystery clung to her like smoke, daring the world to misunderstand her.

And Emma—the anchor. The pragmatist. She lived by lists, rules, control. Where Brianna scattered chaos, Emma imposed order. Where Nadia flirted with fire, Emma carried water.

"Are you seriously still talking about this?" Emma asked, her tone flat with impatience.

"This world was built for men," Nadia declared, tapping her black-painted nails against her coffee cup.

The sharp scent of espresso lingered in the air, blending with the steady hum of voices around them. Their booth by the window was their sanctuary—a place to watch the world and remain untouchable. They'd even christened it: *The No-Judgment Zone.*

"No, listen," Nadia pressed, leaning closer. "Look around. Who owns this café? A guy. Who makes the most money here? Probably a guy. Who—"

"Nadia," Emma cut in, straightening the napkin beneath her untouched tea. "I love you, but you cannot assume every establishment is part of some grand conspiracy."

"Not a conspiracy," Nadia replied, tossing her hair back. "A systemic reinforcement of male dominance."

Brianna grinned. "Okay, let's play: name a female-dominated industry."

"Nursing," Emma answered without hesitation.

"Teaching," Nadia shot back.

"Fashion," Brianna added, smirking.

"Exactly," Nadia said, her voice dropping as though letting them in on a secret. "And guess what they all have in common? They're underpaid. And undervalued."

Emma sighed, though her reluctant nod gave her away. "You're not wrong."

Brianna nudged her with an elbow. "See? You're learning."

Emma rolled her eyes but couldn't hold back a small smile. "Fine. But you still tend to overgeneralize."

"And you," Nadia countered, jabbing a finger like a blade, "have a tendency to live in denial."

The glint in her eyes made Emma pause. It was half-teasing, half-accusatory—but it carried that familiar look Nadia wore when she thought she'd won, lips curving into that sly, almost triumphant smirk.

Then, just as quickly, Nadia's expression shifted, softening as though a thought had surfaced. "Which reminds me—I have something for you."

She dug into her backpack, the faint rustle of papers and clink of keys filling the pause.

Emma's suspicion sharpened. "What is it?"

"Just a little something I picked up at Goodwill with my mom," Nadia said lightly, though the grin tugging at her mouth hinted she was holding back.

Emma's pulse stumbled when she caught a flash of red fur.

Nadia drew it out slowly, deliberately, as if savoring the reveal. She held the doll aloft, twisting her wrist so it rocked from side to side. Its wide eyes caught the light with each tilt, and in the shifting shadows its fixed plastic grin seemed to warp—too broad, too knowing.

A chill threaded down Emma's spine. The thing looked like it wanted to be watched.

She recoiled, smacking Nadia's hand away. The doll wobbled in her grip, its glassy stare leering as it tipped sideways, as if mocking the movement.

Emma swallowed against the unease tightening her throat, forcing her voice dry, almost bored. She cut her gaze to Brianna. "Told you—she's evil."

"No way. Not doing it." Emma's voice cut like glass through the phone, leaving no room for negotiation.

"We need to talk to her," Brianna insisted, urgency sparking in her tone like a live wire.

"Brie, you just got home. You were in the hospital, for Christ's sake. Focus on getting better."

"This fallout has gone on long enough. We should talk to her—together."

Emma pressed her fingers to the bridge of her nose, her head bowing as if memory itself were dragging her under. Anger was easier—it gave her something solid to grip, a harbor in the storm Nadia had left behind. But beneath those jagged edges lay something harder, something she dared not speak aloud:

She missed her friend.

Brianna's voice tightened, conviction crackling. "Nadia knows about this kind of stuff. She can help us figure out who conjured the curse."

Emma's grip on the phone whitened. "What makes you so sure Nadia isn't responsible? For all we know, she's behind Oscar—behind all of it."

Silence stretched—long, heavy.

"Do you really believe that?" Brianna asked at last, her voice softening. "Do you honestly believe Nadia is capable of something like this?"

"Absolutely," Emma said, without hesitation. But even as the word left her lips, she knew it was anger talking. Was Nadia capable? Yes. Would she actually do it? That was another question entirely.

"We can't just forget what she did—what she said about us," Emma added, her voice sharpening to cover the crack beneath.

"Why not?" Brianna countered. "Isn't that what forgiveness is about?"

Emma's eyes narrowed.

She knew exactly what Brianna was doing—prodding, softening, needling her into surrender. But Brianna didn't understand the iron thread woven through her—not completely. Stubbornness wasn't just a trait. It was inheritance. A gift—or curse—from her father, a man infamous for standing his ground until the ground itself gave way.

And yet, beneath the steel and bristling pride, she longed to hear Nadia's voice. To scrape away the bitterness gnawing at her edges. To mend the crack that had split their trio apart. Maybe, in some quiet, unspoken way, she had already forgiven her. But forgiveness wasn't readiness. It wasn't pretending the wound had healed when it still pulsed raw beneath the surface.

"People can't just be cruel without consequences," Emma said flatly. "She needs to understand she was wrong. It's called a rebuke."

"Emma—of all people, you should be—"

"I should what?" The words snapped out, hot and unrestrained. "Know better? Do better?"

The sound of her own voice jarred her, the irony sharp on her tongue. Her father had raised her on scripture, on sermons about grace, on parables that bent always toward mercy. But she had also watched him stand unflinching at the pulpit, his spine steel even when the cost was high.

"Because why?" she pressed. "Because I'm a pastor's daughter? Because I'm supposed to be held to some higher standard?"

Her breath shuddered out. The truth gnawed beneath the heat of her anger: the edge she carried, the fury that bristled—it was her father's voice, living in her. But misdirected or not, right now she didn't care.

"Em, please," Brianna pleaded. "I know you're—"

"No." Emma cut her off, firm and final. "I have every right to be angry, Brianna. So do what you want. But leave me out of it."

She ended the call and let the phone slip from her hand. Her head dropped, shoulders folding inward as silence closed in around her. The irony wasn't lost—preaching forgiveness while gripping rage like a weapon. But if forgiveness was virtue, stubbornness was survival. And survival was the only thing she trusted to carry her now.

Chapter Thirty

BRIANNA SAT ON THE EDGE of her bed, knees tucked tight against her chest, the phone a weight that seemed far heavier than plastic and glass had any right to be. She had sworn she wouldn't call Nadia—had promised herself that her feelings, Emma's feelings, meant more than reopening old wounds.

But promises fray in the quiet.

Pride, once sharp and protective, had thinned with every hour of silence, unraveling into something brittle. Now, Nadia's absence pressed down harder than the sting of betrayal, heavier than the echo of words left unsaid.

She stared at the screen, thumb hovering but unmoving, her reflection faint in the dark glass. To call would be surrender; to remain silent would be a different kind of defeat.

Her thumb hovered over the phone's keypad, the screen's glow painting her hesitation in stark light.

Just press it.

Just one button.

Do it.

But even the simplicity of speed dial felt monumental, as though the tiny act would crack open everything she'd tried so hard to hold together.

With a sharp breath, she forced down the knot in her throat and pressed six on speed dial.

The sound of ringing filled her ear, a hollow rhythm that seemed to echo inside her chest.

Once.

Twice.

Three times.

Each ring dragged her deeper into a sinking dread.

She pressed the phone tighter to her ear, willing the silence on the other end to break, praying for the scrape of Nadia's voice. But nothing came.

She put the phone down.

No answer. Of course not.

She expected nothing less. Not after how they left things. Not after the words thrown like knives, the silence that followed, the wound still raw between them.

Alone in her room, the silence pressed in, louder than any argument they'd ever had. Her mind slipped back to the last time she and Nadia stood face-to-face...

Brianna spotted them at their usual table from across the cafeteria—a storm taking shape in plain sight. The lunchroom buzzed with chatter, laughter, and the clatter of trays, but Emma and Nadia cut through the noise like jagged glass against a blurred backdrop.

Emma sat ramrod straight, shoulders squared, her posture rigid with a brittle defiance, as if bracing for a blow no one else could see coming. Beside her, Nadia's fists pressed white against her thighs, every muscle coiled, vibrating with the kind of restless energy that begged for release.

Even from a distance, Brianna could feel it—the tension pouring off them in waves, magnetic and volatile, pulling her forward with the inevitability of a fuse burning toward its charge. Something was about to break.

"What the hell is going on?" Brianna muttered, weaving through the maze of tables.

Brianna wasn't the only one who sensed it.

Conversations faltered, laughter thinned, and glances darted nervously toward the table. The tension radiating off them was impossible to ignore—like the low hum before lightning splits the sky. Nadia, especially, carried the kind of stillness that made people instinctively wary, the way prey senses a predator is near.

The sound reached her before she did—Nadia's palm slamming against the table so hard it cracked through the room like a gunshot.

Conversations froze mid-sentence.

Heads turned.

Even the air seemed to pause.

Before Brianna could reach them, Nadia spun on her heel, jaw set like stone, her boots striking the floor in hard, furious beats as she stormed away.

Nervous murmurs rippled in her wake.

"Don't look at her," someone whispered.

"She'll hex you," said another.

Uneasy chuckles followed, brittle and hollow.

"Assholes," Brianna muttered, pushing forward until she reached Emma.

"What happened?" she asked, her voice steady but sharpened with urgency.

Emma shook her head, eyes fixed on the space Nadia had left behind. "I don't know. She just felt... distant. I asked what was wrong, and she just—lost it."

Brianna set her tray down and slid into the seat beside her. "Are you okay?"

Emma nodded too quickly, the lie written all over her face.

"I'll be right back." Brianna was already moving, coat in hand. Whatever had detonated between them, Nadia needed her more than Emma did. She could feel it, an invisible pull tugging at her ribs.

"Nadia, wait!" she called, jogging until she caught up. "What's wrong?"

Nadia didn't slow. Didn't even glance back. Her reply cut sharp over her shoulder, threaded with agitation—and something closer to betrayal.

"For fuck's sake, not you too."

The words landed like a slap.

Brianna faltered, her steps stuttering.

What did I do?

The sting cut deeper because it wasn't anger Nadia hurled—it was *disappointment*. Like she'd already decided Brianna had joined the ranks of people who didn't understand her, didn't believe her, didn't stand with her. And worse still—didn't love her.

"Nadia," Brianna called again, her voice cracking despite her effort to hold steady. "What are you talking about? What's your problem?"

That stopped her.

Nadia spun, dark-lined eyes blazing, voice low and lethal. "You really don't fucking know, do you?"

The words pierced Brianna like needles.

"I'm sorry," she stammered, careful now, searching Nadia's face for the smallest crack in the armor. "I really don't."

And for a fleeting second, she saw it—something raw flickering behind the rage. Hurt. Betrayal. A sorrow so sharp it wore fury like a mask. But it vanished just as fast. Nadia's lips curled into a humorless smirk. "I should've never wasted my time on either of you."

Then came the whisper—venomous, deliberate, aimed like a dagger:

"Fucking Holy Rollers."

It wasn't just an insult. It was a charge—meant to land, meant to scar.

Brianna froze, nausea coiling in her gut, the syllables echoing long after Nadia had turned away. Her shoulders were squared, boots striking a hard, deliberate rhythm down the hall, each step pounding the message deeper:

This wasn't anger...

It was exile.

When Brianna turned back, Emma stood pale under the cafeteria lights, stricken.

"What happened?" Brianna demanded as she dropped into her seat again.

Emma shook her head, dazed. "I have no idea."

"She called us 'Holy Rollers,'" Brianna said with a humorless laugh. "What the hell is that supposed to mean?"

Chapter Thirty-One

T HE WHISPERS FROM THE CRUEL kids in the cafeteria clung to her like burrs, sharp and unshakable. Their laughter echoed, warped in memory until it felt louder than it ever had been in the moment. And then Emma's words—cutting in their own way—twisted into the chorus, tangling together until

Brianna couldn't tell where one accusation ended and the other began. They circled in her mind like vultures, shadows with beating wings, drawing closer and closer. The noise swelled until it wasn't just sound but pressure, drowning out reason, smothering every thought with the weight of humiliation and doubt.

What makes you so sure she isn't responsible?

She'll hex you.

For all we know, she's behind Oscar—behind all of it.

The words hissed like warnings, sharper now than when she'd first heard them, needling under her skin, impossible to ignore.

Nadia.

The name carried weight now—a wound, a spark, a shadow. The sheer act of thinking about it felt like pressing on a bruise: tender, raw, impossible to forget.

Brianna shot upright, sheets tangling around her legs as her breath caught. She didn't hesitate. Her feet hit the floor before her mind caught up. Each step down the hallway toward the living room was driven by urgency, the thought beating through her head with terrible clarity.

Byron lowered his book; Diane set aside the folded laundry in her lap. Both looked up, startled.

Brianna drew a steadying breath, locking eyes with them. "Mom, Dad—I know who's behind this."

"Behind what?" Byron asked.

"The curse, Oscar."

Diane's eyes hardened. "There is no curse, Brianna. Don't start down that road."

"Just listen," Brianna pressed.

"It can wait. I need to speak to you first," Diane said, her tone clipped.

"No, it can't wait!" Brianna's voice cracked, desperation spilling through every syllable. Her hands shook as she clasped them together, as if trying to anchor herself against the storm inside. "Please—just listen. This is important."

Diane's words snapped like a whip.

"No, you listen to me."

Her arms folded tight across her chest, a barricade, as she thrust a yellow pamphlet onto the coffee table. The slap of paper against wood landed with finality.

"Read this."

Brianna snatched it up, irritation flaring hot. One glance at the cover—*Coping Techniques for Empaths*, complete with a stock photo of a woman in linen pants walking a golden retriever along a pastel beach—was enough.

Seriously?

She tossed the pamphlet back like it burned.

"Read it," Diane barked, sharper.

Rolling her eyes, Brianna picked it up again and read aloud, her voice dripping sarcasm.

"*Welcome to a brighter, better you...*"

She snapped it shut with a thwack.

"I like who I am, thanks," Brianna replied.

"Keep reading," Diane ordered, her voice leaving no room for refusal.

So she did:

Grounding exercises.

Breathing techniques.

Visualization.

Crystals.

Emotional awareness.

Each word landed flatter than the last, her delivery thick with disdain. She bit down hard on her lip, forcing herself to continue as the phrases grew more absurd:

Summon the light.

Imagine yourself in a protective bubble.

No way this works, she thought.

She let the pamphlet drop with a hollow thud.

"Done. Happy now?"

Diane leaned in, eyes narrowed. "Oh, you are far from done. You *will* practice these exercises every single day. Consider it your job," her mother said. "And since you practically live on your computer, you'll use it to research every method for controlling your emotions."

Her voice was as firm as Brianna had ever heard it.

"Okay," Brianna muttered, arms folding tight across her chest.

"I'm not finished," Diane pressed, unrelenting.

"I expect a daily email from you outlining exactly what you've learned—and how you're putting it into action. Do I make myself clear?"

"Yes, ma'am." Brianna's jaw locked, her voice steady despite the heat rising in her throat.

"Do you understand your assignment?" Diane asked.

Brianna forced her expression into stillness, resisting the urge to roll her eyes. Respect was non-negotiable, and she knew better than to give her mother any reason to see defiance. Besides, her mother's demands weren't lost on her—the academic rigor, the relentless reliance on data and analysis, the instinct to treat every problem as a puzzle to be solved under a microscope—she recognized so much of it in herself.

"I understand," Brianna replied. "Now, may I please say something?"

At last, Byron stirred, his calm presence slicing through the tension.

"Diane," he said firmly, "you've made your point. Now let her speak."

Diane exhaled audibly, lips pressed thin. She gave a curt nod. "Say what you have to say."

Brianna's pulse hammered as her gaze flicked between them.

"Like I was trying to tell you—I know who's behind the curse."

Byron tilted his head, studying her with a look that always made her feel like she was ten years old again.

"Do you really believe something supernatural is happening here?" he asked.

Diane snapped. "Well, it isn't!" Her voice rose, sharp and unyielding, her fists clenched in her lap. "You need to get control of yourself before you hurt someone—or yourself!"

The irony scorched Brianna, but she swallowed it back, refusing to yield ground.

"Diane," Byron said, his tone firmer now. "You said she could speak."

"I can't just sit here and listen to—" Diane's voice cracked. She shoved back from her chair, the scrape against the floor loud as a blade drawn from its sheath. Storming down the hall, her footsteps thudded in angry echoes, muttering trailing after her until it faded into silence.

The quiet throbbed in her absence.

Brianna drew a shaky breath. "I've been thinking about what Dr. Ellis said. Someone must have conjured a curse. I think it was Nadia. And she used Oscar to do it."

Byron's eyes narrowed. "Sweetheart," he said at last, his voice heavy with caution. "Nadia is your friend. I've seen her with you and Emma. She's harmless."

He leaned back, gaze never leaving hers. "Besides... what could possibly drive Nadia to do something like that?"

Brianna hesitated, her throat constricting. When she finally spoke, her voice dropped to a whisper.

"Because we had a falling out. She called us 'Holy Rollers.'"

"And?" he pressed.

Her voice rose, sharp as glass. "Come on, Dad, connect the dots. She's mad at me and Emma. She knows we go to church."

"A lot of people go to church. Besides, that isn't new," he said. "You think she just woke up one morning and suddenly decided to be angry with you about your faith—"

Brianna's eyes stayed locked on him. She watched as realization flickered across his face, his words faltering.

"What?" she demanded.

His expression hardened. He turned sharply toward the kitchen, his voice dropping low, commanding.

"Diane! Get back in here!"

Chapter Thirty-Two

DIANE STEPPED BACK INTO the living room, agitation rolling off her in sharp waves. Her movements were brisk, clipped—shoulders squared, chin lifted as though bracing for a fight. But the moment she crossed the threshold, she faltered. Something in the air had shifted. It carried a weight, thick with words unspoken, charged in a way it hadn't been when she left.

Her gaze swept the room—the rigid line of Byron's jaw, the pulse hammering visibly at Brianna's throat. The silence pressed closer, crowding the space between them.

"You called?" Diane asked at last, her tone clipped, her composure rehearsed. But the mask didn't hold. For a flicker of a heartbeat, unease broke through—betraying that she felt it too, that she knew whatever had been said in her absence had changed everything.

Byron stood rooted in the center of the room, his stance unyielding, eyes fixed on Brianna. "It seems she and Nadia had a falling out." His tone was even, but a blade-edge hid beneath the calm.

"Since when?" Diane's eyes darted between them, searching for an answer she wasn't sure she wanted.

Brianna gave a shrug that passed for casual, but the cracks betrayed her—the tremor in her fingers, the evasive flick of her gaze, the hitch in her voice.

"Last week. Before we started winter break."

A coil of guilt twisted through Diane. How had she missed this? Brianna, Nadia, and Emma had been inseparable, bound tight for months—and yet this fracture had slipped past her unnoticed. The thought of her daughter carrying that quiet ache, losing someone she once called a friend, carved at her.

Her voice softened, the sharpness draining away. "What happened? You two were so close."

Brianna hesitated. Just for a second. Then her eyes flicked toward Byron. A glance, nothing more—but Diane caught it. Felt it like a splinter sliding under the skin. Suspicion unfurled inside her, slow and cold.

Byron tilted his head, his voice calm but edged. "Diane," he said carefully, "I wondered if you might have had anything to do with it."

Her body stiffened, muscles bracing against the accusation. "Me? Are you serious?"

The silence that followed wasn't empty. It pulsed, heavy with meaning.

A sharp breath escaped her, half anger, half defense. "Where is this coming from? Why would you think I had anything to do with this?"

Her eyes swung to Byron, seeking support. But he only stood there—measured, unreadable. Silent.

Frustration ignited into something hotter, edged with desperation. "Why would I invite Nadia's mother to church if I had an issue with—"

The words strangled in her throat as memory surged...

The wind howled against the siding, rattling the windows in their frames. Rain lashed the glass in uneven bursts, a relentless percussion filling every pause in conversation. From the kitchen doorway, Diane poked her head out, wiping her hands on a dish towel.

"Can I get you girls anything?" she asked.

"Stay put for a sec. I want to meet her," Diane added, her voice light but edged with curiosity. She stepped through the living room, her shoes soft against the wood floor, and moved toward the front door.

The hinges groaned as she pulled it open.

Elara stood there, rain dripping from her hair, her black clothes clinging to her frame. Shadows deepened the hollows of her face, and for a heartbeat she looked carved straight from the storm itself.

"You must be Elara," Diane said, steadying her voice as she extended a hand. "I'm Diane—Brianna's mom."

Elara's hand slipped reluctantly into hers. The shake was bony, her skin startlingly cold. Black nail polish flaked from her nails, the chipped edges dusting her skin like ash against Diane's.

Diane's gaze drifted upward—and froze.

Around Elara's neck hung a pendant: an inverted pentagram, glistening with rain. Diane's stomach churned.

Darkness.

Rebellion.

Devil worship.

That's what it meant to her. Not harmless jewelry but a declaration—a mark of allegiance to something twisted, something that opposed everything she held sacred. A chill crawled up her spine.

Her mouth moved before she could stop it, the words spilling out unbidden. "You should come to church with us sometime."

Elara's expression hardened, her reply clipped. "No thank you. I'm firm in my beliefs."

The bitter cold swept between them, a draft curling past the threshold. Elara shivered visibly, damp clothes clinging to her frame. She rubbed her arms briskly. Whether she was trying to warm herself or holding something darker in check, Diane couldn't tell.

Still, her own voice pressed forward, too insistent, too sharp—*Why am I saying this?*—as though she didn't even recognize herself. "It could be good for you. For Nadia. A place of community, of truth…"

"Nadia and I are doing just fine."

"Why settle for fine?" The words snapped out before Diane could soften them.

Anger mingled with disgust in Elara's eyes, the look sharp enough to cut. Diane caught it clearly but couldn't stop, her words tumbling in a stream she couldn't rein in:

"God can do more than fine."

"God is great, you know."

"The church welcomes sinners—all types."

"He will change your life."

"You just have to let Him in—"

Elara's voice cracked through hers like a whip.

"*Nadia!*"

◦ ◦

Diane flinched, the sound of Elara shouting for Nadia still ringing like a gavel in her mind.

I pushed too far.

But beneath the prickle of guilt lurked something colder, harder to name.

How could I behave like that?

Why couldn't I stop myself?

She sank onto the couch, the dishtowel still clutched in her hands.

"I upset Nadia's mother."

The words sounded like an understatement in her own ears.

"I must have really pissed her off."

Byron's slow nod felt like a verdict.

"Mmm-hmm. I thought she looked unsettled when I walked up to you two that evening."

"How do you know she's pissed off?" Brianna asked carefully.

"I invited her to church when I couldn't even be bothered to invite her into my home," Diane admitted. "When I saw her necklace, something just came over me."

The dishtowel twisted tighter in her grip, the fabric wringing beneath her restless hands.

Brianna exhaled sharply. "Mom, that sounds really pushy. Hateful, even."

"I realize that," Diane said, regret seeping into her voice.

"Nadia must be punishing us," Brianna said.

Diane leaned back, folding her arms across her torso as if bracing against the storm unraveling in her mind.

"I just don't get it," she murmured.

Her gaze drifted past Brianna, past Byron—fixing on nothing and everything at once.

If Nadia really is behind this—if that girl unleashed something through Oscar—then punishing Emma and Brianna would make sense. They're practically an extension of me...

Guilty by association.

"Why would she punish Janie? She's completely innocent," Diane asked.

"It's not just Janie," Byron said. "Something's come over Jonah, too."

Brianna's head snapped toward him, eyes wide. "What happened to Jonah? Is he okay?"

Byron nodded, but the tight set of his jaw betrayed him. His silence carried more than words ever could.

"So... what do we do now?" Brianna asked.

Byron exhaled, rubbing the back of his neck. "I'm not sure. I'll ask Emmanuel to come over—we'll figure it out together."

Chapter Thirty-Three

BRIANNA PACED THE LENGTH of the living room, her footsteps quick and uneven, the carpet showing a faint trail beneath her restless stride. Her arms wrapped tight across her chest, then dropped, fists clenching before she shoved them back into her pockets. Stillness was impossible. The thought gnawed at her, burrowing deeper with every turn.

Nadia.

The name was a blade, sharper each time it echoed in her mind. Someone she had laughed with, trusted, shared secrets with. Someone she thought saw her more clearly than anyone else. And now—the possibility that Nadia had twisted that bond into something poisoned, that she might have wished harm—was unbearable.

"Is it at least plausible that a curse is involved, and that Oscar has something to do with it?"

"Yes," Emmanuel said without hesitation.

Brianna blinked, caught off guard by his quick, unflinching response. She had braced for skepticism, for the usual dismissive tone. Instead, his certainty landed with weight, pressing into her.

"We were already discussing the possibility," Emmanuel continued, "before your dad called me over."

She stopped cold. "You were?" The words slipped out before she could stop them, surprise and suspicion bleeding through.

He nodded once, deliberate.

"Sometimes," Emmanuel said, voice low and steady, "the Holy Spirit nudges us—opens our eyes to spiritual warfare. Those nudges should not be ignored."

Brianna studied him more closely. His eyes weren't hard or critical for once; they were steady, almost gentle. His posture leaned forward, not as a judge but as someone meeting her halfway. She hadn't expected this—him—sitting there with patience, willing to listen. The warmth unsettled her in a different way than anger ever had. It wasn't a trick of the light or a mask of authority. It was real. And it was reasonable.

A cold realization slid through her. She hadn't yet faced what happened at the hospital—her sharp words, her defiance, the way she'd lashed out at him. Guilt pressed heavy in her stomach.

"I'm sorry," she said suddenly, her voice quiet but firm. "For how I behaved—back at the hospital. I... I couldn't help it. At the time, I mean." She glanced at her mother. "I'm working on it."

"No need to apologize. I had it coming," Emmanuel said calmly.

His gaze dropped to her hand.

Brianna followed it, pulse quickening. A dull ache stirred in her palm, as if the burn remembered itself.

"May I see it?" he asked.

Reluctantly, she extended her hand.

His touch startled her—gentle, yet cold. The mark looked the same: blistered, dark, curling into erratic waves.

"What do you see?" Diane asked.

Emmanuel lifted his eyes.

"Demons use these marks the way men use contracts. They carve them into flesh to claim ownership of a vessel."

His tone hardened, sharper now. "I see why the children are suffering. It's no coincidence. I'm sure of it."

Brianna's stomach dropped, the words striking like blows she couldn't dodge.

The children. Suffering. Because of me?

Her fingers curled tight, hiding the mark as if she could smother its existence.

"Children? By that you mean Janie and Jonah?" Diane asked.

Emmanuel shook his head. "I got another call last night."

Byron straightened, tension cutting through him. "Three kids?"

"Four kids now," Emmanuel corrected. "They're being attacked, and it's only a matter of time before—"

He broke off.

"But why them? Why the little ones?" Diane pressed.

"Because they're the most vulnerable," he replied.

Across the room, Emma folded her arms and shot a glance at Brianna. "Told you so," she muttered.

"The pattern is clear now," Emmanuel said, regret thick in his voice. "I only wish I'd seen it sooner."

"Did you say oppression?" Emma asked. Her hands tightened on the hem of her sweater. "As in the second stage of demonic possession?"

He nodded solemnly. "Yes."

"Hold on—time out. There are stages?" Brianna asked.

Emmanuel nodded.

"What's the first stage?" Diane asked.

"Infestation," Emma replied, her tone edged with the certainty of someone who had lived it.

Brianna's eyes widened—and across the room, her mother's did too.

"Don't let fear take root. It will never get that far. God protects His children." Emmanuel's voice grew stronger. "Still, we must act fast to end this before it deepens."

A chill moved through the room, though no one stirred.

"So what are we going to do about it?" Brianna asked, her voice low, resolute.

Emmanuel's gaze shifted to her, then to Emma, before settling on Byron. "We must identify the root of this oppression."

"What if we can't?" Emma asked, her voice small.

Emmanuel narrowed his eyes. "Can't what?"

"What if we can't identify the root?"

Brianna sensed the tremor in Emma's words. She leaned forward gently.

"Em, it's okay. We already have."

She exchanged a knowing glance with her mother.

Diane exhaled audibly, the sound heavy with regret. "I may have offended Nadia's mother," she admitted.

Emma's head snapped toward her. "What did you do?"

Byron cut in before Diane could answer. "That isn't important right now," he said, voice steady. "But we think it may have upset Nadia."

"And we think Nadia planted Oscar to get back at us," Brianna added.

Emmanuel pushed back his chair with a slow scrape against the floor, the sound loud in the taut silence. He rose to his full height, shoulders squared, his presence suddenly heavier, commanding the room in a way that made Brianna's pulse quicken. His gaze swept over each of them, steady and unblinking, before settling on her.

"If that's the case," he said, his voice low but resonant, each word deliberate, "this isn't petty drama anymore." He paused, letting the weight of it hang. Then, firmer, with a finality that cut through the air like a blade:

"*This is spiritual warfare.*"

"This is ridiculous. I'm going to call Elara to apologize," Diane snapped, defensive.

"No!" Brianna and Byron shouted in unison, their voices cracking through the air like a whip.

Diane flinched, confusion flashing across her face.

"Mom, please, you've done enough already," Brianna said, her voice tight with restrained anger.

"Fine," Diane muttered. "Why don't you call Nadia, then?"

"She's not answering my calls," Brianna said flatly. "And she blocked me on social media."

"Same," Emma added quietly, twisting a strand of hair around her finger.

Brianna faced her. "You tried getting hold of Nadia?"

"I've been calling her for days." Emma admitted.

"What if we try calling from my phone?" Diane suggested. "She won't recognize the number."

"That... might work," Brianna said, pulling out her phone and reading off Nadia's number.

Diane dialed, each button press punctuating the silence. She pressed the phone to her ear.

"No answer," she murmured, lowering it.

"What about using your profile to try reaching her on social media?" Byron asked.

"We can try," Diane said, already pulling it up.

Time stretched as Brianna waited.

"Wow," Diane said finally, scanning the screen. "She's popular. Over a hundred likes on her last post."

That doesn't make sense.

Brianna snatched the phone before Diane could react.

Her stomach lurched as she scrolled through the comments, each word blurring as her pulse thundered in her ears. A cold sweat pricked along her hairline, her hands trembling so badly she nearly dropped the phone. Words clawed to get out, stuck fast in her throat.

"I can't believe it," she whispered at last, her voice thin, fractured.

"What is it?" Diane asked.

Brianna's lips parted. The words clung to her throat before tearing free—harsh, final, undeniable:

"Nadia's dead."

Chapter Thirty-Four

T HE ROOM FROZE, DISBELIEF THICKENING the air until it felt impossible to breathe. Faces hung suspended in shock, as though time itself recoiled at the news of a young life cut short. Not just any life—one that had filled this house. That had breathed this air. Sat on that couch. Laughed in this very room. And now, that laughter was gone, leaving silence to echo where it once lived.

"What did you just say?" Diane asked, though the answer had already lodged deep in her bones.

Brianna turned the phone toward her, hands trembling. The screen glowed in the dim light, displaying Nadia's profile—her latest post now a haunting epitaph.

"Nadia died," she whispered.

Diane's gaze swept the page, every line striking like a blow. Condolences stacked one after another, a relentless tide of sorrow. Comments poured in, raw and unfiltered—shocked emojis littered between jagged fragments of disbelief, as if grief itself couldn't find the words. Some messages were frantic and clipped, like *Tell me this isn't true.* Others stretched into aching paragraphs that rambled on. Together, they rose into a digital chorus of mourning—chaotic, desperate, unrestrained—hammering home the reality Diane didn't want to accept.

"How did this happen?"

The question scraped out, barely audible.

No answer came. The weight of the revelation pressed heavier with every second.

Emma's strangled sob tore through the silence, raw and jagged.

The sound split Diane open, her heart splintering under the weight of it. The ache deepened as Brianna pulled Emma close, their arms locking tight, sleeves darkening with shared tears. Grief bound them together in a wordless knot, fierce and unbreakable. Each cry cut through Diane like glass, shattering her piece by piece until even her breath felt stolen, her lungs burning for air.

"I need to know what happened," Diane said suddenly, her voice steady but edged with steel.

She crossed to the dining room table, where Brianna's laptop sat unopened. For a moment she hesitated, then lifted the lid—like an eye straining open after uneasy sleep. The sterile glow filled the room.

An unsent email filled the screen. Addressed to her. The subject line glared in stark letters: *Daily Assignment: Coping Techniques for Empaths.*

Diane skimmed the body—careful, detailed, filled with links and notes. Discipline forced onto a page. A fleeting surge of relief broke through—*Brianna was doing what I asked, obeying.* But the relief soured as quickly as it came.

Not now.

Not with Nadia's death pressing down on us.

She shoved the draft aside, pulled up the search bar, and typed: *Nadia Richardson.*

The results appeared instantly. Diane's breath snagged as she clicked the top headline. Seconds dragged like hours before the article unfolded on the screen.

"She was in a car accident."

Her gaze locked on the accompanying photo: twisted metal wrapped tight around a utility pole, the vehicle mangled past recognition, its frame collapsed like a broken skeleton. Glass littered the slick asphalt, shards glinting beneath the cruel blaze of emergency lights.

"It happened just down the road from the church," Diane murmured, her voice flat, distant, as if the words belonged to someone else.

"But... she didn't drive," Brianna whispered.

"Then whose car was she in?" Emmanuel asked.

Diane's stomach lurched. A flash of red seared through memory: the rain, Elara on their doorstep, soaked to the bone. And behind her, parked in the drive—a red sedan.

"It was her mother's car," she whispered, the realization crashing down.

Brianna's shoulders tensed, her breath quickening.

"Sweetie, are you okay?" Diane asked, rising, concern threading her voice.

"I saw the wreckage from the accident that day," Brianna said, low and unsteady.

Diane stiffened, cautious, taut.

"It was Nadia under the yellow tarp," Brianna said. Her gaze swept the room, eyes meeting theirs one by one. Fear, grief, disbelief—all of it tightened around them like a noose. Diane felt the pressure mounting.

This is too much for her. It's too much for even me.

"Nadia tried to stop her," Brianna whispered.

A low vibration shuddered through the room. The coffee table rattled, a mug tipping and spilling its contents in a dark trail across the wood.

Diane's gaze snapped to Emmanuel.

"Take Emma to the car," she ordered, her voice steadier than she felt.

He didn't hesitate. Arm firm around Emma, he ushered her out.

The hinges groaned, the door slammed, and the echo lingered long after they'd gone.

She edged her hand toward her purse. Every movement was calculated, careful not to draw attention, as though even the scrape of leather might provoke what was building in the room. Her fingers slipped inside, inch by inch, the fabric swallowing her hand as she searched for what she needed.

No sudden movements.

Brianna's breathing grew ragged, heavier with each second. The floor groaned under an unseen weight. Her fists clenched, unclenched. Then her voice came, distant, trance-like.

"Her mother did this," she said.

A picture frame slipped from the wall and crashed to the floor, glass exploding across the hardwood.

Diane flinched. "Sweetie, I know this is a lot, but you need to calm down." Her words came out steady, though her pulse thundered. She stepped forward slowly, deliberate, one hand raised in a gesture meant to soothe.

Brianna didn't move. Didn't even blink.

The room quivered, charged with a pressure Diane couldn't see but felt sinking into her bones.

She cut a sharp glance toward Byron—unspoken agreement flashing between them. Then she lunged, fingers clamping around Brianna's arm.

Brianna gasped as the needle slipped into her skin. Her head snapped toward Diane, eyes blazing with shock, betrayal burning hotter than the storm rattling the walls.

"It's just a tranquilizer, sweetheart," Diane said quickly, her voice trembling despite the reassurance she tried to muster.

Chapter Thirty-Five

THE CLOCK TICKED IN THE DISTANCE, its rhythm merging with the soft patter of snow against the windows. Brianna's eyes fluttered open. Shapes bled together before sharpening into the figure in front of her. Byron sat at the foot of her bed, shoulders hunched, hands locked tight. His head was bowed, face lost to shadow, but the worry etched into him was unmistakable. It lived in the set of his jaw, in the lines carved deep. Worry worn into him like a scar.

Her voice rasped out, fragile, barely breaking the stillness. "Dad?"

His head snapped up, eyes locking on hers. Relief flickered across his face, softening the hard edges, though worry still clung to him. "Hi, sweetheart," he said softly, voice steady but frayed.

He reached for the nightstand, lifted a glass of water, and held it out.

Brianna waved it away, the thought of swallowing anything turning her stomach.

He set the glass back down, the faint *clink* carrying loudly in the silence. "It'll be here for you when you need it," he said.

She tried to sit up. Her body dragged heavy, limbs sluggish. A dull ache pulsed at the back of her skull, disorientation sweeping through her in a wave.

"How long have you been sitting there?"

"All night," he admitted. "Your mom and I took shifts." His hands rubbed together absently, as if trying to shake off what they carried.

The room was too still, as if waiting for her to fill it.

"Is everything okay?"

The hollowness of her own question rang in her ears. He didn't answer right away. A hand dragged down his face.

"You scared us, Brie. Your mom thought it was best to give you something to calm you down."

Fragments jolted back—the news of Nadia's death, emotions spiraling so fast she couldn't breathe. Walls trembling. Glass shattering. The air thickening until it pressed into her bones. Emmanuel's arm clamped around Emma, their figures vanishing as the door slammed behind them. And then the sting of a needle—fire under her skin—her own body betraying her as the darkness dragged her under.

"She tranquilized me," Brianna said, her tone flat—disbelief laced with anger simmering beneath.

"Your mother was afraid for you. We both were. We didn't want anyone to get hurt," he said, gentle but firm, shielding her mother. "Speaking of which, I'm going to tell her you're awake."

He rose slowly, the mattress groaning under his weight. "I'll be back in a minute."

Brianna sank into the pillows as he stepped out, mind racing even as fatigue dragged at her limbs. And then it hit her—

They think I'm unhinged.

They think I'm dangerous.

They're afraid of me.

Her gaze slid to the glass of water on the coffee table. Droplets of condensation streaked down its side, pooling in a ring beneath. She fixed on the surface—smooth, still, almost mocking in its calm.

Her eyes narrowed.

She stared harder, her mind coiling tight around a single thought.

Move.

Seconds stretched...

The silence pressed, broken only by the faint tick of the clock.

Move.

A faint tremor rippled across the surface, the water quivering as though the glass itself had caught its breath.

A mischievous smile threatened to curl across Brianna's lips, the kind that would only confirm their worst fears. She forced it down, biting it back before it could surface, schooling her expression into something still, unreadable.

They have no idea.

Byron stepped back in with Diane close behind him.

"Are you doing okay?" Diane asked, her voice careful, guilt threading its edges. "Is there anything we can do for you?"

Brianna studied her mother. For the first time, she saw it—guilt pulling faint lines around her eyes, softening the iron in her voice. It seemed as though she was second-guessing what she'd done, like the act of tranquilizing her daughter had left its own wound.

Brianna sensed the vulnerability. An opening. She took it. "I want to talk to Nadia's mom," she said.

Diane reached for her phone, but Brianna's voice cut in, steady and sharp. "No. I mean face-to-face."

Diane's composure snapped. "No way. We're not letting that kind of energy—that darkness—into this house."

"We won't be," Brianna countered, calm sharpening her resolve. "Because I'll go to her house."

Byron's voice came heavy, final. "Brianna, you're not setting foot in that woman's house. Not after everything that's happened."

"Please." Urgency edged her words. She met his gaze without flinching. "I want to pay my last respects."

Diane crossed her arms. Brianna recognized the shift—her mother was actually giving it some thought.

"At least give it some time," she said slowly. "That poor woman just lost her daughter. She's suffering."

Brianna bit down, swallowing the thought clawing at her throat.

She didn't care about the kids at church suffering.

Her eyes flicked to the pile of glossy booklets on the coffee table—more pamphlets on coping techniques, breathing methods, grounding exercises.

"Mom, you want me to learn how to cope with my emotions, don't you?" Brianna said evenly. "Facing Nadia's mom might bring me closure."

She waited for a response.

Nothing. Only her mother's eyes pressing on her, heavy as a vise.

"What are you worried about?" Brianna asked at last, voice low, unwavering.

Diane's mask cracked. "I'm worried," she snapped, "that you'll have a repeat of last night and hurt yourself—or someone else!"

"I'll bring Emma with me," Brianna said softly, conviction in every syllable. "You can show her how to use the syringe. If she thinks I'm losing control, she can—" she faltered, the word snagging in her throat, her eyes betraying her doubt, "tranquilize me."

Another heavy look passed between her parents. Her mother's lips pressed thin, her father's jaw ticked. Even the air seemed to hold its breath.

At last, Diane exhaled, dragging a hand down her face.

"Okay," she said reluctantly, glancing at Byron.

"Okay," Byron echoed, his voice tight with unease.

"Thank you," Brianna said.

A flicker of relief swept through her—brief, fragile—before dread surged in to claim it.

The unknown loomed ahead, shadowed and uncertain; she couldn't know what she would be walking into, only that it waited for her.

Chapter Thirty-Six

E XCEPT FOR THE CRASH COURSE Diane had given her on how to use the tranquilizer, Brianna had revealed almost nothing about what waited at Nadia's mother's house. The silence around those details gnawed at Emma, every unanswered question stacking into a weight she couldn't shake.

Beside her, Brianna was locked on the road. Her hands gripped the wheel with steady precision, eyes fixed forward, unblinking, as though her body was driving while her mind roamed elsewhere.

"What do you plan on saying to her?" Emma asked.

Brianna didn't answer. She didn't even blink.

"Brie?"

Still no answer.

"Brie!" she yelled, her voice cracking as she tried to break through the wall of silence, to drag Brianna back from wherever her mind had gone.

"What?"

"What do you plan on saying to her?" Emma pressed. Her voice came out thin and tight, her fingers worrying the hem of her sleeve until the fabric stretched out of shape.

"I don't know," Brianna said flatly. "I'll play it by ear."

Play it by ear?

The words slid under Emma's skin like ice. Walking blind into a grieving woman's home with no script felt like stepping off a cliff.

"You really don't have a plan? Not even an idea?"

Brianna's gaze never wavered from the road.

"Not really. I figured I'd feel it out. See where the conversation takes us."

Emma's jaw dropped. "You can't be serious."

"Look—what I have to say is way less important than what she does," Brianna replied. Then, almost under her breath, she added, "Well... that's not exactly true."

The way she said it—quiet, half to herself—made Emma feel like she wasn't meant to hear. Emma shook her head, her unease spiking.

Brianna's voice sharpened, sudden and deliberate. "Do you think I should I call her by her first name or Mrs. Richardson?"

"What?" Emma asked, incredulous.

"Mrs. Richardson, right?" Brianna gave a short nod, eyes still on the road. "Or is it *Ms.* Richardson? Either way, I should keep it formal."

Emma snapped her arms across her chest, the motion sharp, her posture stiff with disapproval. Her gaze flicked to the backseat—Oscar lay sprawled there, limp and lifeless, its very presence oppressive, thickening the air until it felt hard to breathe.

"Can you at least tell me what you plan on doing with it?" Emma asked, disgust curling her voice.

"No," Brianna said curtly.

Emma scoffed again. She clenched her jaw, eyes locking on her reflection in the rain-streaked window. "This is a bad idea," she whispered.

Silence sat thick between them, but Brianna didn't seem to notice.

"There is one thing we should address before we get there," she said suddenly.

Finally. Some thought.

Emma's head jerked toward her. "What is it?"

"Don't even think about pulling that syringe out of your purse," Brianna said, her voice low and cutting. "Under no circumstance are you injecting me with that thing."

Emma blinked as the memory surged—unwanted, jagged—of what she had seen in Brianna's house, of what Brianna was capable of...

It had begun as the faintest vibration, barely noticeable, a low hum threading beneath her feet. Then it grew, rattling the coffee table until the mug toppled and bled across the wood. The door had slammed shut behind her with a force no draft could explain, the sound cracking like a gunshot as her father ushered her. His grip had been iron, unyielding, dragging her toward the car with urgency carved into every step.

"I'll only use it if I absolutely have to."

"No." Brianna's voice cut sharp. "You're leaving it in the car."

Emma snapped her eyes to her. "Why?"

"Because I'll beat you to the ground if you don't."

Emma stared, searching her friend's face for a flicker of humor.

There wasn't any.

The threat was stone, not smoke.

"Fine," Emma replied. "But you have to know this is already starting to spiral."

The rest of the drive crawled in silence. Every bump in the road seemed louder, more ominous, like the world itself was warning them to turn around.

"This is it," Brianna said finally. She eased into a cracked driveway, killed the engine, and let the quiet settle.

Emma's stomach twisted at the sight of the house. The lawn was a wild snarl, weeds clawing over the cracked walkway like they were trying to drag the place back into the earth. Paint peeled in long, curling strips from the siding, exposing raw wood beneath, gray and splintering. A rusted tricycle leaned half-buried in the dirt, its frame eaten with corrosion, its once-bright paint bleached to a ghostly pale blue. The kind of color that should have meant laughter, childhood, life—now it looked like a relic left behind at a gravesite.

"Take it out and leave it," Brianna said, her gaze fixed on Emma's purse.

Emma rolled her eyes but obeyed, slipping a hand inside and pulling free the bag containing the syringe and alcohol wipes. She dangled it between two fingers, a silent show of defiance, before flicking her wrist and sending it tumbling onto the back seat.

"Oh, I almost forgot," Brianna said, circling to the backseat.

Emma remained seated in the car, gut clenched as Brianna emerged with Oscar in hand.

"Are you coming?" Brianna asked.

Emma lingered, fingers brushing the cool metal of the door handle. Her thoughts pulsed through her like a warning siren:

Stay here.

Let her do this alone.

This is reckless.

This is more than reckless.

This is insane.

Her stomach churned, every instinct screaming at her to climb back inside, lock the doors, and wait until Brianna came running out—if she came out at all.

But another voice pressed harder, steadier, relentless.

I can't let her do this alone.

Her chest ached with the weight of it, loyalty dragging at her like chains. With a breath that trembled in her throat, she pried herself free of the car and forced her feet to move, each step not chosen but compelled, pulled forward not by courage but by duty.

Chapter Thirty-Seven

BRIANNA PRESSED THE DOORBELL, the muted chime reverberating somewhere deep inside the house, a sound both familiar and foreign. She swallowed against the tightness in her throat. Beside her, Emma shifted again, her nervous energy jittering through her small frame like a live wire, every fidget betraying what Brianna was trying so hard to keep contained. Brianna kept her eyes fixed on the door, refusing to acknowledge it.

She couldn't afford to falter now. In her mind, the scene was already unfolding step by step—a script she had memorized, a play she had no choice but to perform. Words, tones, and gestures were all rehearsed in silence, even as doubt whispered at the edges:

If she slams the door, wedge your foot.

If she speaks, control the tone.

If she falters, press the puppet.

Keep her off balance.

Always drive the moment.

She could see it unfold—word for word, beat for beat—until the future felt scripted. She had to own it, bend it, seize it before grief turned Mrs. Richardson's fear into defiance.

At last, the door creaked open, the groan of its hinges stretching out like a whispered warning.

Mrs. Richardson filled the doorway. Hollow, red-rimmed eyes commanded instant attention—swollen, raw, marked by nights surrendered to grief and days drowned in tears.

"Mrs. Richardson!" Brianna's voice rang out, startlingly bright, its forced cheer clashing with the somber air.

"Can I help—"

Her words died the instant her gaze locked on the case in Brianna's grip. Her hand flew to the door, ready to slam it shut.

Brianna's palm struck the edge, halting it mid-swing. She slid her foot into the gap, wedging it against the frame. The rubber sole bit into the wood, an immovable anchor that turned the doorway into a standoff.

"I'm Brianna, and this is Emma," she said, her tone calm but edged with steel. "We were good friends of—"

"I know who you are." Her lips thinned, movements sharp, jerky. "I'm not interested in your company," she snapped, each word clipped to the bone, cold as steel.

She shoved at the door.

It didn't budge—just like I planned.

"What are you doing, Brie?" Emma whispered, fear quivering in her voice.

Brianna shut Emma's voice out, locking it away. Questions could wait—this moment couldn't. She raised the puppet. Its lifeless eyes caught the dim light, hollow, accusing.

"We're here to return something," she said evenly. "It belongs to you, doesn't it?"

For a heartbeat, Mrs. Richardson's gaze lingered on the puppet, as if trapped by its dead stare. Then her face twisted.

"Keep it," she spat, panic threading her words.

She shoved harder at the door, but Brianna didn't give an inch.

"You aren't welcome here." Her voice dropped to a venomous hiss. "I didn't invite you."

Brianna's lips curled into a slow, deliberate smile. "We didn't invite this thing either," she said, holding the puppet aloft like an unwanted offering. "But here we are."

Her eyes narrowed, her voice cold and unyielding. "We have business to discuss."

A flicker crossed Mrs. Richardson's face—resignation, recognition—the look of someone who knew this meeting was inevitable.

"But you already knew that, didn't you?" Brianna asked.

Mrs. Richardson stiffened, her fingers whitening against the frame.

"Leave," she spat, her voice fraying at the edges. "Before you regret it."

Emma tugged at Brianna's sleeve, desperation sharpening her whisper. "Brie, let's go. Please—you're scaring me."

But Brianna didn't flinch.

Her focus tunneled on the woman, a sharp predatory edge coiling inside her.

"Why are you here?" Mrs. Richardson demanded. Her eyes darted to the puppet, then back again. "You don't know what you're messing with."

"Maybe not," Brianna said evenly, her tone like ice. "But you do."

She lunged. Her weight slammed into the door. Wood shuddered beneath the force. The puppet slipped from her hand, tumbling to the porch with a dull thud she barely registered.

Emma's gasp cut through the struggle, but Brianna pressed harder, relentless, until she felt the frame splinter. With a sharp crack, the resistance broke.

They stumbled inside.

Brianna straightened, brushing past the threshold as if the house itself had opened for her.

"Don't worry—this won't take long," she said, her cheer honed to a razor's edge.

Her smile deepened, cold and deliberate.

"That is, unless you'd rather drag it out."

"Get out!" Mrs. Richardson shrieked, her voice raw with fury.

Brianna turned slowly, calm as stone, a faint smile tugging her lips. "We know what you did," she said softly, her words slicing the air.

She advanced, each word, each step deliberate.

"I don't care why you did it. But we're not leaving until you fix it," Brianna said, her footsteps whispering against the floor.

Mrs. Richardson's breath rasped. Her gaze flicked to the porch, to the puppet lying outside—a silent specter of guilt.

"I don't know what you're talking about," she stammered, her trembling voice betraying her.

"You know exactly what I'm talking about." Brianna's voice dropped, low and commanding.

A gust of icy wind tore through the room, slamming the door with a thunderous bang.

Picture frames rattled, dust spiraled upward.

Silence followed—unnatural, taut as a wire.

"Undo it," Brianna demanded, her tone sharp, unyielding.

The air turned frigid.

Curtains billowed though the windows were sealed. A low hum vibrated at the edge of hearing, relentless, gnawing.

Mrs. Richardson staggered, clutching her chest. Her eyes darted wildly. "What... what is this?"

"Oh, did you think you were the only one who could play with fire?" Brianna's smile edged with menace as she stepped forward, her presence radiating control.

Mrs. Richardson backed away, clutching her necklace, as though seeking refuge in it. But Brianna's fingers curled, and the pendant lifted from her neck.

"What are you doing?" Mrs. Richardson cried. "How are you doing this?"

The necklace snapped with a metallic ping, flying into Brianna's waiting hand.

She caught it, raising the pendant like a trophy. "This little trinket—this is what started it all, isn't it?"

Mrs. Richardson stumbled, her face a mask of anger.

"You don't know what you're doing," she spat.

Brianna's smile widened. "Oh, I think I do."

Chapter Thirty-Eight

ELARA'S SHOULDERS SAGGED beneath the crushing weight of memories that surged like a relentless tide. They weren't fleeting images—they were visceral, searing sensations, raw emotions tearing through her with the violence of a storm. Grief clawed at her, merciless and unfiltered, dragging her deeper into its grip.

Her chest rose and fell in uneven, shuddering breaths, as though the air itself had turned to stone. Every inhale was a battle.

My babies.

Her voice cracked into the silence, the whisper unraveling into tears that blurred her vision.

In her mind's eye, she saw them vividly—Nadia and Justin, her children, her brightest stars. Nadia spinning Justin in wild circles, his laughter ringing out, bright and unrestrained, filling the house with a joy so pure it felt indestructible.

"Stop, stop, I'm dizzy!" he had squealed, clutching at her shirt for balance.

"You know the rules!" Nadia had teased, her grin wide, waiting for him to raise a single pinky finger in surrender.

That laughter had once been contagious, the kind that lit up the walls and chased shadows from the corners. Nadia and Justin had been inseparable then—two souls bound by innocence, tethered by a love so pure it had seemed untouchable.

But the memory, once radiant, now seared like an open wound—raw, festering, refusing to heal. The ache of it spread through her body like roots burrowing deep, coiling around her lungs in a merciless grip. It was more than sorrow. It was a crushing knot of grief, guilt, and regret—each thread tightening, each breath a reminder of what she had lost and what she had failed to protect.

And now... it was gone.

That bond, that light—ripped from her grasp, leaving behind only a hollow void that echoed through the silence of the house, an emptiness vast and unfillable.

The memory surfaced unbidden...

Elara's voice cracked through the house, sharp and unrelenting.

"You will do as I say!"

Her throat burned with the force of her words, but the fury driving them was stronger.

Nadia stood her ground, eyes blazing, her own voice rising to meet her mother's.

"No! I won't be part of this!"

The defiance in her tone sliced through Elara like broken glass, jagged and merciless.

Justin stood nearby, small hands clutching the hem of his shirt. His wide eyes flicked between them, confusion clouded with fear. Elara's chest twisted at the sight, but her anger moved faster than her grief. She swooped down, lifting him into her arms before he could retreat, his weight warm and solid against her as she strode for the door.

"Enough!" Elara roared, her hands trembling at her sides. "This is happening—with or without you!"

She spun toward the door, fury propelling her.

The knob rattled under her grip as she yanked it open, a blast of freezing rain slamming against her face like shards of glass. She stepped out, the cold soaking through her clothes in seconds, and threw the door shut behind her with a violent crack that echoed through the storm.

The sound of hinges groaning snapped her head around. Nadia burst out after her, her voice cutting through the downpour, raw and desperate.

"Mother, stop!"

Elara ignored the plea, her movements sharp, mechanical. She swung open the car door and hoisted Justin into the back seat. His small body was warm against her chilled arms, his confusion thick in the way he clutched at her shoulder. The rain pelted down in relentless sheets, hammering the roof of the car as she fumbled with the straps. Her fingers slipped, then tightened, forcing the buckle home with a metallic click.

The case in the backseat next to him loomed heavy with purpose. Each ritual, each preparation, had been exact, binding its power. Nadia's refusal—her betrayal—changed nothing.

"Get in the damn car!" she shouted over the storm, her voice cracking with rage and panic.

"No!" Nadia's scream cut through the night, high and fierce, shaking the air around them.

Rain hammered against the windshield in furious bursts, turning the world beyond the glass into a shifting curtain of gray. The wipers slashed back and forth, frantic and futile. The road blurred ahead, a smeared canvas of asphalt and water, each turn treacherous beneath the slick tires. But the storm outside was nothing compared to the tempest inside the car.

Nadia sat rigid in the passenger seat, arms locked across her chest. Her face was pale, but her eyes burned with defiance. Her voice—usually soft—was taut with desperation as she pleaded, but Elara refused to bend.

"Mom, please don't do this!" Nadia begged, her voice raw. "Please, just... turn around. Let's go home."

Elara's hands strangled the steering wheel, knuckles blanched. Her jaw ached with restraint. She told herself this was necessary—no, inevitable.

It's my duty. Our legacy must endure. Their faith cannot corrupt what we've built.

"You don't understand," Elara snapped, her tone brittle. Her eyes never left the slick road.

"No, you don't understand!" Nadia's words cracked, wet with tears. She leaned forward, defiance radiating like heat.

"This isn't who I am! I don't want this! I didn't ask for *any* of this! I don't want to be like you!"

Elara's focus didn't waver.

"You don't have a choice. This isn't about what you want. It's about what's required of you. Our legacy is bigger than you."

Nadia's fists trembled, her words slicing the air.

"I will not carry this legacy. And I will not let you destroy other people's lives!"

Elara's heart gave a twist, but she buried it deep, locking it down. The mission mattered more.

The church loomed through the rain.

"Mother, I will not allow you to do this!" Nadia cried. She lunged forward, yanking the parking brake with brutal force.

The car shrieked as the tires lost their grip, rubber screaming against rain-slick asphalt. Momentum ripped control from Elara's hands—the steering wheel jerking wildly as the vehicle spun. Water exploded upward in violent sheets, battering the windows until the world beyond dissolved into a dizzying whirl of gray and headlights.

Her scream tore free, raw and guttural, swallowed instantly by the storm. The car careened sideways, weightless for a heartbeat before gravity slammed it back down.

Impact.

Metal folded with a bone-deep crunch, the frame collapsing in on itself like a crushed skeleton. Glass detonated outward in a glittering spray, shards catching the strobe of headlights and emergency flashers as they spun through the air.

Her body snapped forward, seatbelt biting savagely across her chest, the jolt wrenching the breath from her lungs. Her skull slammed against the wheel—pain detonating white-hot behind her eyes, searing through her like lightning.

Then—*silence.*

Chapter Thirty-Nine

T HE AIR VIBRATED WITH A LOW, almost imperceptible hum that crawled across Brianna's skin like static, prickling every hair to attention. It seeped into her bones, a resonance she couldn't shake, as though the house itself was holding its breath. Her heart ached for Nadia—but in that moment, it ached even more for Elara. The woman's grief was no quiet sorrow; it was a living thing, thick and suffocating, raw enough to split the air. Brianna felt it pressing against her chest, bleeding into her ribs until it was indistinguishable from her own.

The grief coiled inside her, winding tighter with every beat, twisting into something heavier, darker. It blurred the edges of her own emotions, as if she were no longer certain where Elara's pain ended and her own began. The walls seemed to lean inward, the ceiling lowering by invisible degrees. The room pulsed with it—every flicker of shadow, every shift in the silence a reminder that grief could hollow a place as surely as fire consumed wood.

Stop it.

Focus.

Breathe.

Visualize.

She forced the words into her mind, clinging to them like an anchor, and willed her body to obey, to steady itself, to slow the frantic rise and fall of her breathing, wrestling her emotions into submission.

A flicker at the edge of her vision snapped her attention—a small, unexpected distraction from the storm raging inside her.

A little boy stood in the hallway. His small frame was outlined by the faint glow spilling from the light behind him, his wide eyes brimming with unguarded curiosity. Soft, round features marked his face, a fragile beacon of innocence that seemed out of place here, set against the dread clinging to the room.

Justin.

Nadia had spoken of his infectious laugh—the way it bubbled up like music that could drive away the rain—and the rules of their tickle fights. And now, here he was, that same light flickering in his eyes, unaware of the darkness circling around him.

"Hi," Brianna said softly, raising a hand in a small wave. Her smile was gentle but deliberate. "You must be Justin."

He tilted his head, gripping the edge of the doorway for balance, his gaze locked on her. For a moment, his eyes lingered on her face, searching.

"Who are you?" he asked finally, his voice small but steady, cutting through the brittle quiet.

Elara seized Justin's shoulder and yanked him close, her body angling between them like a shield. Her eyes burned into Brianna's, fear and fury flashing raw and uncontained.

"Justin, go back to your room," Elara ordered, voice taut.

But Justin didn't move. His feet stayed planted, gaze flicking between his mother and Brianna.

Brianna crouched, lowering herself to his level, her tone calm, coaxing. "It's okay, Justin. We're friends of your sister's. She told us all about you."

His eyes lit briefly before Elara's grip tightened.

"Don't," Elara snapped. "Don't talk to him."

Emma shifted uneasily beside Brianna. "Maybe we should go," she whispered.

But Brianna held her ground, her gaze steady on Justin. "Nadia told us how much she loved you," she pressed, her voice threading past Elara's protests. "She said you have the best laugh in the world."

Justin's lips twitched, the briefest ghost of a smile. Then Elara moved sharply, blocking Brianna's view, her voice breaking as she barked, "I said go back to your room!"

Justin's hand slipped from the doorway, but still he didn't leave. The stubborn set of his stance pulled the room into a tense standoff.

"Did my sister send you?" he asked.

"Yes. Sort of. We're here to talk to your mom," Brianna said gently. "About something really important."

Elara stiffened, her grip tightening.

"Hey, can I show you something?" Brianna asked, holding Justin's gaze.

"Don't you dare," Elara snapped, her voice trembling with panic.

"What?" Brianna asked lightly, feigning innocence. "I was just going to show him a trick his sister taught me."

Justin's eyes widened. "You were?"

"Don't you get near him!" Elara barked.

"That's okay," Brianna said, raising her hands. Her fingers wiggled in the air, slow and deliberate, as though tugging at invisible strings. "I can show him from here."

Justin stiffened.

His small shoulders hitched, his body tightening as if unseen hands darted across his ribs, his stomach, his sides. Every nerve seemed to spark alive at once.

Come on...

A chuckle slipped free, faint and stuttering—like the first raindrop striking glass before a storm.

There it is.

The sound swelled, jagged and wrong, sharpening into laughter that clawed its way out of his throat and ricocheted off the walls.

"Justin?" Elara whispered, her voice fraying. "What's happening?"

The laughter spiraled, manic and merciless. Justin convulsed, his chest heaving violently. His face flushed crimson as tears streaked down his cheeks. He doubled over, clutching his sides, the sound pouring from him no longer childlike—it was jagged, shrill, a scream wearing the mask of mirth. His limbs jerked grotesquely, marionette-like, as if pulled by strings only Brianna could see.

"Stop this!" Elara begged, her voice cracking. She clutched at his arms, trying to steady him. "What are you doing? Stop it!"

But the laughter drowned her out, relentless. It rattled the windows, vibrated the floorboards, reverberated inside Brianna's chest until it felt like the room itself was laughing with him.

Justin fell to the floor, thrashing, spasms wracking him as laughter tore through his lungs. His fingernails scraped furrows into the floorboards.

"Please—stop this!" Elara sobbed, her voice raw, broken.

Brianna stood rooted, gaze fixed on him, her fingers twitching in slow, deliberate rhythm. The air itself seemed to respond, vibrating faintly, alive.

Justin's laughter climbed higher, shrill and jagged, until it pierced the room like shattering glass. The sound cracked at the edges, no longer joyous—splintering into broken fragments that scraped against Brianna's ears. His chest heaved in spasms, lungs fighting for air between the relentless bursts of mirth. Each gasp tore out raw, hollow, like his body was unraveling from the inside. His voice cracked under the strain, thin and brittle, as if his small frame couldn't contain the storm ripping through him.

At last, he lifted his hand—shaking, feeble—only a single pinky raised.

Brianna recognized the gesture...

Surrender.

A mischievous smile unfurled across Brianna's face. This time she didn't bury it. She let it bloom, bold and deliberate, on full display.

Justin's laughter cut off in an instant—severed clean, as if the air itself had snapped shut.

Silence crashed down. Only his ragged, wheezing breaths filled the void. Slowly, Justin dragged a sleeve across his tear-streaked face, smearing wetness into his skin. With a wobble, he pushed himself upright. And then—bright and sudden—he smiled. Wide. Innocent. as though the last few minutes had been erased, nothing had happened at all.

"That was awesome!" he cried, bouncing with excitement.

Elara dropped to her knees, yanking him into her arms. Her shoulders shook with sobs, grief curdling into fury as her gaze cut upward, blazing into Brianna.

"How did you do that?" she whispered, trembling.

Brianna tilted her head, calm, detached, her fingers stilling at her sides.

"It's just a trick," she said softly. "Nadia taught me."

Chapter Forty

UNEASE POOLED IN ELARA'S STOMACH, heavy and unrelenting, spreading through her like ice water in her veins. She struggled to make sense of what she had just witnessed. Only moments ago, Justin had been writhing on the floor in a fit of hysterical laughter, his body convulsing as though seized by some unseen hand—and now he stood at her side, calm, composed, untouched, as if none of it had ever happened.

Her gaze shifted to Brianna. The girl was unnervingly still, her composure unshaken, her very presence radiating a quiet force that pressed against the air. It wasn't loud or dramatic, yet it carried a weight that drew Elara's attention in spite of herself—magnetic, but chilling.

The realization struck her with the violence of a thunderclap, rattling through her bones. Nadia, for all her denials of witchcraft, had not been as isolated as she had claimed. She had found allies—built a coven of her own in secret. But this was no coven Elara recognized. These girls—these strange, inscrutable girls—were not tethered to faith, nor did they bow to the rituals of the old order.

They moved outside both, untethered, answering to nothing but themselves. There was no doctrine to restrain them, no tradition to dictate their boundaries. What they carried was raw, volatile, uncharted—power without compass, authority without anchor. And in that lawlessness, Elara sensed something far more dangerous than witchcraft: the birth of something new, something that did not yet have a name.

These girls are something else entirely.

Something she could neither dismiss nor control.

Her eyes locked onto Brianna, narrowing with suspicion.

"You're not just one of us, are you?" she whispered, the question escaping her lips like a fragile thread. "You're... something else."

Brianna's smile widened, slow and deliberate, but it didn't touch her eyes. They remained cool, watchful, as though she was dissecting the moment, weighing it against some unseen scale.

"What I am isn't important," Brianna said, her voice calm, unnervingly measured.

She took a step closer, her presence radiating an authority that felt almost otherworldly.

"What's important is what you do next."

Her tone softened, yet it carried the weight of inevitability, as if she already knew the outcome.

"What are you going to do next, Momma?" Justin asked, his voice soft but unwavering. "And why is it so important?"

The words struck her like a blow, freezing her in place. She stared at him—her son—his small, trusting face tilted up toward hers, wide eyes glistening with innocence and curiosity. Her chest tightened, the weight of his faith in her pressing like a stone against her ribs.

She flicked her gaze to Brianna, whose piercing eyes seemed to strip her bare, and then to Emma, whose uncertainty mirrored the storm inside her. At last, her eyes fell on the porch. Oscar lay there in the pale spill of light, its lifeless form twisted in silence. The puppet wasn't just a relic. It was a reminder—a testament to what she had done, the power she had unleashed without fully grasping the cost.

"It's important because—" Brianna crouched, her gaze locking with Justin.

Elara tensed, every muscle coiling as Brianna leaned closer.

"You see, some kids we know—they're right around your age—they're having really bad dreams."

Elara's stomach knotted, dread rising sharp and certain.

She's baiting him.

"Really bad dreams?" Justin's eyes widened with recognition, a flicker of understanding passing across his face. "You mean nightmares?" he said, his voice small but serious.

Brianna nodded, leaning in slightly. "Yes, nightmares. Really, really bad ones," she said, speaking slowly. "Have you ever had a nightmare, Justin?"

Justin nodded vigorously. "Uh-huh," he said quickly, his tone almost eager to relate.

"They're no fun, are they?" Brianna replied.

He shook his head and pouted. "No," he muttered, the memory of some forgotten terror flickering in his eyes. "No fun at all."

Brianna leaned closer still, lowering her voice as though sharing a secret meant only for him. "Did you know that if nightmares get really, really, *really* bad, they can make someone sick?" she said, her tone careful, deliberate.

His eyes went wide, his small hands gripping the hem of his shirt as if for comfort. "Really?" he whispered.

"Really," Brianna said, her voice calm, her expression solemn as she nodded. "Before Nadia went to—" She paused mid-sentence, her words catching as if she had walked too close to an edge.

Elara's voice broke the moment, low and hollow, each word weighted with bitterness and grief. "Went to a better place," she said, her eyes fixed on Brianna with a mix of suspicion and pain.

"Yes, thank you," Brianna replied smoothly, recovering quickly, her tone even and measured. "Before Nadia went to a better place, she told me and my friend Emma here that your momma is really good at helping kids get rid of nightmares."

Justin's face lit up, his eyes widening with wonder. "Are you going to help the kids, Momma?"

His tone was light, hopeful, a child's innocent faith in the goodness of the world shining through. But the words landed on Elara like a hammer blow, each syllable striking at the guilt and regret she had buried deep.

"I can try," she said finally.

Brianna's glower sharpened, her calm tone underpinned by an almost imperceptible edge, like the glint of a blade hidden just beneath the surface.

"Such a good momma you are," she said, her voice steady, deliberate. She leaned forward slightly, her eyes locking onto Elara's with a piercing intensity that made the room feel smaller. "I bet you'd never let anything bad happen to little Justin here, would you?"

"Never," Elara replied. "Not in a million years."

Justin beamed, his smile so bright it seemed to chase the shadows from Elara's mind.

Brianna's expression softened. For a moment, it seemed she, too, was caught in the glow of Justin's innocence. "Oh, I almost forgot!" she exclaimed suddenly. She slipped a hand into her pocket.

Elara's gaze clung to Brianna's every motion, suspicion knifing through her like a blade. Too many nights battling shadows had taught her that evil rarely announced itself—it crept in quietly, wearing harmless faces, striking hardest when wrapped in the guise of the ordinary.

"What are you doing?" she demanded, her voice sharp. She stepped back, pulling Justin behind her with a protective grip.

Brianna extended her hand, fingers curled, palm up. The gesture was deliberate, her fingers unfurling with almost theatrical care.

Elara squinted, leaning forward despite herself, her breath shallow as she tried to make out what Brianna was holding.

"Justin, stop!" Elara shouted, tightening her grip on him.

But he twisted free, slipping from her grasp as excitement propelled him forward.

"Awesome!" he squealed.

Elara's breath caught. Her eyes softened, blurring with sudden tears as they landed on the pencil topper in Brianna's palm. *Curious George*—Nadia's favorite. The sight pierced her, tender and sharp all at once.

For a heartbeat, the oppressive weight in the room seemed to lift, replaced by a fleeting warmth—something fragile, nostalgic, almost merciful. But the moment shattered as quickly as it came, slipping through her fingers like sand.

Brianna straightened, her shoulders squaring with deliberate precision. The softness in her gaze vanished, replaced by something harder, colder—her posture rigid, commanding.

"Now run along to your room, Justin," she said, her tone light but edged with authority. "Your momma, Emma, and I have important business to discuss."

Chapter Forty-One

T HE SOUND OF JUSTIN'S FOOTSTEPS faded into the distance. Elara stood rooted in place, grief and guilt pressing heavily against her ribs, each breath a battle she wasn't sure she could win.

For a long moment, she remained still.

The silence stretched thin, taut as wire, before she forced herself to turn back toward the girls waiting in her living room. They felt out of place here, like intruders in a house already broken by loss.

In the corner, the Christmas tree glowed. A tall pine, its branches burdened with glass balls of blue, red, and gold, interspersed with handmade ornaments—photos of Nadia and Justin, taped and glitter-framed by small hands years ago. Tiny windows into better times.

Beneath the tree, the wrapped presents mocked her—promises of joy frozen in bright paper and glossy bows, gifts for a daughter who would never open them.

They are coffins in disguise, Elara thought bitterly, *and I wrapped them myself.*

She tore her gaze away and drew in a breath that shuddered.

"Please, have a seat," she murmured.

The words sounded alien in her mouth, brittle and wrong. Still, she gestured toward the sofa, her hand trembling before it dropped uselessly back to her side.

"No, thank you, Mrs. Richardson," the girls answered together.

The unison pricked her nerves, uncanny in its precision.

Elara let out a sharp exhale, part sigh, part bitter laugh.

Of course they don't trust me. I don't trust them either.

"Call me Elara," she said flatly. "I'm not a fan of the 'Missus' nonsense."

Her eyes skimmed them, catching the sheen of sweat on their brows. "If you won't sit, at least take off your coats."

They complied, and Elara's gaze sharpened. Brianna slipped something from her pocket, tucking it into the back of her jeans. Quick—but not quick enough.

What is she hiding?

Brianna's eyes wandered toward the corner. "Nice tree," she murmured, almost reverent.

Elara followed her gaze, her voice catching on the words: "It's for the kids." She forced the rest out. "That's all it is."

But the truth gnawed at her: there would be no kids to enjoy it. No laughter shrieking through the halls, no wide-eyed wonder at twinkling lights, no tiny fingers tearing into paper with squeals of delight. The house, once a vessel for chaos and joy, now echoed only with absence. The gifts beneath the tree might as well have been gravestones—brightly wrapped memorials to what would never be.

Her jaw tightened. "Let's not pretend we're here for tea and manners."

Brianna's gaze slid past her, snagging on something along the wall.

Elara followed her gaze to a faded frame, its glass smudged, the picture curled at the edges from years of handling. In the photo, women crowded shoulder to shoulder, a wave of faces burning with defiance. At the center stood a young Elara—a spitting image of Nadia—small, tense, her arms crossed protectively. Beside her, her mother loomed, chin lifted, fire blazing from her eyes as she held a sign high above her head that read:

W.I.T.C.H.

We Are Women.

We Are Liberation.

"I think I was nine when that photo was taken," Elara said quietly. "My mom dragged me to that protest. I remember being mortified."

"What does W.I.T.C.H. stand for?" Emma asked.

"Women's International Terrorist Conspiracy from Hell."

Brianna blinked. "You're joking."

"No," Elara replied, her tone flat. "Look it up."

Her gaze lingered on her mother's defiance.

The past isn't gone. It still lives here. And it stares back every time I close my eyes.

She turned abruptly. "Brianna, right?"

She nodded.

"You're good with kids."

"She's good with everyone," Emma added.

Brianna smiled faintly, though sorrow clung to her like a shadow.

Elara studied her, suspicion tangling with something softer, maybe even regret. "Yes... that's why Nadia kept you close. She didn't have many friends."

"She was wonderful," Brianna whispered, voice trembling but measured.

"Yes, well..." Elara's inhale wavered. "That's partly my fault. I don't trust easily."

The girls exchanged a look, shared grief woven silently between them.

"She was amazing," Emma whispered.

"There was no one like her," Brianna finished, heavy and certain.

Elara's throat constricted. Her hands knotted together, trembling. "She was my world," she admitted, words spilling like a confession. "It wasn't supposed to end like this."

Brianna's voice softened, coaxing: "End like what?"

"I'm not a bad person," Elara said suddenly, desperate, her voice breaking. "We are not bad people."

"We never thought you were," Brianna soothed. "And I'm sorry if anything we—or my mother—said made you think otherwise."

The words landed like a balm but couldn't erase the fractures. Elara turned her gaze away, down into the pit of memory—her mother's stern orders, her grandmother's rituals, her own stubborn pride. Misunderstandings became walls. Pride hardened into vengeance. Nadia had paid the price.

"Your mother asked me to come to your church," Elara said.

"I'm so sorry," Brianna blurted.

Elara raised her hand sharply. "Let me finish."

Her voice steadied, though her eyes stung.

"I wasn't angry at your mother. Not completely. Nadia wouldn't stop talking about you two. I thought you were trying to influence her. To pull her into the church."

Emma shook her head. "We understood that topic was off-limits."

Elara studied their faces, their sincerity striking something deep.

"I don't know how Oscar made it to the church," she admitted. "We never made it there. It must have flown out the window during the accident."

"It doesn't matter where it ended up. It finished what you started," Brianna replied.

Elara nodded. "Once unleashed, it has its own will. It forges its own path."

Elara breathed in deep, her emotions threatening to shatter her composure.

"Are you okay?" Brianna asked. Elara sensed it was her true nature shining through.

"I thought Nadia was being weak by trying to shield you two," Elara said, her shoulders sagging under the weight of the admission. "But she was stronger than I ever could be."

Chapter Forty-Two

B RIANNA'S HEART ACHED FOR the woman before her—a mother drowning not only in the loss of her daughter but in the crushing awareness of how profoundly she had misunderstood her. Grief was a living thing in the room, pressing against the walls, coiling into every shadow. It carried the weight of unspoken apologies, words too late to matter, saturating the air until each breath scraped Brianna's throat raw.

She drew in a shaky breath, struggling to steady herself, but the air was thick with sorrow. Her lungs burned with the effort, as though she were trying to breathe through water. Emotions swirled inside her like a storm—her own grief clawing at her ribs, guilt cutting sharp and deep.

Everywhere she looked, Nadia stared back.

Photographs cluttered every surface, fragments of a life severed too soon. Nadia laughing, her eyes alight with dreams she would never realize. Nadia mid-sentence, her joy frozen in time. Smiling faces that now felt like accusations. She was everywhere and yet nowhere—her absence a wound carved wide open, pulsing with unbearable emptiness.

The room thrummed with her presence. It wasn't just the photographs. It was the energy—raw, electric—that clung to the walls and floor, vibrating with anger and loss. It felt alive, as though Nadia's spirit lingered just beyond reach, pacing restlessly, a teenager's voice silenced too soon yet still demanding to be heard.

This is where their argument began.

The tension hung thick, pressing down on her like a physical weight. It was more than grief—it was anger, regret, and words left unsaid, all swirling together in a storm that refused to settle.

The echoes were still there. She could almost hear them: Nadia's sharp, cutting voice, raw with pain and defiance, shouting words she could never take back. Her mother's reply followed, louder, harder, thundering with frustration and hurt. The memories weren't just shadows; they reverberated off the walls, trapped in this room.

Nadia's voice rose, shrill and cracking, filled with the fury of a teenager desperate to be understood.

"You don't get it! You can't do this! They don't deserve this!"

The accusation rang out, piercing, the sound so vivid that Brianna flinched instinctively.

Her mother's voice followed, matching Nadia's anger with her own. *"After everything I've done for you? You're ungrateful. Selfish."*

The words were weapons, hurled in the heat of emotion, leaving wounds that could never truly heal.

The remnants lingered here, embedded in the very walls, replaying on an endless loop. They hadn't faded into memory—they had soaked into the room itself, saturating the air with regret and unresolved pain.

Nadia had tried to stop her.

Brianna staggered under the weight of emotions that weren't hers alone. Nadia's anguish beat against her ribs, sharp and raw—the fury of a daughter silenced too soon. Elara's grief pressed heavy, swollen with regret and the hollow ache of a mother realizing too late how deeply she had failed. Emma's fear surged through her veins—jittery, electric—spiking in waves that made Brianna's pulse race. And then her own grief tangled with theirs, indistinguishable from the rest.

It's too much. Too loud. Too consuming.

Her body shook with the sheer force of it, as though she had become a vessel too small to contain the flood.

Overhead, the lights flickered. The buzzing hum of electricity stuttered in uneven bursts, each surge echoing the storm inside her. The room itself seemed to convulse, trembling at the edges, as if her body weren't the only vessel buckling beneath the strain of four hearts beating as one.

Her breath snagged as the flickering grew frantic, shadows lurching across the walls like predators closing in. Then the bulb above them burst with a sharp, deafening crack. Shards of glass rained down in glittering arcs, the scent of scorched filament burning the air.

"Please, stop! Enough!" Elara cried, her voice breaking, desperation raw. "Just tell me what you want from me."

Brianna inhaled deeply, forcing herself to steady her emotions, though her hands trembled at her sides. "Reverse the curse," she said, her voice firm.

"I can't," Elara replied, her tone resolute yet weary. "Even if I tried. The curse has been passed down for generations. No one knows what's behind it—or how deep it runs."

Brianna's pulse quickened. Her mind couldn't stop from reaching outward, imagining the weight of what Elara had just confessed. A curse passed down through generations. That meant not just Elara. Not just her mother.

Her thoughts spiraled into a vast, tangled lineage—faces blurred by time, hands clasping hands, each one carrying the darkness forward.

How many people fed into this? How many voices whispered over fire and ash, binding themselves to something they didn't understand?

Centuries of choices, bargains, rituals. An endless thread knotted and frayed, passed from one life to the next. A web so vast it could never be unraveled, strands snarled together until no beginning or end could be found. A weight that had lived too long, soaked too deep, its origin lost in shadows.

It's not just her curse. It's all of theirs. Every single one before her.

"If you can't reverse it, then break it," Emma demanded.

Brianna's head snapped up, eyes locking onto Emma. She hadn't expected her to speak, let alone with such conviction. Confusion flashed across her face. "How is that different?"

"Reversing it means undoing it," Emma said, her gaze steady and clear. "Breaking it means it stops now. It ends here—no more harm, no more victims."

Elara nodded. "Sounds like you know a thing or two about curses," she said with a wry edge.

"So will you break it?" Brianna asked.

"I can't," Elara replied. "But I'll help you."

Her gaze shifted between Brianna and Emma, lingering just long enough to convey the gravity of her choice.

"But I want to be clear," she added, her tone firm, posture straightening as if reclaiming her authority, "I'm not helping you because I'm threatened by you."

Her eyes locked on Brianna's, daring her to object.

"I'm helping because I know it's what Nadia would have wanted."

Chapter Forty-Three

U NTIL NOW, EMMA'S UNDERSTANDING of evil—the way it threaded itself through ordinary places, the way it could hide in plain sight—had been nothing but a burden. It clung to her like a second skin, pressing down on her shoulders until she felt permanently bent beneath its weight. It set her apart, carving out a gulf between her and everyone else who moved through life blissfully unaware. While others laughed, pretended, or turned away, Emma was forced to look. Forced to see.

She had spent years resenting it, this unwanted sight, this curse that forced her to notice the rot behind the smiles, the shadows beneath the light. How many times had she prayed for ignorance, begged for blindness, wished to be spared the constant reminder that darkness was never far away? Yet no matter how hard she tried to shut her eyes, no matter how stubbornly she clung to denial, the truths whispered back to her from the corners, echoing in her mind with a persistence that bordered on cruelty.

It made her different.

Lonely.

Afraid.

And in that difference, she had known only isolation—until Brianna. Until Nadia. Until this moment, when the very thing that had set her apart no longer felt like a curse, but the key. The knowledge she had borne so quietly for so long now felt like a blade in her hand, sharp and ready, a weapon forged from pain and truth.

Emma took a steadying breath and looked directly at Elara.

"How do we break the curse?" she asked, her voice firm despite the nervous energy buzzing beneath her skin.

"We have everything we need right here," Elara replied evenly. "But I doubt you have it in you."

Emma exchanged a glance with Brianna.

"Of course we have it in us," Brianna said, stepping forward.

"I wasn't referring to you," Elara said.

Her gaze fixed on Emma with piercing intensity that made her stomach drop. "You. Bring *Oscar* inside."

Emma froze. "Why me?" she whispered.

"It has to be you," Elara said, her expression unreadable.

"I don't... I don't understand," Emma stammered, her eyes darting to Brianna.

Brianna met her gaze with quiet concern.

Elara stepped closer, her presence commanding, her voice low but cutting. "You've felt it, haven't you? That unease, that sickness. The way it creeps in, even when you know you're safe."

Emma shook her head quickly, as though denial could undo the truth. "I don't... I mean, I feel things, but—"

"You are marked," Elara interrupted, her tone slicing through the denial like a scalpel. "Oscar doesn't choose randomly. It seeks. It knows your deepest fears."

Her words landed like blows, reverberating in Emma's mind. Her breathing quickened, the edges of the room blurring as the walls seemed to close in, the air thick and stifling.

That's impossible, she thought, clinging to her father's teachings. *Darkness is cunning and deceptive, but not omniscient.*

"You're lying." Emma said. "It knows nothing. How could it possibly?"

Elara stepped closer, the air tightening with her nearness. "How does darkness ever know, child?"

Her eyes gleamed with a strange mix of pity and triumph. Her tone lilting, playful—like a cat toying with a cornered mouse.

She continued, "It watches. It listens. It waits. And when it finds a crack, it seeps in."

Emma's pulse hammered.

Don't listen to her. She's twisting it. She has to be.

But memories surged, vivid and unrelenting, dragging her back. She could hear Nadia's voice, low and conspiratorial, their lunchtime conversations echoing like whispers through time. Secrets passed across cafeteria tables, fragile truths too delicate for anyone else to hold.

"You see, Oscar doesn't just barge in. It finds the cracks. The vulnerabilities. And you, Emma—you've been primed for it your whole life."

No, she doesn't know that. She can't.

But the images came anyway. The childhood toy she once loved—its cheerful giggle, its bright red fur. Innocent then. Twisted now. She remembered nights when the fabric scraped against her palms, rough and scratchy, when she swore its glassy eyes followed her across the room.

It was just a toy.

But she remembered crying herself to sleep, muffling the sound in her pillow so her parents wouldn't hear. She remembered the way the toy's grin seemed to stretch wider in the dark, the way its laugh warped into something guttural, mocking. The terror she felt then never loosened its grip...

It grew roots.

Emma's eyes narrowed on Elara, fury and grief knotting in her chest until it burned. The woman's knowing smile was hard to watch—that smug curve of her lips, the way she wielded Emma's past like a blade.

A thought sank like a stone in her chest, betrayal flickering through her before unease took hold:

Nadia told her.

The realization slammed into her, bitter and cruel, hollowing her out from the inside. Nadia had been there—standing beside her mother the day she bought a doll as a joke. She'd laughed when she showed it to Emma, her voice light, teasing, with no trace of malice. There had been no cruel intent in Nadia's eyes, only the mischief of a friend sharing a joke.

Elara had taken that innocent moment and poisoned it. She had twisted the memory, sharpened it into a weapon, wielding it with precision until it cut deep. What had once been harmless had been turned against her, reforged into something venomous, something designed to wound.

"You used her," Emma said, her voice low, trembling with anger. "You used your own daughter."

"You're being dramatic," Elara replied coolly. "The truth is, you never know where your words might travel... or into whose hands they might fall. Besides, what kind of mother would I be if I didn't ask about her friends?"

"Stop!" Emma snapped, her voice breaking, too raw to disguise the tremor underneath. Heat surged up her neck, hot and suffocating.

Elara's lips curled into a mocking smile, deliberate, taunting. "Oh, she has a pulse after all."

Emma's stomach twisted. That smile wasn't just cruel—it was triumphant, as if Elara had peeled back her defenses and found exactly where to dig the knife.

Her eyes gleamed with merciless amusement, locking on Emma like a predator circling prey.

"Oscar latches on to those who feel it. Who carry its influence. And you..."

Her voice dropped, soft but venomous.

She pointed directly at Emma, her hand trembling with fervor, her finger like a blade leveled at her chest.

"You let it in."

The words slammed into Emma, cold and jagged.

I would never.

But the protest caught in her throat, smothered by the images clawing back to life—red fur, plastic eyes gleaming in the dark, laughter that wasn't laughter at all.

Chapter Forty-Four

ELARA'S WORDS POUNDED IN BRIANNA'S mind like a relentless drumbeat, each strike sharper, more deafening than the last. Her breath caught, chest rising and falling in ragged bursts beneath the crushing weight of revelation. The room tilted, swimming at the edges, dissolving into a haze of fear and desperation—yet Brianna knew the terror flooding her veins wasn't entirely her own. It carried Emma's shape, Emma's echo. It had bled into her, invasive and consuming, until Brianna could no longer tell where Emma ended and she began.

"Leave her alone!" Brianna shouted.

The words tore out of her throat, raw and jagged, a cry so forceful she barely recognized it as her own.

The house responded. A low vibration groaned through the floorboards, picture frames rattling against the walls, the coffee table shivering as though it might crack in half. The air quaked, dense and electric, saturated with something furious and alive.

Thoughts spiraled through her, jagged, unrelenting, as the truth carved its way into her like a blade:

She hadn't merely absorbed Emma's emotions—she had amplified them until they swelled into something monstrous.

And it didn't stop with Emma.

The children at church—

Their fears. Their whispered nightmares. Their sleepless cries. All of it clung to her like barbed wire, a thousand tiny hooks tearing into her spirit. Their dread had burrowed deep into her marrow, feeding on her even as she unwittingly fed it in return.

The energy roared inside her, not her own, not theirs, but something forged in the collision between them—raw, unrestrained, and terrifying.

Her hand shook as she lifted it, the burned flesh catching the dim light, blistered and curling in unnatural waves. The mark seemed to pulse, alive, as if mocking her.

"Emma didn't let it in—I did," Brianna said, her voice breaking, her confession cutting through the heavy silence. She held her hand out, the scarred flesh exposed, undeniable.

Time seemed to slow as she stood silent, isolated and consumed by her thoughts, drowning in guilt.

"It isn't your fault," Emma said.

"I gave it power," Brianna shot back. Her voice sounded foreign in her own ears, detached, as though the words had bypassed thought and risen from some deeper place. For a heartbeat, she didn't even feel like the one speaking.

Then, like a veil lifting, a sliver of clarity cut through the storm. Her breath leveled, the frantic pounding in her chest easing just enough to let her see a way forward.

Slowly, she raised her head. Her eyes locked on Emma's with quiet resolve. Searching. Pleading. Drawing strength from the bond they shared.

"We need to confront it," she said, each word steady, deliberate. "We need to take away its power."

The room held its breath.

Brianna turned her gaze toward Elara, throat constricting as she forced herself to meet the woman's eyes.

Elara's face was unreadable at first, the shadows carving her grief-lined features into something harder, sharper.

"She's right," Elara said, her voice low but unwavering. "Oscar's grip only grows stronger with time and contact. If you want to end this, it has to be now."

The confirmation washed over Brianna like a cold wave, chilling but steadying her resolve.

Emma's breath hitched, her lips parting as if to argue, but no words came. Her chest rose and fell too fast, fear flickering in her eyes like a trapped flame.

"We'll do this together," Brianna said, firm.

Emma hesitated, then reached out, fingers gripping Brianna's hands. The connection steadied them both—a fragile but unbreakable bond against the darkness looming ahead.

Elara stepped closer, eyes narrowing. "He thrives on fear, but if you don't let him in, you'll never be able to cast him out."

Brianna drew Emma forward. Their steps were slow as they approached the front door, the weight of what lay beyond pressing in like a storm. Emma's energy crackled against her like static, a current of fear, doubt, and stubborn resolve surging through their joined hands. *It's too much. Too much to carry.* But Brianna tightened her grip, anchoring them both.

Oscar sat on the porch in a way that defied logic, propped upright, its head cocked at an unnatural angle. Its glossy black eyes caught the faint light like shards of obsidian. This wasn't how she'd left it. Someone—or something—had set it there deliberately. Waiting. Watching.

Brianna knelt, her knees scraping the rough wood. Her stomach lurched as she reached toward the puppet. The moment her fingers brushed the surface, a chill shot up her arm, freezing the breath in her lungs.

Emma's grip tightened, desperate. "Brianna, don't," she pleaded, voice cracking. "I can't... I can't do this."

Brianna turned to her. For a heartbeat, the raw terror in Emma's eyes almost made her pause.

Her voice softened, though steel edged her tone. "Maybe *you can't*. But *we can*."

She stepped back inside.

The air shifted instantly, as if Oscar's presence warped the fabric of the room. The temperature plunged. The lights flickered, casting jagged shadows that crawled along the walls like living things.

"Brianna, this is insane," Emma said, panic rising. "You don't know what you're doing!"

Brianna set Oscar on the table with deliberate care. The wood groaned beneath its weight. Its glassy eyes fractured the dim light into sharp, broken reflections, mocking.

Ignore it.

Focus.

"This is what it wants. It's been attacking us, trying to control us," she said, low but steady. "Now it's our turn."

"But how?" Emma asked, her eyes darting between Brianna and the puppet.

Brianna stared at Oscar, her thoughts aligning.

"We didn't just let it in before," she said finally, each word heavy with guilt. "We gave Oscar energy—our energy. Now we need to take it back."

"I don't understand," Emma said, brow knitting. "How do we fight it?"

Brianna exhaled slowly. Resistance wasn't the answer. Fear wasn't either. The truth cut sharper.

"We don't *fight* it," she said at last, her voice steady. She met Emma's eyes. "We *face* it. We draw it out and prove we're stronger."

Emma's breath quickened, her hands twitching as if she wanted to pull away. "How?"

"By not running," Brianna said, grounding her with a squeeze. "By not hiding. By showing it has no power over us—unless we give it."

Her words hung in the air, defiant, heavy enough to shift the room.

"This isn't about reversing it or destroying it," she continued, unwavering. "It's about breaking its hold—on you, on us. And we do that by facing everything we fear. Head-on."

Emma swallowed hard, her gaze fixed on the puppet. Its glassy stare seemed to glint with malice, as though it knew.

"Are you sure about this?" she whispered.

Brianna's jaw tightened, her resolve hardening like forged steel. "No," she said. "But we don't have a choice."

Chapter Forty-Five

W*E HAVE NO CHOICE.*

The words carried a different weight now. Once they had been an admission of fear, a surrender. Now they rang like steel—an invocation of power.

Emma's gaze snapped to Oscar.

Its glassy eyes no longer looked dead. A faint light churned inside them, spiraling, gathering strength. The shadows on the walls writhed in response, bending and twisting as though something unseen had been shaken awake.

Her pulse hammered, each beat louder than the last.

There was no scripture she could flip to, no neat verse that spelled out what to do when the dark stared back. But something older than reason stirred in her gut, raw and primal, tugging her forward with unshakable instinct.

"Brianna, something's happening," Emma whispered, inching closer.

The hum thickened in the air, low and vibrating, rattling through her bones.

Emma clamped a hand over her mouth, muffling the gasp that tore free.

"What do we do?" she asked, her voice barely steady, every word trembling against the pull of the storm gathering in the room.

"Breathe," Brianna said calmly. "Slow, deep breaths. Picture roots extending from your feet into the earth, anchoring you. Envision light surrounding you, a shield against the darkness."

Emma inhaled shakily, but the shadows only crept closer—tendrils unfurling from the corners, deliberate and taunting.

"Don't let it rattle you," Brianna said. "Don't give it power."

The words rang hollow.

The temperature plummeted, the air turned sharp, biting. A chill sank into Emma's bones, breath curling in pale wisps before her face. The walls seemed to lean closer, the room shrinking, the weight of it crushing.

Brianna continued, "Take control of your emotions. Choose what you want to feel."

"Take control," Emma whispered.

But doubt gnawed at her with teeth sharp as glass. She hadn't been in control when Diane cornered Elara. She hadn't been in control when Nadia cut her off, leaving her to rot in silence, questioning every word she'd ever said. She hadn't been in control when Elara loosed a curse vast as a tidal wave. And now—standing before Oscar, with shadows thickening around her—she felt like nothing more than prey.

The crack of wood splintering sliced through the silence like a gunshot. With a sharp, unnatural jerk, Oscar's head snapped upright. Its eyes locked on Emma's—glassy, yet alive, black depths swirling with something that should not exist.

"Emmmm-ma... wanna play?" it hissed.

Its grin widened, grotesque, a parody of joy. Its head tilted sharply, as though pulled by unseen strings.

Emma jolted. She stumbled back, breath catching, legs colliding with a chair. Her hands gripped the table, knuckles white, gaze locked on the thing.

Oscar slid from the tabletop, limbs moving with sickening fluidity, dragging across the floor like a stalking predator. Then, impossibly, it began to climb. Up the wall. Effortless. Defying gravity.

Emma's hand clamped over her mouth, muffling the gasp that ripped free. Horror pinned her where she stood.

It clung to the ceiling like some unholy insect. Its eyes glowed hotter, brighter, sweeping the room with predatory calm. The small frame was no longer a toy. It radiated intent—cold, merciless, alive.

It hung there, inverted, studying them. Waiting.

"What are you waiting for?" it taunted, the voice jagged, mocking, vibrating through the air itself as though the house had become its throat.

Emma froze. Her lungs refused to draw air, her heart battering her ribs in frantic, punishing bursts. Every instinct shrieked run, but her body betrayed her—paralyzed, pinned by an unseen weight. The edges of her vision seeped to black, shadows bleeding inward as the room tilted and warped, its shapes bending like heat haze. Reality slipped, elastic and unstable, as though the world itself was about to fold in on her. Through the thickening dark, Brianna's voice strained to reach her—faint, distorted, muffled, like a cry echoing from deep underwater.

The memory surfaced, sharp and vivid.

Emma whispered a prayer as her father stepped out of her bedroom:

"Now I lay me down to sleep, I pray the Lord my soul to keep.

Keep me safe through the night and wake me with the morning light.

If I should die before I wake, I pray the Lord my soul to take.

Amen."

Surrounded by soft pink bedding and plush pillows, she closed her eyes, letting the warmth envelop her as sleep began to tug at her.

The room filled with a sudden cacophony of mechanical whirs and tinny electronic melodies.

Her eyelids fluttered open.

The darkness was pierced by flashing colors from her toys.

"Oh no," Emma whispered, scrambling out of bed. "You'll wake Mommy and Daddy."

One by one, she hurried to silence them.

An unfamiliar sound rose above the clamor—a laugh. High-pitched. Eerie.

The chilling sound rooted her in place.

Her gaze jerked to the source of the sound—the bright red toy her father had insisted on buying. The one she'd never asked for, never wanted.

Tickle Me Elmo.

Its eyes gleamed under the dim light, its wide, plastic grin frozen in place.

She reached for it, her fingers trembling as she laid it face down on her lap. Carefully, she peeled back the Velcro seam on its back, the rip tearing through the quiet. Her breath hitched as she found the battery pack. With a click, the toy fell silent, the laughter cut short.

"There," she whispered.

She returned it to the shelf. Its vacant eyes stared forward.

Climbing back into bed, she pulled the blanket to her chin. Then—an eerie giggle drifted through the dark.

Emma's eyes widened. Slowly, she turned back toward the shelf.

The toy was standing.

Its oversized eyes burned like twin orbs, vacant yet alive, throwing an eerie shimmer into the dark. The grin carved across its face no longer looked playful but grotesque, stretched too wide, a parody of joy. Then came the cackle—a warped, jagged echo of the cheerful giggle it was meant to have, twisting the familiar into something monstrous.

Her throat cinched as thoughts clawed at her mind, frantic and disbelieving:

It's not supposed to stand like that.

Its eyes aren't supposed to glow like that.

The toy extended a fuzzy red arm toward her, the movement stiff, deliberate—as though pulled by invisible strings. Its felt mouth began to work, opening and closing with a grotesque snap.

"Do you want to be Elmo's frrrriend?" it crooned, the voice warped, glitching at the edges—half-childlike, half-demonic—every syllable dragging across her nerves like a blade.

Her stomach dropped as the realization hit.

Its mouth isn't supposed to move.

It cackled again, its body shaking violently—the one thing it was designed to do.

The shaking stopped.

The toy's jaw unhinged, stretching far wider than its felt frame should allow.

"Pllllleeeease," it hissed, the word warped into a serpentine rasp.

Then the flood came. A torrent of roaches poured from its gaping mouth, a black, writhing river that hit the floor with a wet hiss. Wings buzzed furiously, bodies colliding and splitting apart as they scrambled over one another, multiplying as though they had been nesting inside its hollow chest, waiting for this moment. The stench of damp earth and rot filled the room, clawing at Emma's nostrils.

Her stomach lurched. Her legs buckled. She opened her mouth to scream, but terror clamped down like a hand around her throat, strangling the sound before it could escape.

Chapter Forty-Six

T HE CHANDELIER THRASHED, CHAINS GROANING, metal links clanging like a funeral bell tolling overhead. Crystal pendants trembled and clashed, their sharp, discordant chime echoing like a warning. The fixture creaked—a high-pitched whine, as though the frame itself were protesting against the unseen force driving it. Glass rained down in a glittering cascade, shards pinging against the hardwood floor with delicate, crystalline chimes.

"What's happening?" Brianna shouted, her voice sharp with panic. Her breaths came ragged, chest heaving as though the air itself had turned hostile.

"I'm not doing this!" Elara cried, her tone frayed with desperation.

Emma's terror surged outward, spilling beyond her body, coiling through the air like an invisible noose. Each beat of her heart cinched it tighter. Her fear no longer belonged to her—it multiplied, contagious, latching onto Brianna, feeding the shadows until they thickened like smoke.

It's too much. I can't hold it back.

The weight of it pressed harder, suffocating thought, eroding reason. Emma could feel her grip on herself slipping, consciousness unraveling thread by thread as the darkness closed in.

The chandelier thrashed harder, its chains shrieking. The remaining bulbs flickered in erratic pulses, their light sputtering as if being devoured by the darkness.

Brianna's gaze snapped to Oscar.

Its grin was wide, grotesque, triumphant. Its dark, gleaming eyes burned with sadistic delight. In a blur, Oscar slithered across the ceiling—fluid, insect-fast, defying gravity with grotesque ease. Brianna's heart thundered as she tried to track it, but it was too quick, too serpentine. Its presence intensified, its power swelling as it fed on the fear saturating the room.

In a heartbeat—Oscar was gone, swallowed by the shadows of the hallway, leaving only the faint echo of malevolent laughter reverberating through the dark.

"He's going after Justin!" Elara's scream tore through the air, raw with panic. She bolted toward her son's room, footsteps echoing down the hall.

Brianna tried to follow, but her legs felt like lead, her body rooted to the floor. An icy paralysis spread through her limbs, locking her in place as if cold tendrils bound her muscles. She gasped, lungs burning, willing herself to move.

Her mind screamed at her to move, the command cracking through her skull like a lightning strike.

But her body betrayed her—frozen, helpless—as the darkness surged forward.

Her hand crawled toward her back pocket, every inch a battle, as though invisible hands dragged it down.

Then, with a sudden lurch, Brianna lunged. Her fingers clamped around Emma's wrist in a desperate grip.

Emma's wide eyes dropped to the object in Brianna's hand—the syringe.

"I'm sorry," Brianna whispered, her voice taut with regret.

The needle pierced Emma's skin. Her breath hitched, pupils blown wide, shock flashing across her face. She tried to speak, to protest, but the words choked in her throat, drowned by the fog already pulling her under. Her head lolled, features softening as panic drained away. Her breathing steadied, a disturbing calm settling over her. Her knees buckled as the tranquilizer took hold, robbing her of resistance.

Freed from the chokehold of Emma's fear, Brianna caught her before she crumpled. She eased her to the floor, arms trembling with guilt more than exertion.

The sound of hurried footsteps snapped her head up. Elara appeared in the doorway, Justin clutched tightly in her arms.

"It didn't reach him," Elara gasped, breathless with relief, her grip on Justin iron-tight.

She looked down at Emma sprawled on the floor.

"Momma, is she okay?" Justin asked.

Elara kissed the top of Justin's head, her voice soft but steady. "Yes, baby—she's just taking a nap," she assured him. Her eyes cut to Brianna, sharpened with determination. "How long do we have before she wakes up?"

Brianna glanced at Emma, then back at Elara. "A couple of hours, maybe."

"Good." Elara nodded decisively. She shifted Justin in her arms and pressed another kiss to his forehead. "I'm taking Justin to the neighbor's. He isn't safe here."

Brianna nodded. "I understand."

Elara hurried out the front door, clutching Justin tight. "I'll be back before you know it—I think I can help."

As the door closed behind them, the realization struck Brianna like a tidal wave, flooding her with chilling clarity. Her so-called gift didn't just magnify emotions—it gave them form, shaping fear into monsters that could walk and strike. Every fear, every spike of panic, every shred of doubt she absorbed didn't stay confined inside her. It spilled out, shaping itself into something tangible. Something dangerous.

Her stomach knotted as she turned toward the hallway. The air thickened there, charged with a static weight that prickled along her skin, raising every hair on the back of her neck.

Oscar lay sprawled before Justin's bedroom door, its wooden frame twisted, limbs splayed in a grotesque parody of rest.

Not lying, she thought. *Waiting.*

Her fists clenched at her sides. She forced her breath into rhythm, drawing in the fear and burning it down until only resolve remained. The paralysis that had gripped her cracked and fell away. She understood now—what she carried, what it meant. Her abilities weren't a curse. They were a weapon.

Every muscle in her body coiled, drawn taut as a bowstring. Her gaze locked onto the puppet's grin, daring it to move, daring it to strike.

"You won't win," she said, low and steady, her voice tempered into steel. She could hear the strength in her words—stronger than a warning. More reverent than a vow...

A declaration of war.

Chapter Forty-Seven

T HE PLAN WAS ALREADY BREWING in Elara's mind as she rushed back to her home. She'd sensed it from the moment she laid eyes on her. Emma was terrified before she had even stepped foot in her house. Unless Emma could build up the courage to face Oscar, they didn't stand a chance.

She stormed inside, her movements swift and deliberate, without pausing to acknowledge Brianna and Emma, who lay restless but still unconscious.

There was no time for therapy or modern medicine. She rushed to her bedroom, her resolve hardening with each step. There, Elara flung open the closet door, revealing an array of objects that spoke of a life steeped in ritual and magic. Her eyes darted to a box of delicate glass vials filled with liquids in colors that defied nature: glowing green, deep violet, and molten gold. Each vial was etched with cryptic symbols, whispering of ancient potency.

Tucked beneath the closet shelves was a small chest with iron hinges. Black candles, wax seals, and a set of brass charms engraved with protective symbols lay inside. Her gaze settled on a particular glass jar.

"Ah," she murmured, her lips curling into a satisfied smile. "This should work."

Her fingers skimmed past a dried poppet bound in red string and a jar of iron nails. Her eyes locked on a small, intricately carved wooden box. She lifted the lid, revealing a set of courage charms—amulets infused with spells of bravery, each one glinting faintly in the dim light.

"This," she breathed, holding up a lion's-head charm, its eyes glowing with a faint, unnatural fire. "This is what Emma needs."

Clutching the charm tightly, Elara rushed back into the living room, her arms laden with the tools she would need. The air around her seemed to hum with anticipation, the promise of ancient magic awakening once more.

Emma's head rested on Brianna's lap like a pillow, her small face pale and drawn with exhaustion. Brianna brushed damp strands of hair from her forehead, her touch careful, almost hesitant.

"What is this?" Brianna asked, rising from the floor. She stepped closer, her eyes widening as she peered into the ornate box. Inside lay bundles of sage, sweetgrass, and rosemary nestled beside polished crystals that caught the dim light, glittering faintly.

"You're not putting a spell on Emma," Brianna said, her tone sharp, defiant.

Elara held her gaze, steady, unflinching. "Smoky quartz for protection," she explained, lifting a dark crystal, its surface gleaming like trapped smoke. "And tiger's eye for courage." Her hand slipped deeper into the box and emerged with the one object that mattered. Her voice lowered, reverent. "But most important of all—the Witches' Magic Jar."

The vessel stood a foot tall, fashioned from translucent, smoky glass. Patterns seemed to stir faintly beneath its surface, like currents shifting under water. Tiny imperfections marred its smoothness, as though shaped by ancient hands.

Brianna scoffed, arms crossed. "The Witches' Magic Jar? That's what you call something this... fancy?" She hesitated. "What does it do?"

Patience steadied Elara's voice.

"Fear is powerful," she said, reciting words that had lived in her memory for years. "But courage is stronger. This jar doesn't banish fear—it draws out the courage buried within. But only if you believe."

She watched curiosity flicker in Brianna's expression as she leaned closer.

Inside the jar, a golden mist churned, alive, shot through with shards of obsidian, flecks of gold, and dried marigold petals. Light refracted in dizzying patterns across the glass. When Brianna's fingers hovered near it, the mist swirled faster, sensing her.

"This is Emma's only chance," she pressed, her voice softening. "Will you trust me?"

Brianna's eyes dropped to Emma's pallid face, her chest lifting in shallow breaths. Then back to the jar. Finally, to Elara. "Alright," she whispered. "Do what you need to do."

Elara tapped the jar lightly. Its glow brightened, as though stirring from slumber. She set it at the table's center, careful with her hands. Along the base, an inscription curved in looping, ancient script.

"What does it say?" Brianna asked, her skepticism loosening.

"Courage lies within," Elara murmured, her eyes tracing the familiar letters.

Brianna's gaze lingered on Emma's fragile body. "Will it last? Or is it temporary?"

"That depends entirely on Emma," Elara said gravely. "Her choice. Her will."

Emma twitched, breaths coming uneven and shallow.

Elara's chest tightened with urgency. *No more time.*

"She could wake at any second," she warned. "It's now or never."

Silence held them a moment before Brianna relented. "Okay," she said, steady. "Let's do it."

"Help me carry her."

Together, they lifted Emma onto the table. Brianna flinched at its hardness, but Elara moved with practiced precision, arranging candles around the girl and placing the jar at the center. Its glow pulsed in rhythm with Emma's fragile breaths.

"Help me place these." Elara pressed cool gemstones into Brianna's hands. As they circled Emma with them, the sharp scent of rosemary and sage filled the room, earthy and biting. Brianna coughed, but Elara did not pause.

"What now?" Brianna asked, folding her arms.

Elara clasped her hand gently. "We chant."

Brianna blinked. "You're kidding."

"It's the only way." Elara's voice was firm. She began, steady and low:

"I am in control. Courage is mine. Light within, unbroken. Darkness will not have me."

Brianna's voice joined hers, faltering at first, then stronger as the words gained rhythm.

"I am in control. Courage is mine. Light within, unbroken. Darkness will not have me."

The golden mist spun faster, the crystals glowing in time with their chant.

"I am in control. Courage is mine. Light within, unbroken. Darkness will not have me."

Emma stirred, her body shifting.

"I am in control. Courage is mine. Light within, unbroken. Darkness will not have me," they repeated, voices rising.

The mist whipped violently now, light bursting across the room in fractured flashes. The gemstones blazed, feeding the charged air.

Emma's chest convulsed once, twice—then her lungs dragged in a ragged, desperate gasp.

Elara's eyes locked on her, unblinking, following every fragile rise of her ribs, every twitch of her lips. The world narrowed to that single sound of breath fighting its way back. Her own heart hammered so violently it drowned out everything else.

"Don't you dare give up now," Elara whispered, the words tearing raw from her throat.

Chapter Forty-Eight

T HE EDGES OF THE ROOM BLED into shadow, sounds collapsing into muffled echoes as though the world itself were sinking underwater. Sleep dragged Emma down, sudden and weightless, a plunge beneath a dark lake she could not resist. Her body grew heavy, pinned as if by unseen hands, while her mind blazed unnaturally bright—more awake here, in descent, than it ever was in daylight.

The dream folded in on itself, sharper than any memory. Emma was no longer drifting but placed, set down in a moment she thought she had lost forever.

Color struck first. Everything appeared vivid, hyper-saturated—shadows sinking deeper than they should, light glinting so sharply it seemed to cut. Small details flared with impossible clarity: a single bead of water trembling on a leaf, the grain etched into a wooden door, the fleeting flicker of her father's expression caught and held too long.

Even the air had weight, carrying the echo of something she had breathed before, a half-forgotten texture clinging to her lungs. It pressed against her skin like a second body, thin and invasive, sliding straight into her chest until every breath felt lined with ice.

Emma felt unmoored, as though she had slipped free of herself. She hovered just above her own shoulder, watching the body below march forward with unnerving precision—the jaw set, the grip on the case unyielding, the swing of her stride mechanical in its determination. The scene unfolded like a play she both performed and observed, déjà vu laced with dread.

Just before the church threshold, her body halted.

She floated above, watching her own hand loosen its grip and lower the case to the ground. The hollow thud of wood on stone echoed in the cold air, final and deliberate.

"It stays out here," she heard herself say, her own voice steady, unfamiliar.

Brianna's eyes narrowed, but she gave a single nod.

Emma's body moved again.

Emma felt herself pulled forward, compelled, each step into the church precise, deliberate, unstoppable. Her limbs carried her as though they belonged to someone else entirely, yet with a steadiness she had never known. Beside her, Brianna matched her stride, shoulders squared, her posture echoing Emma's unnatural resolve.

The weight of the dream clung to her as she lifted her hand and knocked on her father's office door. The sound cracked through the hollow silence, final as a gavel. Without waiting for an answer, she pushed the door open, carrying herself inside.

"Dad, we need you to come outside and check something out," Emma said.

Her father looked up from his desk, surprise flickering in his eyes. An open Bible lay before him, its pages splayed wide, the thin pages whispering in the draft. His hand hovered over it, pen poised above a half-finished line of notes.

"Can it wait?" he asked. "I'm busy preparing for next week's sermon."

"No, it can't."

Her voice didn't waver. It carried a weight she hadn't known she possessed. No hesitation. No apology. No fear.

Her father studied her, his brow tightening, but he didn't question. He rose, and the quiet strength in his movements seemed to bolster her own resolve.

Outside, Oscar waited.

"What is this?" he asked, his gaze narrowing on the battered case, scuffed, its latches tarnished to a dull brass. A faint hum seemed to hang in the air around it, a whisper of something ancient, patient.

He crouched, curiosity sparking in his eyes—the eagerness of a man perched on the edge of revelation. His fingers hovered above the latch.

"Don't," Emma said.

Her voice cracked like a whip, commanding.

He froze. The scholarly gleam in his gaze vanished. A shadow passed over his features, his jaw tightening as if even being close to the case carried a risk.

"You opened it?"

His voice was hard, incredulous. His expression shifted, anger flashing across his face.

Brianna stepped forward, shoulders squaring as though to shield her, but Emma cut in first.

"It was moving when we found it," Emma explained. "I had to make sure whatever was inside was okay."

Her gaze locked on the fury in her father's eyes. This time she refused to let it pierce her, refused to let it carve its way into her mind. That fury was not hers to bear—it no longer carried her name. It belonged to something else: the evil that had birthed Oscar into existence, the shadow that had carried it here.

"Mija, do you know what you just did?" her father asked finally, his voice low, almost reverent.

Beside her, Brianna's chin lifted. Emma caught the pride softening her friend's face, the steady way her eyes met Emmanuel's.

"She stopped it," Brianna said.

Chapter Forty-Nine

EMMA'S EYES FLUTTERED OPEN, the faint, earthy scent of sage swirling around her like a hazy memory. For a moment, disorientation held her captive. Her gaze darted around the dimly lit room, searching for familiarity but finding only shadows dancing across the walls, their shapes both comforting and alien.

She groaned softly, pressing a hand to her lower back as she shifted on the hard surface beneath her. Her muscles ached as if she had been still for hours. Her limbs felt heavy, her thoughts foggy, like she was waking from a dream she couldn't quite grasp.

Fragments returned in pieces—a blur of voices, flashes of light, a distant hum of energy—but none of it made sense. Time felt distorted, stretched and twisted. She couldn't remember how she had come to be here.

But that didn't matter now. What mattered was the weight no longer pressing on her chest, the fear that, for the first time in forever, had loosened its grip. She inhaled deeply, letting the warm, sage-laden air fill her lungs and ground her.

Her eyes fell on Brianna and Elara, standing nearby, their faces taut with both worry and relief.

Emma sat up abruptly, her head jerking as she scanned the room.

A ring of flickering candles encircled her, their golden flames casting jagged shadows on the walls. Scattered gemstones glimmered faintly in the dim light. At the table's center, an ornate jar stood, golden mist swirling inside, alive and mesmerizing.

Her breath came faster, a knot of unease tightening in her chest. She scanned the glowing jar, the trembling candles, and at last, Elara.

"What did you do to me?" Emma demanded, her voice sharp, her posture rigid with suspicion.

Brianna stepped forward, hands raised in a calming gesture. "Emma, wait. Just breathe," she said quickly, her voice steady but edged with worry. "She didn't hurt you, I swear."

Emma swung her legs over the table, her movements abrupt, defensive. Her eyes flicked between Elara and Brianna, confusion hardening into anger.

"What is all of this?"

Elara stepped closer.

"You were trapped, Emma. Not just by fear, but by something darker—something trying to control you." Her eyes flicked to the jar. "We used its energy to help you find your strength."

"My strength?" Emma repeated, her voice taut with disbelief. Her gaze locked on the tall, ornate candle at the table's center, its base etched with an inscription she didn't recognize. She turned back to Elara, realization twisting her features. "You used magic? You used magic on me?"

Elara didn't flinch. "Yes. It was the only way to free you from whatever was gripping you."

Emma's breath caught. She turned to Brianna, betrayal flashing in her eyes. "How could you let her do this to me?"

"I'm sorry, Emma. I didn't know what else to do."

Emma swallowed hard, fury prickling beneath her skin like fire begging to spread. Her first instinct was to lash out, to demand answers, to scream at Brianna for letting it get this far. But she forced the anger down, grinding it into silence.

If she stood by and allowed this to happen, it must have been for a reason.

She drew in a shaky breath, the sound ragged in the charged air. Brianna's choices scared her, unsettled her—but she trusted her. She had to.

"How do I know if it worked?" Her voice softened, uncertain. She looked down at her hands, flexing her fingers. Energy coursed through her veins—stronger, sharper. Different.

The lights flickered, the candle flames sputtering as though responding to her awakening. A cold shiver swept through Brianna, her face draining of color as her eyes shot to the hallway.

"It's not there," Brianna whispered, her voice hollow, distant.

Emma followed her gaze, muscles taut as the shadows leapt across the walls. *Not there—what does she mean, not there?*

"What do you mean, it's not there?" Emma's voice cracked sharp, brittle. She slid off the table, eyes locked on the yawning darkness.

"It was there," Brianna stammered, trembling. "It was lying there after everything happened. It's gone."

From the shadows came a whisper—thin, malevolent—too faint to be human yet too deliberate to be ignored. It slithered into the room like smoke, like a cold breath against the back of the neck.

The lights sputtered once, twice, then flared in protest, as if the house itself choked on the presence invading it. The air thickened, heavy in Emma's lungs, every breath scraped thin by unseen hands.

The candles shuddered violently. Their flames bent toward the hallway, straining in unison as if pulled by a tide too vast to resist. The shadows stretched with them—long, clawed fingers dragging across the walls, reaching for the open threshold like the mouth of something hungry.

The hallway yawned before them, darker than darkness, swelling outward with slow inevitability.

Emma's feet edged backward, her pulse pounding against her ribs. "It's not gone," she said, voice breaking into the silence. "It's loose."

A soft, eerie laughter rippled from the void—sharp, mocking—rising until it filled the room, vibrating inside her bones.

Brianna's grip clamped on her arm, nails biting, a desperate anchor. "We have to get out of here," she whispered, her words shaking. "Now."

But the laughter didn't fade. It multiplied, crawling along the walls, echoing back on itself until it was everywhere. The darkness pulsed, alive, shadows writhing like veins through the air. They swarmed the candlelight, clawing to smother the last fragile sparks of warmth.

Oscar was no longer bound.

He was loose. And he was coming for them.

Chapter Fifty

ELARA CLOSED HER EYES, SUMMONING the strength buried in her bloodline, an inheritance carved from generations of ritual and defiance. It wasn't power she wielded often—or lightly—but with darkness pressing in, she had no choice. She had to fight the very thing she had unleashed.

Her steps fell with ritual weight as she circled the table, hands outstretched. The chant rose from her throat in steady cadence, each syllable vibrating through the air like a struck chord. Sage smoldered in her grasp, its smoke curling into a barrier of protection. The sharp scent rooted her, pushing against the encroaching dark with relentless defiance.

The shadows writhed, recoiling as the chant swelled. Energy rippled outward, weaving through the room, bolstering Emma's resolve and fortifying the barrier Brianna had begun to build.

Elara didn't stop.

She couldn't.

She was fighting for what Nadia would have wanted—demanded.

Her voice rose, sharper, fuller, carrying weight older than herself—an authority dredged from bloodlines and rituals long buried. The words thrummed through the air, ancient power coiled in every syllable. For a heartbeat, even the shadows seemed to flinch.

But Elara knew...

It wasn't enough.

The darkness drank in her command like water on stone, soaking it up, leaving nothing changed.

Her head snapped toward the girls.

"You must fight it!" Elara shouted, the words tearing raw from her throat. Her voice cracked with urgency, desperation threading through her command. "Both of you! Now!"

"Where is it?" Brianna demanded, her voice taut as her eyes swept the corners, scouring the walls and floor. Her pulse hammered in her ears. "Where's Oscar?"

Then came the sound—skittering, sharp and unnatural, like claws dragging across bone. It scraped along the ceiling above them, a metallic rasp that set their teeth on edge.

Their heads snapped upward in unison.

Oscar clung to the ceiling, skittering with a grotesque, spiderlike gait—jerky, inhuman, its limbs bending at impossible angles. Each step landed with a faint tap, reverberating like nails on wood. Dust sifted down with every movement, carrying the faint stench of rot. Its joints twitched as if jerked by unseen strings, the failing light warping its silhouette into monstrous shapes that stretched and twisted across the walls.

Elara's gaze flicked to Emma. The girl's eyes followed Oscar, not in terror but with unsettling curiosity, as though dissecting something vile beneath a microscope. Her face remained steady, disturbingly composed, while the creature crawled overhead in its grotesque defiance of gravity.

"Emma?" Elara called, her voice tight, fraying at the edges. *Please don't break now.* "Are you all right?"

Emma didn't answer at first. Her gaze remained locked on the thing above them, unblinking, as if caught in its orbit.

"It's... different," she said at last, her tone calm.

Oscar's head snapped toward her, joints creaking like splintering wood. Its eyes burned with a glint—wild, yet disturbingly familiar, as though some fragment of humanity still lingered behind the gloss.

"I see... fear," Emma whispered, sorrow weaving through her words. "That's what it fed on. That's how it controlled us."

Elara's breath caught as the truth sunk in...

Emma—the mousy girl—from before was gone. In her place stood someone tempered by fire—rooted, sharpened, unyielding. Her voice now carried the weight of someone who had stared into the abyss and, against all reason, refused to flinch.

"It worked," Elara murmured, though her words trembled with the dread of what lingered still. She exhaled a shaky breath. Relief flickered across her face, brief as a spark, before her eyes darkened again. The shadows along the walls were still moving—slithering, curling like snakes disturbed from their nest.

The air grew taut with their hiss, restless, waiting. Elara turned to the girls, her gaze fierce.

"I can't fight it alone. It's too strong. I need your help. We need to harness our power together."

"But, I can't," Emma said. "I'm not a witch!"

Elara seized her hand. "Today you are."

"Are you afraid?" Brianna pressed.

"No," Emma answered, steady.

"Me neither," Brianna said, her grip tightening. Their joined hands radiated warmth, grounding them, a conduit of shared strength. "Now summon the light."

"What does that mean?" Emma asked.

"It means whatever you want it to mean!" Brianna's voice flared with urgency.

Emma inhaled deeply, steadying herself. When she spoke, her words rang with power. "Oscar, you have no place here. I rebuke you in the name of Jesus!"

Brianna's eyes widened. "What are you doing?"

"I'm summoning the light," Emma replied. "Now pray with me!"

Brianna drew a breath. "Darkness has no place here. Fear has no place here." Her tone wavered with uncertainty, but the energy binding them was undeniable.

"Keep going!" Elara urged.

"I don't know what I'm doing!" Brianna shouted.

Emma locked eyes with her. "You know the Our Father, right?"

Brianna nodded.

"Do you believe it?"

Another nod.

"Then say it with me—like you mean it."

They began:

"Our Father, who art in heaven..."

The words were barely spoken, yet already the house recoiled. The walls trembled, dust sifting down from the ceiling in thin, ghostly streams. Curtains lashed out like sails caught in a violent wind, though no breeze stirred the air.

"Hallowed be Thy name. Thy kingdom come..."

A cold current blasted through, burning their skin like ice.

Oscar's grin warped into a rictus as it shrieked without sound, claws tearing at the plaster in a frenzied scramble.

"Thy will be done, on earth as it is in heaven."

The floorboards buckled. Frames crashed from the walls. Pressure bore down on them, crushing until their bones seemed to hum under its weight. Still, the girls stood firm.

"Keep going," Elara gasped, awe breaking through fear.

The hiss rose again, scraping across the air like metal on bone.

"Give us this day our daily bread..."

Light burst between their joined hands, radiating outward in pulsing waves.

Oscar twisted, its body elongating, head wrenching around at an impossible angle, eyes blazing with fury.

"And forgive us our trespasses, as we forgive those who trespass against us..."

The sound built to a roar. Not thunder, not wind—something deeper, tearing at the fabric of the room.

"And lead us not into temptation, but deliver us from evil."

The final words detonated like a cannon blast. A shockwave surged outward, a living force. The light was intangible yet crushing, pressing against the shadows, driving them back.

Oscar shrieked in silence—its limbs elongating grotesquely, its body contorting as it scrambled across the ceiling. Its head twisted unnaturally to glare down at them, mouth stretched wide in a soundless scream.

But the girls did not flinch.

They stood with hands raised, radiating defiance as the light swelled brighter, filling the room—banishing the darkness that had held them captive.

Elara collapsed to her knees, the weight of the moment crashing over her like a tidal wave. Tears streamed down her face, carving raw paths of anguish. Her fingers clawed at the floor, digging into the cold wood as though searching for an anchor while the storm of emotion threatened to consume her.

She lifted her face to the faint golden light lingering in the room. Her tear-streaked cheeks caught its glow, her eyes glistening with a fragile mix of relief and sorrow. Yet beneath that fragile flicker, grief pressed heavier still—omnipresent, unbearable, a weight she hadn't known the soul could endure.

Her breath hitched, sharp and ragged. A groan tore loose, raw and guttural, born of sorrow so deep she had no idea how to release it.

"It's over," she whispered, her voice splintering, barely audible.

Her head bowed, shoulders shaking as she curled inward. "Nadia... my sweet baby girl... I'm so sorry."

Each word fell jagged, another shard of her heart breaking free.

"It's over—I promise you... it's over."

Chapter Fifty-One

T HE ROOM FELT DIFFERENT NOW—lighter, brighter, as though some oppressive veil had finally lifted. Shadows no longer clung to the corners. The air itself seemed clearer, easier to breathe, charged not with dread but with fragile relief. It should have been a moment of triumph, a victory won after so much terror.

But Brianna's relief fractured the instant her gaze slid to Emma. Her shoulders hunched, her body taut, eyes lowered to the floor as if wishing she could vanish into it. The contrast struck Brianna hard—victory had been claimed, but Emma looked anything but victorious.

She watched Elara notice it too—saw the shift in her expression, the way concern overtook exhaustion. Maternal instinct surged through the woman; Brianna could feel it like a pulse in the room.

Elara rose and crossed the space toward Emma.

"What's the matter?" Elara asked gently, crouching down until she was level with Emma. "Oscar is gone. You're safe now."

"It's not over," Emma whispered. "You have no idea what you've done."

Worry deepened the lines on Brianna's forehead. She knew exactly what they had done. The truth pressed against her chest like a stone, heavy and immovable. Her head dropped, shame pulling her gaze to the floor. She hadn't stopped it. She hadn't fought harder to protect Emma from Elara's ritual. She had allowed it.

Elara leaned closer, her voice patient, coaxing. "Emma, please. You can tell me."

From Brianna's vantage point, she wasn't the same woman who had stood in this room when they first walked in. The ache was still there, the raw grief etched deep into her features—but something had shifted. The sharp edges had dulled. Her presence no longer felt like a wall but like a doorway, soft around the edges, almost welcoming. For a fleeting moment, Brianna wondered if it was because they reminded her of Nadia—two girls still standing, when hers was gone.

Brianna stepped forward, arms crossed in a gesture of defense, though her voice didn't carry the same bite.

"She's worried about the spell you used on her," she said, steady and firm. "It's not something she would've ever agreed to willingly."

"Is that what this is about?" Elara replied, her tone cool, almost dismissive.

"Emma's father says there are consequences for toying with things like this," Brianna said, her voice steady but tight. "He says it gives the devil a foothold."

Brianna had heard the phrase *the lesser of two evils* before—tossed casually in sermons, in half-remembered stories, a warning packaged as cliché. But now, in this room, with the air still vibrating from the ritual, the phrase wasn't abstract. It had teeth.

"It's not what I believe," Elara murmured, voice quiet but deliberate. "But I understand your concern."

"No, you don't." Emma's voice cracked, sharp with fear. Her hands balled into fists in her lap. "My father is going to kill me."

Elara reached out, brushing a tear from Emma's cheek with a tenderness that caught Brianna off guard. The woman who had towered in anger and grief hours ago was different now.

"Emma, I need you to listen to me," Elara said, her tone low, coaxing. "Your father's choices—his beliefs—aren't yours to carry. They never were. Remember that. You are more than his mistakes. More than his shadow."

In the cadence of Elara's voice, in the way her eyes flickered before settling on Emma's, Brianna caught it—this was more than advice. Each word dragged a chain of history behind it. A confession cloaked in counsel. A shard of Elara's own past, raw and uninvited, slipping through despite her restraint.

"I'm so sorry, Em," Brianna whispered, her voice thick with regret. "I didn't know what else we could do."

The truth pressed down on her, heavy and undeniable. By allowing Elara to perform the ritual—by standing there and letting the chant coil around Emma's fragile body—she had crossed a line that could never be uncrossed.

The lesser of two evils.

Brianna had chosen for Emma.

And now, all she could do was hope that when the scales tipped, she hadn't damned them all.

Chapter Fifty-Two

ANXIOUS THOUGHTS SLIPPED INTO EMMA'S mind uninvited like old companions she couldn't quite shake. Rehearsed too many times, they traced the same worn paths they always did:

What if my dad finds out?

What will I do?

What will I say?

Emma could see it as clearly as if it were unfolding before her: her father's face darkening, jaw clenching, voice rising with the fury she had known since childhood. His anger would come swift, blistering, laced with scripture and shame, every word a hammer meant to crush her back into obedience.

But as the image burned bright in her mind, something inside her shifted.

The fear that once made her small, that kept her quiet, wasn't the same anymore. She realized with startling clarity—it wasn't her father that terrified her now. What twisted in her chest, what made her stomach coil tight, was something far heavier...

She was afraid of the truth—that they had touched something vast and untamed. That by stepping into it, by letting it coil around her, she might have opened a door that could never be closed.

"There must be something we can do," Emma said, her voice breaking at the edges. Desperation thinned it, stripped it bare, so it came out half-plea, half-demand. Her eyes darted between Brianna and Elara, wide and glistening, as if searching their faces for an answer neither of them had.

Elara moved slowly, reaching for a glass of water. Her hand was steady as she offered it.

Emma hesitated, trembling fingers closing around the glass. She stared at the rippling surface, clutching it like the only solid thing she could hold.

Elara smiled gently, laying a hand on Emma's arm.

"I have a story that might help—passed down in my family for generations," Elara said, her voice low, almost soothing.

Emma's breath snagged, unease flickering across her face before she could hide it.

"Nadia knew it well. May I tell it?" Elara asked, her voice gentler now, almost reverent.

Emma glanced toward Brianna, searching. Brianna met her eyes, steady, unflinching, and gave the faintest nod. With a reluctant tilt of her chin, Emma nodded too.

Elara eased onto the couch, settling between them. Her presence felt heavier than the room, grounding, steady as an anchor in a storm.

"There was once a boy named Kamau," she began, her voice lowering into a steady rhythm, the cadence of a tale told many times before.

"He was no older than you two. A boy who lived in a small village, tucked far from the eyes of the world. From the day he could walk, fear clung to him like a shadow. He was afraid of storms, of the dark, of the silence between one breath and the next. He was even afraid of his own heartbeat, the way it thundered too loudly in his chest."

Emma shifted closer without realizing it, her eyes catching on the glow of the jar at the table's center. The golden mist swirled as though listening, keeping pace with Elara's words.

"One day, a witch came to Kamau's village. She was an old woman, cloaked in black, her hair streaked with silver. The children scattered when they saw her, whispering of curses and hexes. But Kamau—he was too tired of fear to run. He followed her to the edge of the forest, where the shadows grew tall and the air smelled of rain.

"The witch looked at Kamau and said, 'You want freedom, don't you, boy? You want to be rid of this fear that strangles you.'

"Kamau nodded, desperate. So the witch reached into her satchel and pulled out a jar. Simple, ordinary glass, no bigger than his fist. She placed it in his hands. 'Inside this jar,' she told him, 'is magic. When fear grips you, open it, and the magic will protect you.'

"Kamau clutched that jar like it was life itself. And from there on, he didn't run when thunder rolled across the sky. He didn't cower when shadows stretched too long. He carried the jar everywhere, sleeping with it beneath his pillow, holding it tight when the wind howled through the cracks of his house. And slowly, people began to notice—Kamau stood straighter. He didn't tremble as much. His voice grew louder."

Elara's lips pressed into a line, her voice weighted with significance. "But here's the truth—"

Emma leaned forward without thinking, her body moving closer, caught in the pull of the story. Beside her, she sensed Brianna doing the same, as though they were children again, listening by firelight.

"The jar was empty."

Emma's brow furrowed. She turned, her eyes locking with Brianna's in confusion. The look on her face asked the question her lips couldn't form.

"The witch had given him nothing but belief," Elara said, her tone slow and deliberate. "The courage was his all along. He just needed something to hold onto, something to convince him it was real."

The golden mist inside the Witches' Jar pulsed once, as though answering her words.

Emma's pulse quickened. Empty. It had all been empty.

Brianna's voice broke the silence. "So... there was no spell?"

Elara's lips curled into a sly smile. "Nadia spoke of you both often. I developed a sense for what was off-limits."

Brianna blinked, still trying to process. "But we chanted together."

Elara leaned back, a sly shrug lifting her shoulders, mischief flickering in her eyes. "More mantra than spell," she said. "Words of empowerment."

Emma sat quietly, her hands folded in her lap, fingers twisting together. Her lips pressed thin as the truth seeped in. Elara hadn't poured magic into her veins, hadn't forced power into her body—at least not in the way Emma had feared. The ritual, the chanting, the glow—it had all been smoke and mirrors. And yet... it had worked.

Elara's gaze lingered on Brianna, her voice soft but deliberate, like a teacher setting the next challenge before a student. "Now that I've told you my secret," she said, "tell me yours."

Chapter Fifty-Three

B RIANNA FELT THEIR GAZE on her—searching, unrelenting, heavy with expectation. It pressed against her chest like a hand, harder than words, holding her still. Even the room seemed to lean in, as if the house demanded answers too. She considered brushing Elara off—keeping the truth tucked away for later, saving it for the quiet safety of the car ride home, when the shadows of this house were behind them. She imagined deflecting, letting silence shield her secret just a little longer.

But Elara's stare cut through that fantasy. Steady. Unblinking. It was the kind of look that said *I know you're holding something back.*

The words clawed their way up before Brianna could stop them.

"I was diagnosed with something called spontaneous psychokinesis," she admitted at last.

Elara leaned in, her expression sharp with interest. "What does that mean, exactly? You can move things with your mind?"

Brianna shook her head. "It's not that clear cut. I can't just decide to pick up a book or slam a door across the room. It only happens when my emotions spiral—when they get too big for me, too much for my body to contain. Then... it spills out."

The articles she had devoured late into the night surfaced in her mind. Their sterile language blurred into the same refrain: *spontaneous psychokinesis, often tied to heightened emotional states.* Forums filled with strangers speculating about *energy bodies* and *thoughtforms.* Videos of experiments she had replayed again and again, studying every twitch, every flicker of movement, trying to see herself in them.

Emma's eyes narrowed, suspicion flashing like a knife.

"I know what I saw—what you did in this house. That wasn't spontaneous. You controlled it."

Brianna hesitated only a beat before nodding.

There had been long hours no one had seen. The hospital stays, the sterile rooms where machines beeped steady and unforgiving, where she lay awake staring at white ceilings, counting her heartbeats just to stay still. Nights curled in bed, forcing her lungs into even breaths, visualizing calm washing over her like water, holding it tight until her body obeyed. Every moment she could, she practiced controlling her breathing. Visualizing. Boxing herself in until the storm passed.

"When we found out Nadia died, I was just so upset..." She swallowed hard, tears threatening. "That's when I learned I could control the spillover. I didn't stop it—I harnessed it."

Emma's gaze sharpened, a flicker of recognition flashing there. "The door slamming shut behind me... when my dad and I left your house—"

Brianna nodded. "I controlled it."

Elara's voice cut in, low, certain. "What you did to Justin—"

Another nod. Her chin lifted, trembling but defiant. "I controlled it."

Elara leaned forward, studying her with an intensity that made Brianna's skin prickle. There was no ridicule in her gaze, no dismissal—only recognition.

"You've taken what most people would call a weakness," Elara murmured, "and bent it to your will." Her lips pressed thin, her eyes glinting in the candlelight. "That's rarer than magic."

The words landed deeper than Brianna expected. A smile tugged at her lips—small, uncertain, but real. She hadn't thought of it like that before. Her mother had framed it as a burden, something she struggled to contain. But hearing it reshaped as strength—as rarity—it felt different. It was something she could be proud of.

Emma's lips parted, closed, then parted again, as though she wanted to swallow the question but couldn't. When it finally slipped out, her voice was fragile, almost careful not to disturb the air between them.

"So... you're not a witch?"

Brianna shrugged. "Who's to say?" Her smile faded, giving way to a dry laugh—low, humorless, brittle at the edges. "Nadia seemed to think so."

The inspiration for Oscar, along with the church children he terrified.
1985, Temple of Light and Peace
San Antonio, Texas

KEEP READING

An Excerpt From the Author's Next Book

La Llorona – The Awakening

MARY ROMASANTA

Water seeped cold between her toes as she ripped the curtain aside. The tub yawned before her like an open grave, water rippling in eerie silence. And there—adrift like a discarded doll—was Mi-Ra. Her body hung weightless, pale face tilted toward the ceiling, eyes wide and unblinking, glassy orbs staring through the wavering surface as if already fixed on another world.

"Mi-Ra!"

The scream tore from Ruth's throat as she plunged in, pulling dead weight from the water's clutch. On the tiles, cold as marble, Ruth laid her out, pressing fingers to neck, cheek, chest.

No breath. No beat. Just stillness.

Ruth's chest felt like it might collapse under the weight of her fear, but she didn't hesitate. She tilted Mi-Ra's head back, pinched her nose, and sealed her lips over Mi-Ra's, forcing two breaths into her lungs. Then she placed her hands on Mi-Ra's chest, one on top of the other, and began compressions.

"One. Two. Three." Ruth's voice shook. "Come on, Mi-Ra. Breathe. Please." She pressed down hard, her arms aching with the effort, her mind a chaotic blur of prayers and instructions she barely remembered from a CPR class she'd taken at work years ago.

Seconds stretched, each compression a plea, each breath a desperate hope. Ruth refused to give up, even as her arms burned, and her breaths grew ragged. Finally, Mi-Ra's body jerked, a weak, choking gasp escaping her lips. Water sputtered from her mouth as her chest heaved. Ruth turned her onto her side, patting her back to help her expel the water.

"Mi-Ra, can you hear me?"

Mi-Ra convulsed with violent coughs, her body jerking with each ragged gasp. Her eyes fluttered open—glassy, unfocused—scanning the room as though caught between dream and waking. Dazed, she blinked slowly.

"Ruth," she croaked.

"You're okay," Ruth whispered, her own hands trembling as she cradled Mi-Ra's face. "You're going to be okay. Just keep breathing."

Mi-Ra's head sagged, her strength slipping away, but her breaths steadied. Ruth grabbed a towel, clumsy with panic, wrapping it around her shoulders before fumbling for her phone. Her fingers shook so badly she nearly dropped it as she dialed 911.

"You can't help me," Mi-Ra rasped. Her gaze slid past Ruth, vacant, as if addressing the room instead. Her head lolled to the side, eyes glassy. "It would've been better," she whispered, voice splintering, "for both of us."

"You don't get to decide that," Ruth snapped, desperation sharpening her tone. "Not for me. Not for John. Not for anyone."

Mi-Ra didn't argue. She only stared past Ruth, hollow and unseeing.

"You don't have to do this alone," Ruth urged, her voice gentler now. "But you have to let me help you."

Mi-Ra's hands clenched in her lap, nails biting into the damp fabric, her stare fixed on the wall. "I don't deserve it," she whispered.

Ruth cupped her cheek, her palm steady despite the tremor in her chest. "Look at me."

Mi-Ra's gaze finally met hers, and Ruth saw the truth written plainly: hollowed cheeks, bruised shadows beneath her eyes, and the vacant stare of a soul buckling under unbearable grief.

"John loved you with his entire hear and soul," Ruth said, her voice low but steady, weighted with equal parts anger and desperation. "That tells me you deserve it and much, much more."

The words lingered in the silence, fragile but insistent. Ruth leaned closer, searching Mi-Ra's eyes for any flicker—acknowledgment, defiance, anything.

Then her breath caught. Reflected in Mi-Ra's glassy stare was a silhouette. A man. Familiar in the way of an old photograph brought suddenly to life. The set of his shoulders, the tilt of his head—details Ruth recognized before she could name them.

She froze, pulse spiking, though fear wasn't the only thing rising in her chest. There was a strange calm threaded through it, a hush that felt almost protective. The figure behind her didn't radiate menace but something closer to memory—comforting and unsettling at once, as if grief itself had conjured him.

Slowly, she turned, braced for what she already knew she wouldn't see. Nothing.

When she looked back, Mi-Ra's gaze locked with hers, unnervingly serene. "Did you see him?" Mi-Ra asked.

Ruth swallowed. "See who?"

"Greg," Mi-Ra whispered. Her lips trembled, but her eyes were steady. "He's calling for me."

MORE FROM THIS AUTHOR

Twenty-nine-year-old Emma is an intelligent, strong-willed, and ambitious PR exec, who has always relied solely on herself. But when her recurring nightmares start taking a toll on her health, she turns to renowned University of Chicago psychiatrist and oneirologist Dr. Edward Clark for help.

Dr. Clark learns that Emma's nightmares all revolve around her past love interests, a theme not uncommon among his patients. But, as they delve deeper, they discover a disturbing truth—Emma is losing touch with reality. The traumas from her nightmares are bleeding into her waking life, leaving her trapped in a waking nightmare.

In a race against time, Emma and Dr. Clark uncover the dark secrets buried deep within her psyche. As they unearth violence, control, and manipulation from her past, they realize that her diagnosis is more horrifying than they ever imagined. They must fight for Emma's life or risk succumbing to the relentless grip of unspeakable evil.

A brilliant neurologist at the University of Chicago, Dr. Prasad Vedurmudi, makes a mind-bending discovery: a hidden region of the brain that acts as a gateway to the next dimension. If repaired before death, it could unlock humanity's most coveted mystery—the ability to control the afterlife itself.

Together with psychiatrist Dr. Edward Clark, Prasad ventures into uncharted territory, chasing undeniable proof of life beyond death. But as their research deepens, they awaken forces determined to silence them.

Blending suspense, science, and the supernatural, *The Eternal Secret* pulls you into a twilight realm where the line between life and the afterlife blurs. Prepare to be captivated—and haunted—by secrets that may change everything we believe about existence.

Infestation by Mary Romasanta is a chilling tale where the cost of salvation could very well be the soul itself.

Struggling to keep the doors of his church open, a young pastor moves his family into an abandoned house across from a cemetery just outside of Chicago, where darkness unfurls its tendrils through the splintered frame of the home. Amidst the decay, ancient whispers breed within the walls, and six-year-old Emma's innocent eyes see a world veiled to others. Her gift, a rare discernment of spirits, reveals a spectral horde as vast as the cemetery itself. Her warnings fall on disbelieving ears until each unsettling encounter with the unseen erodes their reality, pushing them to the brink of madness.

When the distinction between the living and the oppressed is no longer discernible, the family's hope to save their church becomes a desperate battle to save their souls from a home hell-bent on their destruction. With the last hour ticking mercilessly close, they must uncover the secrets rooted in the house's dark core before they find themselves permanently entwined in its insidious branches.

In *Deliver Us*, Mary Romasanta pulls back the veil between story and reality to reveal the true supernatural encounters that shaped her most chilling works.

Raised as a pastor's daughter in a home across from San Antonio's largest cemetery, Mary's childhood was steeped in spiritual realities others dismiss as coincidence or imagination. From demonic manifestations and generational curses to spiritual oppression and deliverance, these stories are not fiction. They are lived. Witnessed. Endured.

With boldness and faith, Mary recounts the encounters that inspired her novels—and the God who carried her through them.

These stories aren't written to entertain. They are written to expose. To equip. To remind us that the battle is real... and so is the victory.

Acknowledgements

To my husband and children, your unwavering support has been my foundation. Thank you for believing in me, for cheering me on, and for giving me the courage to pursue my dreams.

Thank you to my parents for the invaluable lessons and for never hesitating to instill them in me, even when they were hard to hear and harder to accept. Your guidance shaped me in ways I'll forever be grateful for.

To my brother, for sharing in my fears and helping me outgrow them through countless horror movie marathons that, thankfully, are more laughable now than terrifying.

To my friends and family, thank you for your encouragement, your belief in me, and your endless support throughout this journey. I couldn't have done it without you.

About the Author

Mary Romasanta is an author, technologist, and mother of three young boys. After twenty years in her corporate career, she transformed her lifelong passion for storytelling into reality, blending psychological thriller, science fiction, horror, and the paranormal.

Raised in San Antonio, Texas, just steps from the city's largest cemetery, she grew up surrounded by the mystique of the supernatural. The daughter of a pastor and a florist, she draws on her childhood fascination with the spiritual and the ethereal to create vivid, haunting backdrops for her novels.

Through her distinctive fusion of genres and her dedication to cultural depth, Romasanta invites readers to explore the human psyche, question reality, and confront the terror that lurks in the shadows.

FOR A COMPLETE
LIST OF BOOKS BY

MARY ROMASANTA

VISIT

MaryRomasanta.com

Follow Mary Romasanta on Instagram

@AuthorMaryRomasanta